NOT PRETENDING ANYMORE

PENELOPE WARD
VI KEELAND

NOT PRETENDING ANYMORE
Cover designer: Sommer Stein, Perfect Pear Creative
www.perfectpearcreative.com
Edited by: Jessica Royer Ocken
Formatting and proofreading: Elaine York,
Allusion Publishing www.allusionpublishing.com
Proofreading: Julia Griffis

NOT PRETENDING ANYMORE

CHAPTER ONE

Molly

"So, what do you do for a living?"

The woman drummed her fingers on her thigh. "I'm a musician."

I glanced down at the renter's application in my hand. *Lyric Chords* was the name listed at the top.

I bit my tongue and tried to keep an open mind. This was the twelfth woman I'd interviewed as a prospective roommate. Just because she had a few safety pins in her eyebrow and what looked like a dog collar around her neck didn't mean I should rule her out.

"Oh. That's nice. Are you a singer?"

Lyric shook her head. "Drummer. Do you know the dimensions of the bedroom I'll be sleeping in? I have two sets of drums I need to fit."

"Umm... I think it's fourteen by fourteen. But you don't practice at home, right? I wrote in my ad that I'm looking for a quiet roommate because I work nights."

"I do. But no worries. I'll practice in my room."

My bedroom and my potential roommate's bedroom shared a wall, so that was the end of interview number twelve. I sighed and forced a smile. "Thank you for coming. I have a few other people left to meet with before I decide. I'll let you know."

"Great." The woman stood. "Also, I know your ad said two months' rent up front, but I'm running a little short right now. Would one be okay?"

I smiled. "Sure, no problem." *Since you're not going to be living here.*

After Drummergirl, I interviewed two more candidates. One wanted her boyfriend to move into the room with her, even though my ad had specified I was only looking for a single. And the other arrived twenty minutes late, reeked of alcohol, and slurred her words... at three thirty in the afternoon.

Why in the hell was it so difficult to find a roommate in a city of almost three-million people? I needed my last interview of the day to be a miracle, or I was going to have to shell out money for another ad and start the entire process all over. And I definitely didn't have the time or the funds for that. Rent was due in two weeks. If I got stuck paying the full amount on this place myself again, I'd be eating cat food for a month.

When my last appointment knocked right on time, I took a deep breath, looked up at the ceiling, and asked the big guy in the sky for a little assistance.

Opening the door, I blinked a few times.

Uhhh. I think you answered the wrong prayer, God.

A man stood in my hallway—and not just any man, an absolutely gorgeous one with a perfect, straight nose, cheekbones to die for, a masculine, square jaw, full lips, tanned skin, and the sexiest chocolate brown, almond-shaped eyes I'd ever seen in my life.

"Uh. Can I help you?"

He flashed a killer smile, one that I immediately suspected had made countless women remove their panties.

"Hi. I have a four-thirty appointment with Molly Corrigan."

"You do?" I had the last application in my hand and looked down at the name on the top. "I don't think so. My appointment is with a D. Tate?"

He extended a hand. "That's me. Declan Tate."

"But...you're...not a woman."

He smiled again. "You're correct. Very observant. I am *most definitely* not a woman. But my last roommate told me I should've been because I use moisturizer at night and cried at the end of *Marley and Me*. And if I'm being honest, I also got a little watery at the end of *Toy Story*, so maybe I'm a bit of a wuss. Either way, I think you should consider those my positive feminine qualities."

I was thoroughly confused. "Umm... I'm sorry. You must've missed that my ad said *female only*."

"Actually, I didn't. But if you'll give me just five minutes, I think I can convince you I would be a better roommate than a woman."

I chuckled. "Let me get this straight... You hid your first name—what did you say it was again?"

"Declan."

"Right. Declan. Anyway, you applied to an ad for a female roommate, intentionally deceiving the person who is going to decide if you get the room by leaving your first name off. And your strategy is to convince me I don't really know what I want in less than five minutes? Do I have that right?"

3

He flashed that boyish charm again. "You sure do."

I debated how to handle the situation. On one hand, he was going to waste my time, and I had done enough of that today. But on the other, my curiosity was definitely piqued. Something about his grin told me this could be amusing. *Screw it*. I had nothing better to do anyway.

I opened the door wider and stepped aside, holding my hand out for him to enter. "I'm setting the timer on my phone, and I'm getting a glass of wine before you start. I like a drink while I'm being entertained."

Declan smirked and strolled into my apartment.

I motioned to the couch. "Have a seat. I'll just be a minute."

When I got to the kitchen, he called after me, "Hey, Mollz?"

I turned back. "Yes?"

"How about you make that two glasses of wine?"

I chuckled. "Sure. Why not, *Decs*."

I poured a couple of glasses of pinot grigio and returned to the living room.

"Here you go. Hope you like white."

"You see? We're perfect together already. I prefer white over red."

I brought my wine to my lips. "Yes, perfect. A match made in heaven. I think we might even be soul mates."

Declan showed me his pearly whites once again. He really did have a great smile, nice teeth, too. Too bad he also had *a penis*. I knocked back half the contents of my glass and placed it on the coffee table. Picking up my cell, I swiped to the timer app and set it for five minutes.

I showed him the screen. "You ready?"

"I'm always ready."

I pressed start, placed the phone face up on the coffee table between us, and folded my hands. "Go."

"Okay. Well...what's your favorite color?"

"My favorite color?"

Declan pointed to the timer. "Time's a ticking, Molly. I'm going to need you to not repeat questions."

I laughed. "Fine. My favorite color is pink."

Declan reached into one of his pant pockets and pulled out a set of keys. The keychain had a bunch of pink beads with white letters between each one. The letters spelled out his name. "Mine too."

I arched a brow. "Did you make that yourself?"

"No. My niece, Arianna, made it for me."

"So how do I know that isn't just Arianna's favorite color?"

"Good point. Let's move on. Your ad said you work nights."

"That's right. I'm a nurse. I work the night shift on the maternity ward."

"So you sleep during the day, then?"

"I get off at seven, and I try to get to sleep as soon as I get home."

He held his hand to his chest. "I work days. I leave for the gym by six and usually don't get home until after seven at night. So the apartment will be quiet when you need it to be."

I nodded. "Okay. I'll give you that that would make you a good roommate. But most people work days, so it's not really something that makes you too special."

"Do you cook?" he said.

"Does macaroni and cheese count?"

"I grew up in a multigenerational Italian home. My nonna taught me how to make sauce from scratch."

5

"So you're going to cook for me?"

"If that's what it takes to get this apartment, yes."

"As tempting as that might be, there's an Italian restaurant around the corner that makes great food. Funny enough, it's called Nonna's Place, and an *actual nonna* makes most of my meals. Not a knockoff."

Declan took an exaggerated breath and blew it out. He glanced at the cell on the table. "Three minutes and thirty-eight seconds. I can see you're not going to make this easy. How about you tell me why you can't have a male roommate so I can address that head-on. Is it because of the toilet-seat thing? Because I have four older sisters, so I'm appropriately trained. When I was eight, I made the mistake of leaving it up once, and my sister sat down where I'd accidentally left a little pee. She dunked my head in the toilet bowl *before* she flushed. That was the last time I left the seat up." He held up three fingers. "Scout's honor. It won't be an issue."

I smiled. "It's not because of the toilet thing."

"Alright. So why don't you want a male roommate, then?"

I'd actually never given much thought to why my roommate had to be female. It just seemed natural to have another woman sharing the apartment. "Well...I don't really have a specific reason. I would just be more comfortable living with another woman. For example, I sleep in a T-shirt and underwear. When I get up to start the coffee, I don't get dressed. It would be weird to do that in front of a man."

"Why?"

"Why would it be weird to walk around with my ass cheeks on display in front of a man and not a woman?"

6

"Yes."

I shrugged. "I don't know. It just would. I guess because the women I've lived with aren't attracted to other women, so it doesn't feel sexual in any way."

"Ah. Now we're getting to the crux of your issue. So you're afraid of some sexual tension going on between you and me? Is it because I'm so handsome?"

"What? *No!* And aren't you full of yourself, assuming I think you're handsome, and I'm worried I won't be able to control myself."

"Just keeping it real, Mollz. You're only giving me five minutes, so I'm trying to get to the heart of the reason."

"I guess I just don't want to feel like I have to cover up to come out of my bedroom. When I dry my hair, I wear a towel or a bra and underwear—that type of thing."

"Would you feel you had to cover up if I told you I was gay?"

That question gave me pause. *Would I?* I wasn't sure. "Are you?"

"Fuck, no. I was just trying to pinpoint your issue. Is it the fact that I'm a man, or the fact that I might admire your ass if it were on display? Sounds like it's the latter. So let me put your mind at ease: I won't."

I felt oddly offended. "What's wrong with my ass?"

He chuckled. "I wouldn't know. I haven't looked. You know why?"

"Why?"

"Because I'm in love with someone else."

As insane as it was, I felt a pang of jealousy. "Oh. Well, why aren't you moving in with her?"

"Because she doesn't return the feelings...yet. So basically, if your concern about having a guy for a roommate is that he's going to be checking you out, you have nothing to worry about with me. I'm a one-woman man. If you want, I can give you the numbers of some of my exes for references. I'm no cheater."

Hmmm... "I don't know..."

Declan looked down at the clock. Thirty-one seconds were left. "We're running out of time, so we need to speed things up. How about if I just give you the facts you need to know?"

"That would be good."

"I'm twenty-eight years old. I make six figures. My credit score is eight hundred and ten, and I have references from previous landlords. I'm neat and clean up after myself. I'm not home a lot, but when I am, I'm pretty quiet. I'm also damn good with a hammer." He glanced around my apartment and pointed at a hole I'd accidentally made in the wall when I flung the closet door open too hard. "I can spackle that and put on a door stopper so it won't happen again." He pointed to the kitchen. "And those cabinets are pretty tall. I'm six foot one. No more having to stand on a chair to reach something on the top shelf. And—"

The timer on the stopwatch buzzed.

"Can I just say one last thing?"

"Sure. Why not?"

"I'll share my Hulu and Netflix passwords. I have *the premium* Hulu account."

I laughed. "Well, those are some pretty enticing qualities for a roommate."

He smiled. "So I'm in?"

I sighed. "I'm sorry. While I appreciate your tenacity, unfortunately, you're not. Though I interviewed fourteen other people today, and I have to say, you do seem like you'll make some other lucky person a fantastic roomie."

Declan frowned, but nodded. "I figured it was worth a shot. This is a great building, and I work right around the corner. It's hard to find an apartment where it's only a six-month commitment."

"My lease is up then, and I haven't decided if I'm going to extend or not."

"See? That's another reason I'd be perfect. I'm only in town for six more months."

"I'm sorry. This is definitely a case of *it's me and not you.*"

He picked up his wine and guzzled it down before standing and extending his hand. "I appreciate you giving me your time. And thanks for the pinot."

We shook. "It was nice to meet you, Declan."

After I walked him out, I shut the door and leaned back against it. What a shame; he really seemed like a nice guy and the best candidate I'd met *by a mile.* I was just about to go wallow in another glass of alcohol when there was a knock at my door. Checking the peephole before opening, I found Declan standing there.

"I forgot something important," he said.

"Oh? What's that?"

He took out his wallet and produced a photo of a nun. "This is my sister Catherine, and it's not a costume from Halloween. She's a legit nun. How bad can a person be if his sister is a nun?"

I laughed. "Is this the sister who dunked your head in the toilet?"

He grinned. "It is, actually."

"Well, I'm not sure there's a direct correlation between your sister deciding to dedicate her life to the church and you being a good person. Though, even if I take your word for it, it still doesn't change my answer."

Declan's shoulders drooped. "Had to try. She tells me her being a nun won't get me into heaven. Thought maybe it was good for *something*."

"Goodbye, Declan."

"Later, Mollz."

. . .

"So...how's the roommate search going?" Emma poured a cup of coffee and sat down at the small table in our break room.

I sighed. "Why is it so hard to find a normal person these days? I've interviewed more than a dozen people, and not one suitable candidate."

"Did you post an ad on the employee bulletin board, like I suggested?"

I shook my head. "I don't want another nurse or tech. It makes it weird at work if things don't work out."

"Maybe Dr. Dandy will apply." She wiggled her eyebrows. "I heard he's sleeping on Dr. Cohen's couch until he finds a place."

That information certainly perked me up. "Really? Will and whatshername broke up?"

"Yup. Lisa in X-ray told me Dr. Cohen told her he's staying with him. Apparently he and the wannabe actress are finito."

"Wow."

Emma smiled. "Yup. And fair warning, my friend... I'm allowing a ten-day grace period for him to grieve the end of a year-long relationship. But after that, I'm going to be up your butt making sure you let the man know you're interested. He's not going to be on the market for long, and you missed your opportunity last time he was single. You can't keep pining for the guy."

Of course she was right. And while I felt elated that Will was back on the market, the thought of coming clean to him about my feelings made me want to throw up. Will Daniels—or as Emma called him, *Dr. Dandy*, because of his last name and uncanny resemblance to a male model named David Gandy—and I had been good friends for four years now. We'd started on the very same day at the hospital and had gone through orientation together. I'd had a boyfriend back then, and he'd been seeing a girl from med school at the time, so even though I'd always thought he was insanely handsome, things didn't bloom until two years ago. And most of the time since then, he'd been seeing one woman or another. Emma was right that the man never seemed to stay single for long.

"He's going to be at happy hour this Friday night," I said. "A few of the crew from CCU are meeting up over at McBride's. I'm curious to hear what he says about the breakup."

"Does he know you're looking for a roommate?"

"I don't think so."

"Well, he needs a place to sleep, and you need a roomie." Emma shrugged. "Timing is everything. Maybe it's fate and he'll move in and take care of *two* of your needs."

"I think your imagination might be getting ahead of itself. Why don't we start by seeing if things are really over with him and whatshername? They've split up a few times, but he always winds up going back."

"Okay. But I have a good feeling about you two."

"Could you possibly have a good feeling about me finding a roommate instead? I just had to pay for another damn ad."

Emma shook her head. "I can't believe you didn't find one decent candidate."

Remembering my last interview, I said, "Actually there was one who would've been perfect—great credit score, neat, cooks, leaves early in the morning, and works long days."

"So why didn't you take her?"

"Because *she* was a *he*."

CHAPTER
TWO

Molly

Interview number fifteen took the cake.

The girl was a professional yodeler and announced that she often had to practice for competitions. She wanted to know whether the room was echoey.

Why couldn't I find anyone quiet? There was no way I wanted to have to listen to that. So as nice as she was, I let her out of the apartment knowing I'd never see her again.

After we said goodbye, I noticed something on the ground outside my door. It was a covered Tupperware container with an envelope taped to the top.

I took it inside and ripped open the envelope.

The note read:

I noticed the room is still listed for rent. Sorry you're not having better luck. In the meantime, enjoy these cupcakes I made. Maybe they'll help relieve some of your stress. If there's anything else I can do—you know,

*like take the room off your hands—you have
my number.
Declan
(Full disclosure, though: I still have a penis.)*

Covering my laugh, I opened the green lid to reveal eight large cupcakes with white frosting. A different word was written on each one. I soon figured out they were meant to create a sentence:

Do. It! Eat. One. And. Thank. Me. Later.

Frustrated, I grabbed the "one" cupcake and took a huge bite off the top. I always ate the tops off cupcakes and left the bottoms. Without the frosting, the cake was dead to me.

I had to admit, it was delicious. The frosting was buttery, and not too sweet. It was creamy, not hardened with sugar.

Did this guy really think he could win my heart—or entry into my apartment—with cupcakes, though?

I laughed to myself and grabbed another one, licking the frosting first before devouring the entire top. They were really delicious. I would've assumed he'd bought them from a bakery were it not for the Tupperware container, and also the fact that the shapes were somewhat imperfect.

I'd seriously lost my mind if was I considering giving this guy a chance because his cupcakes tasted so damn good.

Within ten minutes, I'd eaten the tops off all of the cupcakes except two.

I looked down at the words on top of the ones that were left.

Do. It!

Do it!

Was it a sign that I should give him a chance?

And was I desperate enough to look for wisdom from baked goods?

The answer was yes. Yes, I was.

I let out a long breath, conceding what I knew in my gut: the search was over. Declan Tate was going to win by default. I needed the money. He was the least crazy person to walk in my door. And the truth was, I had *peni-lized* him—punished him for having a penis. I'd thought about that a lot over the past couple of days, and oddly, I'd thought about *him*. His charisma, how he'd made me laugh—there were worse traits in a roommate.

But before I considered this for real, he and I needed to have a discussion, set some ground rules.

I picked up the phone and dialed the number I had for him.

He apparently knew it was me.

"Hey, Mollz! How's it go—"

"Okay. You can have it," I blurted.

"Seriously?"

"Those cupcakes were so damn good. You won me over, which was obviously your intent."

"Cupcakes plural? Did you have more than one?"

"No comment."

He laughed and spoke to himself, "Take note, Declan. The way to the new roomie's heart is through her stomach."

Roomie.

I sighed.

What am I doing?

He must have sensed my frustration. "Don't be so down about it, Mollz. It'll be fun, and like I said, you're barely even gonna have to see me. Our schedules work out perfectly for avoidance."

"When do you expect to move in?"

"You tell me. I can leave my buddy's place this afternoon and be there by five. He's eager to have his privacy back anyway—something about not wanting me in the room when he fucks his girlfriend. Can you believe that?" He laughed. "Anyway, do you have to work tonight?"

Tonight? That seemed so soon, but honestly, I might as well just get it over with.

"Actually, no. Tonight is my night off. I'm not working the next couple of days."

"Perfect then. I'll pack up my stuff and come on by."

I grabbed the "Do" cupcake and took a bite. "Great," I said with my mouth full.

• • •

A few hours later, there was a knock at the door.

When I opened, I was greeted by Declan's blinding set of gleaming teeth.

"Howdy, roomie."

I moved out of the way, allowing him to enter. "Hey."

A whiff of his scent floated by me. *Amazing.* I couldn't say I minded the idea of my apartment becoming saturated with whatever cologne he wore. The vibe in my place was about to be bombarded with masculine energy.

The bag on his arm dropped to the floor with a thud. He looked around before wheeling his suitcase to a corner of the room. Then he walked back toward me and caught me off guard when he reached for my face.

I flinched as he swiped his finger along the corner of my mouth. It grazed my bottom lip, giving me goose bumps.

"You had some frosting there."

I touched the same spot. "Oh."

A few minutes before he arrived, I'd demolished the "It!" cupcake top—the last one. All that was left now were eight stumps of naked cake.

He examined my face. "You okay?"

"Yeah. I'm fine," I said, feeling flushed.

I wasn't sure if all the sugar was going to my head or what, but I was more on edge than I thought I'd be.

"Stop freaking out about me being here." He chuckled. "I take it you've never lived with a guy before?"

"You'd be correct. My parents divorced when I was sixteen. So, after my father left, it was just my mother, me, and my sister, Lauren."

"Well, I promise, I don't bite."

I swallowed, unnerved by the fact that he was so attractive. Almost *too* attractive. I would never want to be with a guy like that. Deep down, he was probably full of himself, even if he didn't show it. There was no way he didn't know he was good-looking.

"We have to set some ground rules, okay?"

He straightened his posture and nodded once in an exaggerated manner. "Shoot."

"This should go without saying, but what's mine is mine and what's yours is yours. I don't share my personal items, like toiletries or food."

"Got it. But it should work both ways. Like...if I happen to cook up something delicious and you partake, you'll let me have something in return."

My brows furrowed. "In return? What exactly are you insinuating?"

His eyes widened. "Not what your dirty little mind is venturing to right now. We already established that I'm into someone else, remember? I just meant, you know, like, if you eat my food, you owe me something of equivalent value. Don't dish it if you can't take it kind of thing."

I squinted. "What makes you think I'm going to eat your food?"

"You might not. But you seemed to like the cupcakes, so..."

He had a point. But the cupcakes were a gift. I supposed I could agree to his stipulation and just vow that I wouldn't ever touch his food. *Pfft!* I didn't need his food.

"Okay." I shrugged. "Fine. It works both ways."

He leaned against the small island in the center of my kitchen. "What other rules you got for me?"

"You can do whatever you want when I'm not here, but no bringing people into the apartment when I'm sleeping. Our schedules should make that pretty easy since you have three nights a week when I won't be here."

"Fine. Done. Hit me with the rest."

"I like everything nice and organized. So, if you see something arranged a certain way, don't change it."

"You mean like the pastel M&Ms you have in those jars on the counter? Don't mix the pink with the mint-colored ones, that kind of shit?"

"I only like certain-colored M&Ms, so I order them online. But yes...don't mess with anything I might have arranged a certain way."

"Okay." He chuckled. "You're a trip, you know that?"

18

"Everyone has their quirks. Mine include liking color-coordinated candy and a neat and organized apartment. So sue me. I like what I like."

"What kind of a man does a woman who likes all pink M&Ms in one jar go for? A dude who wears pink Lacoste shirts and loafers?"

"No. I like a man who's got a good head on his shoulders and who's—"

"Dull and pretentious as fuck?"

"No," I answered defensively.

"I'm kidding, Molly. Just messing with you."

Letting out a long breath, I said, "I know."

"You're single?" he asked.

"Yes. But...hopefully not for long."

"Oh yeah? What's going on there? Who's the lucky guy?"

Ugh. Why did I even say that? Now I have to explain it.

Might as well admit to my crush on Dr. Daniels. That way Declan would know I was completely unaffected by his charms.

"There's this doctor I work with. I've had a crush on him for some time, and he just became single. I'm actually meeting him and a bunch of other people for happy hour tomorrow night. So, I'm hopeful something will develop there."

He smiled. "Good for you. Going for it."

Feeling embarrassed, I cleared my throat. "What about you? What's the deal with this girl you said you're into?"

"Well, she's a co-worker, too, actually. We work for the same advertising firm. We're both from California, where the company is based, but we came to Chicago to

19

work on a campaign for a major client out here. That's why I'm only in town for six months. She and I work on the account together."

"Does she know you like her?"

"That's the thing. She's sort of dating this douchebag back home. He did *not* want her to come to Chicago. Things are always up and down with them. So, I'm hoping one of these days they go all the way down, and I can move in for the kill. I wouldn't be a dick and try to make a move when she technically has a boyfriend. So, at the moment, I'm just waiting in the wings."

"Okay, but does she know you like her?"

"I don't know. I bet she suspects, though. We're friends...for now. But I want more. Not only because she's gorgeous, but she's intelligent and sweet, too. The whole package. And I do think we're compatible."

The hint of jealousy I felt was unnerving. I think it was more just wishing someone felt that way about *me*. It certainly *wasn't* because of an attraction to Declan. He was good-looking and all, but not my type.

"What's her name?"

"Julia."

"Pretty name."

"What about Hot Doctor?"

Smiling shyly, I answered, "Will."

"What kind of doctor?"

"He's an OB-GYN."

"Oh, that's right. You said you work in a maternity ward. Makes sense. At least the whiny babies you deal with are cute—unlike my clients." He pretended to reach for my M&M jar, then backed his hand away with an impish smile. "Any other rules, Molly?"

"Well, obvious stuff, like no walking around naked."

He wriggled his brows. "Worried you might get turned on?"

"No." I looked down at my feet. "It's just not appropriate."

"Same goes for you, then. But that's just to be fair." He lowered his voice. "Between you and me, I'm not gonna complain if you do."

I rolled my eyes. "I thought you only had eyes for one woman?"

"I'm smitten, not dead, Mollz." He grinned. "If it happens, I'm probably gonna sneak a look. But I won't say anything or be creepy."

My cheeks felt hot as I changed the subject. "Is your sister really a nun?"

He chuckled. "Yes."

"That's so...unique."

"Why? Because her brother is the devilish antithesis of holy?" He flashed a mischievous grin.

"Well, that, plus you don't hear about too many people becoming nuns nowadays."

"Catherine was always different from the rest of my sisters, always looking for a greater purpose. But it was pretty shocking when she told us."

"Are your parents religious?"

"They're Catholic and go to church every Sunday, but they're not obsessed with religion or anything. My mother cried when Catherine told her she was joining the convent. She'd always envisioned a different future for her. But you know, in the end, people are gonna do what they want. And she's happy."

"Good for her."

"Funny how kids can grow up together and all be so different. Catherine's living in a convent, praying, doing good deeds, and most nights I'm fucking around on the Internet or watching Hulu. Same parents. What happened?"

"You seem pretty successful. I'm sure they're proud."

"They'd like me to settle down at some point, but yeah, they haven't disowned me yet." He changed the subject. "So what's the game plan for tomorrow night?"

"What do you mean?"

"Going in for the kill with Dr. Dickalicious. What's your strategy?"

Why did I tell him about Will? "Am I supposed to have a plan?"

"Well, you want him to know you like him, right?"

"Yes. But I don't want to be too forward. He just got out of a relationship. By the same token, guys like him don't stay single for very long."

"Okay, so you know you need to kill him with unattainability."

"What does that mean?"

"Everything with men is about reverse psychology. If we think we can't have something, we want it ten times more. We're like toddlers that way."

"Is that why you're so into Julia—because she's taken?"

He scratched his chin. "On a subconscious level, that could be fueling the fire. It's not even close to the main reasons I like her, though."

"What are you suggesting I do?" My tone was dismissive, but a part of me actually *did* want to hear what he had to say. It wasn't often I got a man's perspective on such things.

"Don't show him you like him. Show him *why* he should like *you*."

My ears perked up. "And that consists of doing what?"

"Looking fucking hot as hell, which I know you can pull off easily. Inserting yourself into conversations with everyone nearby but him—show him what he's missing. Then when he inevitably comes around, talk to him, but then move your attention on to someone else. That will leave him hanging and wanting more. We love a good chase."

"Doesn't that risk making it look like I don't like him?"

"Trust me. If he wants you, he's going to make a move at some point. The more disinterested you seem, the harder his dick will get."

"Well, thanks for that visual, I think."

"You're welcome. You'll find that I'm pretty blunt and don't like to beat around the bush." He looked around. "Are we done with roomie rules?"

"Yes. I think so—until I think of something I've forgotten."

"Good." He walked over to his gym bag and opened it, taking out a couple of bottles of Gatorade. "Mind if I throw these in the fridge?"

"Not at all."

After he placed his drinks in the refrigerator, he noticed the Tupperware container and opened it.

"Damn. I guess you liked them?"

"I got a little carried away. They were really good."

"Is that another one of your quirks—decapitating cupcakes evenly?"

"The frosting is my favorite part."

"You won't eat the bottoms now?"

"Not without frosting, no."

"Well, see? I knew we were a good match. I hate the frosting. I normally eat around it. Between this and our mutual affinity for white wine, I'd say this is gonna work out." He grinned. "Are you a muffin-top person, too?"

"Yes."

"Bingo. See? I'm a bottom." He rolled his eyes. "Okay, yeah, that didn't come out right, but you know what I mean."

"You're nuts." I shook my head, unable to contain my smile. "Thank you again for making the cupcakes, though. That was very thoughtful."

"Well, obviously you know I had an ulterior motive."

"One that clearly paid off."

His eyes wandered in the direction of the bedrooms. "Mind if go unpack?"

"Go right ahead."

"Sweet. Lead the way."

Declan rolled his suitcase as he followed me to his new room.

I ventured into my own room to give him some privacy, but felt unable to concentrate on anything other than the fact that he was here.

As I listened to the sound of Declan humming along to the tunes he played on his phone while he unpacked, I couldn't help but smile. I'd been dreading having to get a new roommate, losing sleep over it. But for the first time in a long time, I felt like I was going to get a good night's rest.

He startled me when he popped his head into my room. "Okay to hang my toothbrush next to yours?"

"Did I give you the impression that it wouldn't be?"

"You said what's yours is yours. So I didn't know if that extended to the toothbrush holder."

24

"I'm sorry if I came off a little harsh at first. I just need to get used to this. That's all. I'm already feeling better about you being here."

"Good." He suddenly made himself comfortable on the end of my bed, lying flat on his back as he looked up at the ceiling. The sight of his long body splayed across my bed was...something else.

He rested his hands behind his head and turned to me. "You said tomorrow's your day off, right?"

"Yeah."

"You got eggs and bread and stuff?"

"Yes. Though I think they're going to expire soon."

"Cool. I'll make breakfast for us in the morning—a little inaugural celebration. No strings. You won't owe me anything." He winked. "For this one."

"You're not gonna hear me complain about someone making breakfast for me. Ever."

"But I'm warning you, I like to play music when I cook, shake my ass around to the beat. Sing a little. Might use a spatula for a microphone. You okay with a little kitchen karaoke?"

"As long as I'm awake and you're clothed, go for it."

He hopped off my bed, spun around like freaking Michael Jackson, and disappeared down the hall.

This is going to be a long six months.

CHAPTER THREE

Molly

The next morning, I woke to the smell of bacon.

After I washed my face and brushed my teeth, I let my nose lead the way to the kitchen. Declan stood at the stove singing Darius Rucker's "Wagon Wheel." He had earbuds in, so he didn't immediately hear me walk out. It gave me a chance to listen to his voice, which was...*pretty damn bad*. For some reason, that made me smile. A man who looked the way he did and was blessed with so much charisma had to have some flaws. Plus, I liked the fact that he didn't seem to care that he couldn't carry a tune.

I walked straight to the coffee pot, opened the cabinet above it, and grabbed a mug. Declan took out one earbud and smiled.

"Morning, roomie. I hope I didn't wake you with my singing?"

I wasn't generally a morning person—mostly because I worked the night shift—so I had a hard time falling asleep before two in the morning on my days off. Nevertheless, I felt chipper today.

"You didn't." I poured coffee and raised my mug to my lips. "And is that what that sound was? You were singing? I thought maybe someone was strangling a cat."

Declan squinted. "Are you trying to tell me I don't have a good voice?"

"I can't possibly be the first to break that news."

He smiled like I'd given him a compliment instead of insulting him and nodded his chin toward my mug. "You drink your coffee black. Me too. Told you we were meant to be roommates."

I chuckled and stepped closer to the stove. Declan had three burners going, including the one that hadn't worked since I'd moved in. "How did you get the left front burner to turn on?"

"You had a clog. I took it apart and used a toothpick to clean out some dried grease stuck in the burner holes."

"Oh. Wow. Well, thanks."

"Glad to be of service. Now why don't you take a seat? Breakfast is almost ready."

A few minutes later, Declan placed a perfectly formed omelet, bacon, and hash browns in front of me, along with a glass of orange juice.

"This looks amazing. Because of my schedule, I don't tend to eat a lot of breakfast. If I'm hungry after I get off work, I usually just grab a yogurt or something. I don't sleep well on a full stomach. But this is actually my favorite type of meal. I prefer breakfast foods to most dinners. It's probably the thing I miss most about a normal morning schedule."

Declan sat down and cut into his omelet. "Why do you have to miss it? Just make breakfast for dinner, before you go to work."

I wrinkled my nose. "I couldn't do that."

"Why not?"

"I don't know...because breakfast is morning food."

"Who says?"

"Umm...everyone?"

"Let me get this straight. Breakfast is your favorite food, but you don't eat it because traditionally people eat it in the morning and you're usually sleeping during that time."

"You're making it sound silly. But it makes sense."

He perked a brow. "To whom?"

I laughed. "To me."

Declan tsked. "*Molly, Molly, Molly*. Not everything needs to have a specific time or place. It's a good thing I'm here. You need my help."

"Oh I do? Exactly what kind of help is it that I need?"

"You need to loosen up a little."

We'd been joking around until now, but his comment hit a nerve. My last boyfriend had called me uptight on more than one occasion. So I felt a bit defensive. "I don't think you know me well enough to make that type of judgment. I'll have you know, I'm not uptight."

Declan tilted his head. "No?"

"No."

"Alright, Molly. Whatever you say..."

Now he was just pacifying me. "Don't say *alright, Molly*. You're making me sound rigid. But I'm not. I didn't say I *wouldn't* eat breakfast at night if the opportunity presented itself. It just hasn't. That's all."

"Okay. Sorry if I upset you."

I'd effectively killed the mood. What had started as a fun morning had now turned into breakfast in silence. By the time we were done eating, I felt like a giant ass.

"That was really delicious. I'm sorry I snapped at you."

Declan forced a smile. "It's fine."

"No, it's not. You went to all this trouble, and I jumped down your throat. It won't happen again."

He smirked. "Oh yes it will. I tend to say things that should probably be kept to myself. So it most definitely will be happening again."

I chuckled. "Okay. Well, maybe you can work on that, and I'll work on not snapping at you so easily."

"Sounds good, Mollz. You have any plans for today? You're off, right?"

I picked up my plate and started to clear the table. "Yeah, I'm off. I worked three twelve-hour shifts in a row, so now I'm off for a couple of days. Though I don't have any big plans really. Today I'm going to go food shopping and to the dry cleaner. And then later I'm meeting some friends from work at happy hour. I mentioned it last night."

"That's right. Tonight you're seeing Doc in the Box."

"Do you mean Will? He works at the hospital with me, not one of those roadside urgent-care places."

"Oh, I know. But he's an OB, right?"

"Yes...but.... *Ohh*, doc *in the box*." I chuckled. "Cute."

Declan and I cleaned up the kitchen together. I loaded the dishwasher while he put away all of the things he'd used to cook, cleaned the kitchen table, and wiped down the stovetop. When we were both done, I dried my hands on a towel before blotting at my wet shirt. The damn kitchen faucet had a leak that sprayed whenever the water was turned on more than a trickle. I'd had a piece of electrical tape wrapped around the neck as a temporary fix, but it must've fallen off.

Tossing the dishtowel on the counter, I looked up and found Declan staring. I quickly realized why. Last night I'd slept in a white T-shirt and no bra, and now the top half of my shirt was completely see-through. Not only that, the wetness was cold against my skin, so my nipples were fully erect, practically piercing through my invisible shirt.

Folding my arms, I attempted to cover up. "The... uh...water faucet sprays a bit."

Declan's eyes lifted to meet mine. He swallowed and cleared his throat before looking away. "I'll take care of it today."

"Oh. It's okay. It's been that way for a while. I can just call the super again. You don't have to fix it."

He grumbled. "Yeah, I do. I *absolutely* freaking do."

• • •

Later that evening, I was a little disappointed that Declan hadn't been home before I left for happy hour. I'd gotten myself more done-up than usual, and could've used his bluntness to find out if I looked like I was trying too hard. I mean, *I was*, but I didn't want it to look that way.

My four outfit changes had made me late, so most people were already at McBride's when I arrived. Noticeably absent was *whatshername*, who usually came to happy hour to hang on Will's arm. Feeling unusually nervous, I walked straight to the bar and stood next to Daisy, a new physician's assistant. I'd met her a few times on the unit, but this was the first time she'd come to one of our twice-a-month meetups.

"Hey," I said. "I'm glad you came."

"Hey, Molly." She did a quick sweep over my outfit. "I love that green on you. You look so different without scrubs and a ponytail."

I smiled, now glad I'd made that last wardrobe change and sprung for a professional blowout this afternoon. The emerald color of my silk blouse was a bit bold for me, especially against my pale skin and dark hair. But I'd paired it with dark jeans and simple wedges to try to keep it casual. "Thank you. You look really nice, too."

The bartender walked over and set down a napkin in front of me. "Hey, Molly. How's it going? What can I get for you today?"

"Hey, Patrick. I'll have a Stoli vanilla and ginger ale, please."

He nodded. "You got it. Coming right up."

"Mmm..." Daisy said. "That's the drink that tastes like a cream soda, isn't it?"

"It is. You want one?"

She looked at the bottle of beer in her hand, which was almost empty. "Sure. Why not?"

I looked at the bartender. "Can you make that two? And hers is on me."

"You want to start a tab?"

"Yes, please."

After Patrick walked away to make our drinks, Daisy said, "You didn't have to do that. But thank you."

I smiled. "No problem. So tell me how you like being at Chicago General? How long has it been now? Has to be almost a month already, right?"

She nodded. "Five weeks, actually. I really like it. Not that I have too much to compare it to. This is my first job after graduating. Some of the doctors can be really intimidating."

"You mean like Dr. Benton?"

Daisy grimaced. "Especially *Dr. Benton*. God, that man makes me so nervous. He walks into a room and I start to freeze up."

"I'll tell you a little secret about him that might help."

"What?"

I leaned in. "Smile a lot. It freaks him out."

She chuckled. "Are you serious?"

"Yup. Anything he asks you, just respond wearing a giant smile. It's like it disarms him or something. I have a theory that he barks at everyone so they won't be able to smile, because smiles are kryptonite to him."

"Wow. Okay. I'll try it. That's really great to know. What else you got?"

"Have you met Dr. Arlington?"

"Yeah. He's pretty grumpy, too."

"He'll try to dump his interns on you and take off for hours if you let him."

Daisy's eyes widened. "He did that to me the other day. Told me to show them the ropes. I had no idea what to do with four interns. They've been at General longer than I have. They would've been better off showing *me* the ropes."

"Yup. So next time he attempts to leave you with them, you say '*Actually, I need to go see Edith in the nursing office.*'"

"Even if I don't need to go see her?"

I nodded. "Yup. He's terrified of Edith."

"He is? But she's so tiny and sweet."

I pointed at Daisy. "Until you piss her off. Then she's pretty damn scary. Even the threat of Edith will scare Dr. Arlington. She once laid into him for dumping his interns, and now if you just mention her name, he backs off."

She laughed, probably assuming I was exaggerating, but I wasn't. We worked with a real cast of characters. Patrick, the bartender, walked over and delivered our drinks. While we sipped, the two of us looked around at the group. Tonight was a nice turnout.

Daisy lifted her chin and pointed to where Will was talking to an anesthesiologist at the far end of the bar. "What about Dr. Daniels? What's his story?"

"Will's one of the good ones. He's pretty nice to everyone. You won't have any problems with him."

She bit her bottom lip. "I meant *what's his story*. Is he...single?"

Oh. *Ugh.* Shit. "Umm... I'm not sure. He's off and on with someone. Are you...interested?"

Daisy sipped her drink with a coy smile. "He's really good-looking."

Yeah, he is. I shrugged. And of course, just then, he had to walk over to us.

He kissed my cheek. "Hey, Molly. I didn't see you come in."

Daisy straightened her posture.

"I just got here," I said.

He nodded and turned his attention to the woman next to me. "It's Daisy, right?"

She lit up with a megawatt smile. "It is. It's nice to see you, Dr. Daniels."

"Please, call me Will."

"Alright, Will. You know, the other day I happened to notice you getting into your car in the parking lot. You have a Northwestern alum sticker. Is that where you went?"

"It is."

"Me too." She made a fist and pumped it into the air. "Go Wildcats."

"Oh yeah? I'm a huge fan. I still keep season tickets."

Daisy pouted. "I'm so jealous. I couldn't afford them this year. I was a cheerleader for four years, and I miss the excitement of game days."

Ugh.

Will sipped his beer. "You'll have to come along for a game then sometime."

Her pout curved to a smile. "I'd love that."

Double ugh.

Little Miss New Girl just got herself invited to a day alone with Will in thirty seconds, right in front of me. I really sucked at flirting.

The two of them slipped into a conversation about some new quarterback for the upcoming football season, and I was left attempting to smile at appropriate times while feeling like my heart was being ripped out. Normally, I wasn't one to take out my cell phone when I was with people, but when it buzzed in my pocket, I decided to make an exception.

I was surprised to find Declan's name on my screen.

Declan: How's it going? Are you playing hard to get?

I sighed and typed back.

Molly: Apparently easy to get is more Will's style. A woman basically just made a date with him right in front of me.

The dots on my phone jumped around for a minute, then stopped, then started up again. Eventually, my phone rang in my hand. Declan's named flashed with an incoming call.

Excusing myself from the conversation I really wasn't part of anymore, I stepped away from the bar to answer.

"Hey."

"I thought this might warrant an actual conversation. What happened?"

I shook my head. "A new PA basically just told me she has the hots for Will, and when he walked over to say hello, she got herself invited to a football game within thirty seconds."

"Okay. Are they still talking?"

I glanced back at the bar to find Daisy flipping her hair and giggling. Frowning, I said, "Yes."

"What are you wearing?"

I looked down. "A green silk blouse and jeans."

"Nice," he said. "I don't even have to see it to know you look phenomenal in green with your hair and skin color. Are the jeans tight?"

"Sort of."

"Heels?"

"I have wedges on."

"Okay, so you're looking smokin' hot. This is good... very good. Here's what I want you to do. Is it warm in the bar?"

"Umm...it's comfortable, I guess."

"Alright. Well, you're warm. Go back to the conversation, and while Dr. Dickalicious is talking to—what's this woman's name?"

"Daisy."

He scoffed. "Dumb name. Anyway, go back to this conversation, and while he's talking to Violet, lift the back of your hair and sort of fan it up and down like you're warm. Then order a glass of ice water from the bar. When the bartender brings you the water, accidentally spill it on your shirt."

"What? *No.* Why the heck would I do that?"

"Just trust me and do it."

"Half of my closet is on my bed because I struggled to find exactly the right outfit to wear tonight, and you want me to ruin it?"

"You won't be ruining it. But let me ask you something else—how big is your purse?"

I looked down at my hand holding it. "I don't know, about twelve inches long by ten inches tall, maybe. Why?"

"Okay, perfect. So before you go get your water, make a quick trip to the ladies' room and slip off your bra. You are wearing one, right?"

"Have you been drinking, Declan?"

"No. But I might hit that bottle of wine you have open in the refrigerator when we hang up if you don't listen to me."

"Declan, I am not taking off my bra and intentionally spilling a glass of water on myself."

"Take a chill pill, Mollz. It's no big deal. You want this guy to notice you in a new way—that will definitely get him to take notice. Trust me, he'll forget all about Rose."

"Daisy."

"Whatever. Now, are you going to take the horse by the reins or what? This is the way to do it."

"I thought the way to do it was to play hard to get."

"I'm calling an audible."

"A what?"

"It's a football term. One that Little Miss Marigold who's going to the game with your doc probably knows. But that's unimportant now. Just trust me on this."

I shook my head. "I don't think so, Declan. That's not the way I want to be noticed."

"Alright. But I'm telling you...it would work."

"Goodbye, Declan."

"Later, Mollz."

CHAPTER FOUR

Molly

As the evening wore on, Will and Daisy continued to reminisce about Northwestern, and I wanted to vomit.

"Did you ever get to paint the rock?" she asked.

"Yeah, actually, my fraternity brothers and I did one night. We painted it pink for breast cancer awareness because of my buddy's mother. We stayed up all night guarding it."

"That's so sweet," she gushed.

I cleared my throat. "What's the rock?"

Will smiled. "It's a Northwestern tradition. It dates back to the forties or fifties, I believe. There's this giant rock in the center of campus. Students paint it to advertise causes or post info on events. Then they have to guard it for as long as they can to keep someone else from painting over it."

"Ah. Very cool." I slurped the last of my drink.

Daisy continued to twirl her hair and flirt with Will.

I couldn't take it anymore, so I got up. "Excuse me," I said before walking to the bathroom. Once inside, I looked at myself in the mirror, feeling defeated.

It felt like I was close to losing my only chance. There was a very short window for nabbing a guy like Will Daniels. He was a magnet for all single women around him. But I'd be damned if I was going to lose him to the newbie physician's assistant. I'd put in my time—time spent flirting and obsessing over this man. Maybe I would lose, but it wasn't going to be to someone who'd been here a matter of minutes and hadn't earned her stripes.

I thought about Declan's suggestion. The small amount of alcohol I'd consumed was already getting to me, and I concluded that desperate times called for desperate measures. Reaching under my blouse, I unsnapped my bra and pulled it out. Then I stuffed it into my purse. The cold air in the bathroom immediately made my nipples perk up. It was too soon to flaunt them, so I turned on the hand dryer, applying heat to my chest.

This would be a miracle if it worked. Daisy had Will so enraptured in nostalgia, I wasn't sure anything could snap him out of it. I positioned my hair over my breasts so that my braless state wasn't so obvious yet.

When I ventured back out to the bar, more people from work had shown up. Will was now mingling with some of our other co-workers, with Daisy still glued to his side as she laughed at everything he said.

Burning with jealousy, I asked, "Is it just me or is it hot in here?"

It seemed my theatrical presentation had begun. I raised my hand to call the bartender and ordered a water. After sipping, I set it in front of me and waited for the perfect moment to go in for the kill.

Daisy excused herself and walked toward the bathroom. A minute later, I slid my arm in front of the glass and knocked it over my chest, pretending of course that it was an unfortunate accident.

Feigning shock, I said, "Oh no. I'm such a klutz!"

I looked down at myself. *Jesus*. The thin silk of my shirt was much more susceptible to the water than I'd anticipated. My first inclination was to be mortified—mostly at my own behavior.

Until...

Until Will's eyes nearly popped out of their sockets as they wandered down my chest.

He rushed over and handed me a napkin. "Here you go, Molly."

"Thank you," I said, wiping myself down in sloppy strokes, because of course my intent wasn't to *actually* do the job appropriately.

After Will stole one more peek, his eyes lifted and lingered on mine.

"It's nice to see you out again with us. The past couple of times you've skipped." He smiled.

Slowing the strokes over my chest, I said, "I'm surprised you were keeping track."

"I'm always aware when you're around—at work or otherwise."

Holy shit. Is it really this easy? Declan is a freaking genius!

By the time Daisy returned from the bathroom, Will and I were already immersed in conversation. He spent the next half hour at my side. Then I remembered one of Declan's earlier pieces of advice.

"The more disinterested you seem, the harder his dick will get."

It was a risk, and it felt completely unnatural to push myself away when I had finally hooked him, but I said, "Excuse me."

"Of course," Will said, seeming caught off guard by my stopping the conversation.

I then proceeded to fetch myself another drink and mingle with some of my other co-workers. Daisy moved in on Will again, but oddly, I kept noticing his eyes veering in *my* direction. Okay, maybe it was the fact that my nipples were still protruding, but nevertheless, his attention begged to be on *me*, not on Daisy.

In another bold move, I downed the last of my drink. Then, loud enough for Will to hear, I announced, "Well, it's been nice, peeps, but I have to leave."

Will suddenly put his beer down, seeming disappointed. "Going so soon, Molly?"

"Yes. I have...plans."

"A date?"

I paused. "Something like that."

"Okay." He nodded. Then he looked at me for a moment before leaning in to my ear. "Listen, I'd love to have coffee sometime. Maybe the next time our shifts collide?"

I acted cool. "Sure...maybe."

Maybe?

As if.

Heck yeah!

"Good. Okay. Have a good night, Molly."

"You, too," I said before strutting out of there, feeling on top of the freaking world.

• • •

I couldn't wait to get home and tell Declan his little plan had actually worked.

To my surprise, when I opened the door to my apartment, Declan was in the living room, but he wasn't alone. A gorgeous woman with bright auburn hair was sitting on the armchair across from him. There were white papers splattered atop the coffee table.

Declan stood. "Oh, hey, roomie. I didn't think you'd be back so soon."

"Well, I wasn't planning to be home so early, but I took your advice tonight."

Declan looked down at my still-braless chest. "I can see that."

"Not *just* that. Although, it did work like a charm." I crossed my arms over myself. "Anyway, what I meant was, I remembered what you said about seeming disinterested. I actually left early, told him I had other plans. He asked me to have coffee sometime on my way out. So both of your strategies worked."

"I had no doubt." He turned to the woman. "Sorry to be rude. I should've introduced you. This is my roommate, Molly. And Molly, this is Julia." He turned to me and winked to make sure I knew she was *the* Julia. "Julia and I work together. We have a deadline for our client's latest campaign, so she came by so we could brainstorm."

"It's nice to meet you," Julia said, holding out her hand but staring at my chest.

"Likewise." I shook her hand and looked around, feeling awkward. "Well, don't let me interrupt your work."

42

"It's no interruption," she said.

"Yeah," Declan said. "Pretty sure we were just wrapping up."

When Julia looked down at my chest again, I said, "I'm sure you're wondering why I'm not wearing a bra."

"It's because of me," Declan said.

Her eyes widened. "Really?"

"Don't take that the wrong way," I clarified. "Declan just gave me some advice that was a little daring but brilliant."

I then told Julia about my crush on Will and my experience at happy hour.

"So, it's all thanks to Declan that I now have an informal coffee date with Will."

Julia looked between Declan and me. "Well, you two seem to be getting along really well for two people who just moved in together."

"I have to say, it *is* going pretty well. He's growing on me."

Declan smirked. "She's lying. Her affinity toward me was instant."

"My affinity toward your *cupcakes* was instant."

As she watched us interact, Julia's smile seemed forced. Was she uncomfortable? It made me wonder if perhaps she was jealous of how well Declan and I got along.

I knew how he felt about her, but now I was starting to suspect the feelings were mutual, even though she had a boyfriend.

Julia looked over at my color-coordinated, pastel candy jars. "I've never seen M&Ms so nicely organized."

"Mollz is a bit of a perfectionist."

"I'm really not. As much as I like things a certain way, I'm far from perfect."

"Give me an example," Declan challenged.

"Well...for one, my original plan was to be a doctor, but I never had the guts to go to medical school. Not that there's anything wrong with being a nurse—I'm very proud of what I do—but my fear of failure prevented me from pursuing a bigger dream. So while I may be organized, I'm far from perfect."

His expression softened. "You never told me that."

"Well, seeing as I've only known you a matter of days, that shouldn't be surprising."

He winked. "Feels like longer."

An awkward silence lingered in the air.

Declan clapped his hands together. "Anyway, who's hungry? I could cook something for us. Although Molly can't eat any unless she's willing to pay up."

Julia's eyes widened. "Pay up?"

"Just a little arrangement we have. She thinks she can resist my cuisine. She'll have to owe me something if she gives in to temptation."

"I already ate," I lied. I was actually starving but wouldn't be eating with them for a couple of reasons. One, I didn't want to prove him right, and two, I figured maybe he wanted some privacy with his crush.

"You two have a nice dinner. I'm gonna go to my room and finish binge-watching this show I'm into on Hulu, thanks to my roommate sharing his premium password with me."

"I told you you wouldn't regret letting me move in," he called.

I waved. "It was nice meeting you, Julia."

"Great meeting you, too, Molly."

As I lay in bed watching the show, I listened to Julia laughing as the smell of whatever Declan was cooking wafted through the apartment. It seemed like only a matter of time before she would succumb to his charms.

My emotions were all over the place tonight, ranging from satisfaction over having garnered Will's attention, to a strange discomfort over Julia. I told myself I was jealous of how Declan felt about her, not because of any feelings *I* harbored toward Declan.

• • •

The following day, it was almost noon by the time I rolled out of bed. I never slept that late. My body clock was screwed up in general because of the overnight hours I worked, and I tried to stay up during the day rather than sleep on my days off.

When I went out to the kitchen, there was a note on the counter from Declan.

Good morning (or afternoon, sleepyhead). Went into the office to get some work done. See you later.

Working on a Saturday? That was dedication. Or maybe he was just looking for an excuse to spend more time with Julia. That had to be it.

My stomach growled. I hadn't eaten since yesterday afternoon. Whatever Declan made last night had smelled amazing...

I opened the fridge and saw a glass dish of leftovers staring me in the face. There was a sticky note attached to the top.

Best mushroom risotto I ever made. Might even be worth the consequences. You decide.

I shook my head and laughed. Was it strange that I almost wanted to eat it just to see what his consequences were?

Unwrapping the cellophane, I took a whiff. It smelled garlicky and delicious with lots of herbs and spices. *Maybe just a small bite.* I scooped some onto a plate and popped it into the microwave.

Taking the leftovers back to the couch, I crossed my legs and shoveled a giant bite into my mouth.

Damn you and your food, Declan.

CHAPTER FIVE

Declan

Julia and I sat in the empty conference room. We'd spent the morning practicing our pitch for a new campaign. We were taking a break, enjoying some coffee from the kitchen.

She stirred some cream into her cup. "Your roommate seems to like you."

"What makes you say that?"

"I can just tell."

"We're friends, yup. We get along well."

"Okay, but I mean I think she might *like* you more than you think."

"Did you not hear her say she's into that doctor from work?"

"Well, yeah, I mean, that's what she says...but I think she also might like *you*. I mean, why wouldn't she? You're a catch."

Well, well, well...

In all the time Julia and I had been friends and co-workers, she'd never come close to complimenting me like that. She'd also never exhibited anything that remotely resembled jealousy. Yet given the redness of her cheeks, if I didn't know better, I would've thought she was jealous. *Well, I'll be fucking damned.* Maybe there was a chance for me after all.

"She also could have totally put her bra back on before she came home," Julia added. "I think it was an excuse to flaunt her tits around you, to be honest."

It was hard not to show my amusement.

I decided to push the envelope. "Well, she does have a nice figure. I'll give her that." I shrugged. "I don't know, maybe she *is* into me. You could be right."

Then the craziest thing happened.

"What are you doing tonight?" Julia asked.

"No plans. Why?"

"When we're done here, we should grab some dinner."

Okay, then.

"Yeah. Sounds good."

Julia almost never initiated hanging out with me outside of work. It was always me suggesting it. *Holy shit.* Maybe I *was* onto something. I'd been giving Molly advice on how to get Dr. Dickalicious to like her—by seeming disinterested. But maybe it was even more powerful to seem interested in someone else.

• • •

That night, I opened the refrigerator to find that my roommate had polished off the majority of the leftovers. Molly was lying on the couch reading when I decided to taunt her.

"You bad girl, Mollz. I see you couldn't resist my risotto."

She closed her book and sat up. "Actually, I could. But I chose not to. I was also curious as to what the punishment might be. How do I know if resisting your cuisine is worth it if I don't know what the consequences are?"

I chuckled. I didn't know what the consequences were myself.

"I'll come up with something. The penalty will be posted on your door tonight."

"Ah, something to look forward to. You said your grandmother taught you to cook? Is your mom a good cook, too?"

I wasn't about to explain the complicated story of my family dynamic, or how my mother wasn't always enough in her right mind to care for her kids. Instead, I shrugged. "Everyone took turns cooking in my house. But I mostly learned from my grandmother." Opening a bottle of Gatorade, I changed the subject. "So, how is everything going? Did you hear anything from Hot Doc?"

"No. And unfortunately, I found out from my friend that Will got pretty cozy with Daisy again after I left the bar."

"Yeah, but that's only because you weren't there."

"I guess I'll have a better gauge as to where things stand at work this week. He said he wanted to grab coffee. Let's see if he pursues it."

"Daffodil won't stand a chance once you get in the game again."

"Let's hope."

"So...something interesting happened on my end," I began, eager to share my experience today.

"What?"

"Julia and I were working at the office, and she started randomly talking about you. I sensed a little jealousy."

"Really? It's funny you say that, because I thought I sensed the same last night. What did she say?"

"She said she thinks you like me." I flashed a cocky grin. "I mean, we both know you do. But it was interesting that she picked up on it." I winked. "I'm kidding. Well, not about her *thinking* you like me. The hint of jealousy I sensed from her got the wheels turning in my head."

"About what?"

"It made me realize the only thing better than showing disinterest as a strategy might be the threat of someone else."

"Interesting. Well, glad I could be of help."

"Your nipples helped more than anything, I think. Thank them for me."

Molly blushed. "Wait—she thinks I did that for *you*? But I told her about Will."

"Yeah, but she said you could have put a bra on before you came home. She felt like you were flaunting them."

"She thinks I'm a slut. Great. I didn't think to put my bra on because I was coming straight home and thought you'd be out."

"Well, *you* know that, and *I* know that, but *she* doesn't. So, let her think it. Let her think I like looking at you, too. That may be what finally works." *And I do like looking at you, but that's not the point here.*

Later, after Molly had gone to sleep, I left a sticky note on her door.

That risotto got you in a quandary, because now you must do my laundry. I'll have a basket ready by tomorrow evening. ;-)

• • •

Molly and I didn't cross paths again until she called me from her shift the next day. I'd been in the middle of a late-night workout in my room and stopped to talk to her.

"What's up, Mollz?"

"Seriously? Your laundry?"

I wiped my forehead with a towel. "I'm in the middle of pumping iron as we speak. Lots of sweatiness for you to wash."

"Oh joy."

"I'm excited because I bet you'll color coordinate my underwear." When she fell silent, I said, "Hey, I might as well milk it. Is that why you called? To complain about my punishment?"

"No, actually, I wanted to tell you something interesting."

I took a swig of water. "I'm always up for that."

"Remember when you were telling me Julia seemed jealous when she was talking about me?"

"Yeah?"

"Well, I think you're on to something. Will and I just had coffee together during our break. He asked me what was new, and I told him all about my new roommate. I started raving about you, as if you were God's gift to women."

"So it wasn't much of a stretch. Okay. Go on."

"Whatever." She laughed. "Anyway...his mood seemed to change as I was going on about you. He seemed interested in our relationship."

"Did he ask you out?"

"No. But I'm wondering if maybe he needs something to light a fire under his ass. Maybe I need to make him believe I *am* interested in you."

I scratched my chin. *This could work. Better yet...*

"Maybe I could visit you at the hospital. If he saw me, he'd be even more threatened."

"Conceited much?"

"Just trying to help."

"Actually..." she said. "I have a better idea. Why don't you come to the next happy hour?"

"I could totally swing that. But on one condition."

"Why are there always conditions with you?"

"This one is only fair."

"What is it?"

"You do the same for me. I haven't figured out the logistics, but I want to make Julia jealous. I think we should pretend there's something happening between us."

After a brief pause, she said, "Okay, but we have to figure out what this entails."

Wow. I was a little surprised she was going for it. She must be really hard up for Willy Dick.

"It entails whatever it takes to make the other person jealous," I said. "If we're supposed to be seeing each other, that means—"

"We have to, like, touch...and kiss?"

I chuckled at her reaction. "If you think that's too much, we don't have to. We can just seem *really, really* into each other in some bizarre way, like constant creepy staring and telepathic communication."

She sighed. "No, I...think we should make it believable."

Well, this is going to be fucking interesting.

• • •

I didn't see Molly for the next few days. She worked her three, twelve-hour shifts, and our schedules didn't align. But I knew today was her day off, so this afternoon I'd texted to ask if she'd be home for dinner and stopped at the grocery store after work to pick up some things I'd need to make one of my specialty dishes.

She came in and tried to peek over my shoulder as I was mixing ingredients in a bowl. I turned so she couldn't get a look at what I was making.

"No looking before dinner's ready," I said.

She pouted, but I saw the smile beneath those full, downturned lips. "What if I don't like what you're making?"

"You'll like it."

"How do you know?"

"Because I'm making it, and it seems you'll eat whatever I cook."

She rolled her eyes. "Don't get all full of yourself. I only stole your leftovers again yesterday because I was too lazy to go to the store and get cold cuts."

I grinned. "It's okay to admit you like my cooking, you know."

Molly shook her head. "From the short time I've known you, I'm positive you don't need anyone stroking your ego and making it bigger."

"You're right. I got something better than my ego that grows when you stroke it." I winked.

She started to blush, but turned away so I wouldn't see. I don't know why, but I loved when she pinked up and tried to hide it.

"How long do I have before dinner is ready?" she asked.

"That depends...how long do you need?"

"Well, if we have fifteen minutes, I'm going to call my mom back before we eat. She called while I was a few blocks away, but I try not to talk on my phone and drive at the same time anymore. I had a little fender-bender a few months back. I'd been arguing with my credit card company about a charge that wasn't mine and not really paying attention."

"Take as long as you need."

"Fifteen minutes should be good. If I'm still on, just loudly mention that dinner is ready. That'll help me get off. My mom *really* likes to talk."

I smiled. "You got it." I actually only needed a few minutes to finish up what I was making, so I figured I'd wait until I heard her get off the phone to start again. But almost half an hour went by, and Molly still hadn't come out of her room. So I knocked lightly. Maybe she hadn't been exaggerating earlier and needed help getting off the phone.

"Hey, Moll? Dinner will be ready in a few minutes."

"Okay. I'll be right there."

Ten minutes later, she finally emerged from her room. I had two plates all ready on the kitchen table and was just about to tease her for making my dinner cold when I looked up and saw her face all red and blotchy. She'd definitely been crying.

I rubbed my breastbone. My chest felt like I had heartburn or something. "What's going on? Is your mom okay?"

Molly sniffled a few times. "Yeah. She's fine. It's not my mom. It's my dad."

"What happened?"

"He's sick. Apparently he was diagnosed with lung cancer, and the long-term prognosis is not good."

"Shit, Moll. I'm sorry. Come here." I pulled her into a hug. She started to cry again in my arms. Not knowing what to say or do, I just held her tight and kept petting her hair and telling her everything was going to be okay. Once she calmed down, I led her over to the couch.

"What can I get you?" I said. "Do you want a glass of wine, or water, maybe?"

"No, it's fine. You made dinner, and it's probably already getting cold."

"Don't worry about dinner. Tell me what you need."

Her face was so red that it made the blue in her eyes really stand out. Mascara or some other kind of makeup streaked down one of her cheeks. I wiped it away with my thumb. "You want wine?"

She nodded. "I think I could really use a glass, yeah."

In the kitchen, I poured two white wines and took the bottle with me when I went to sit next to her again. Passing her a glass, I said, "My dad had prostate cancer when I was a teenager. I was terrified and thought he wasn't going to make it. But he pulled through. Medicine improves every day. Sometimes a bad prognosis can change."

"I know. It's just that my dad and I... We have a complicated relationship."

I nodded. "I get it. My relationship with my mom isn't simple, either."

Molly sipped her wine while staring down at her feet, seeming lost in thought. I gave her some time to decide what she wanted to share with me. Eventually, she continued.

"When I was sixteen, my father left my mother. He's a dermatologist, and he married his nurse barely a year after he walked out. Kayla, his wife, is only six years older than me. I think I took the breakup and his recoupling harder than my mother did." She shook her head. "I was just so mad at him. He basically started a new life without us. The entire thing was so stereotypical and cliché. My mom had worked two jobs to help put him through med school. He paid her back by trading her in for a newer model a month before her fiftieth birthday—and his nurse, no less. I actually have a little sister who people think is my daughter."

"That sucks. I'm sorry, Molly."

"Thank you. Anyway, it's been almost twelve years now. My mom is over it. She's dating a really nice guy now. But I never let go of the grudge, and it's really put a strain on my relationship with my dad over the years. He calls me every few weeks, but our conversations are like two strangers talking—*How's the job? How's the weather? Any good vacations planned?*"

"Does he live here in Chicago?"

She nodded. "He lives over in Lincoln Park." She stayed quiet for a few minutes again, and then said, "I've wasted so many years harboring bad feelings over something that wasn't even about me."

"Well..." I took her almost-empty wine glass and refilled it. "The good thing about forgiveness is that it doesn't have an expiration date. You can give it anytime."

Molly forced a smile. "Thanks."

"Is he in the hospital?"

She shook her head. "Apparently he had some tests done, and he's starting chemo in a few days. He called my mom because he left me a message last week, and I haven't gotten around to calling him back yet. Apparently neither did my older sister."

"Does your sister live here in Chicago?"

"No, Lauren lives in London. She did a study abroad during her junior year in college and met a guy. Moved there to be with him the day she graduated. They're both professors at a university, so she only comes back once a year to visit."

I nodded. "How are you going to handle things? Will you call him or go over and see him?"

"I don't know. I guess I should do both—call him back and then go speak to him in person. Though, to be honest, the thought of that makes me feel sick. It's been a long time, and I'm not sure how to go about fixing things, especially now."

"I'll go with you, if you want."

Molly blinked a few times. "You will?"

"Of course. You're my roomie. I got your back."

"I appreciate that. I really do. But it would probably be weird to bring along someone he's never met before. I think I need to mend this fence on my own."

I nodded. "Okay. Well, how about I drive you over to Lincoln Park when you go? I'll park around the corner and wait for you. I can bring my laptop to do some work. That way you don't have to drive if you get upset, and you'll have someone to keep you calm on the way there."

"That's really generous of you. I know I'll be too preoccupied to pay attention to the road. So I might take you up on that, if you mean it."

"I do. And consider it done. You just let me know when, and I'll be there."

Molly smiled, and it felt like the hand clutching my heart had loosened its grip a little. "Thanks, Declan."

She was quiet for a few minutes. "Did your parents have a messy divorce, too?" She tilted her head.

My forehead wrinkled, and Molly noticed.

"You said you have a complicated relationship with your mother," she explained. "So I thought maybe you had a similar situation to mine."

I shook my head. It was much easier to talk about my dad's bout with cancer than my mom's illness, especially these days. Plus, I'd finally lightened the mood a little. Molly didn't need me bringing her down any more. So I tried to downplay what I'd said earlier. "Nah, just some family crap." I stood. "Why don't you finish your wine and relax for a bit? I'll go get dinner ready. It'll take me ten minutes to make a new batch."

Molly looked over my shoulder toward the kitchen. "What did you make?"

"Belgian waffles with ice cream. Figured part of my job as your roomie was to help you break your aversion to morning foods at night. And I'll tell you what—since you had a tough evening, this meal's on me. You won't even have to do my laundry or pick up my dry cleaning."

She shook her head, but chuckled. "Thanks."

I tossed the cold waffles and melted ice cream in the garbage and whipped up a fresh batch. It made me happy that Molly dug in and seemed to forget about her dad for a little while.

"So, how are things going with Julia?" she asked as we ate.

"Good, I guess. We had dinner after work the other night."

"You went on a date?"

"Not really. We work together and travel a lot, so we often share meals together. But this time it felt sort of different."

"Like how?"

"She complained about Bryant, her boyfriend, a lot. They've been together for almost a year, and she's never done that before."

"So she wants you to know there's trouble in paradise?"

I shrugged. "I thought the timing was interesting. She suddenly lets me know for the first time that maybe things aren't so great in her relationship, right after she suspects something might be going on between me and my hot roommate." Right after I said it, I realized calling Molly hot might not be appropriate. I liked to tease her, but I didn't want to make her uncomfortable. "Sorry. I shouldn't have called you that. I mean, obviously you're beautiful, but I don't want you to think I'm checking you out when you're walking around the apartment or anything. It's just the way I talk."

The truth was, I did check Molly out when she wasn't looking. It would be pretty damn hard not to. But she didn't need to know that.

She smiled. "It's fine."

"Anyway, the timing could be a total coincidence. But I don't think it is. How about you? How are things with you and the good doc? Anything new on that front?"

"Not really."

"Well, maybe seeing us together will give him the push he needs, like it seems to have for Julia."

Molly swept the last of her waffle around her plate, dipping it into the melted ice cream. "Why does it need to be such a game? If Will likes me, why would he only act on it if he thinks he might lose his opportunity? Same with Julia. The entire thing seems so immature. To be

59

honest, I still can't get over what I did the other night at the bar. Taking off my bra and pretending to spill water on myself to get a man's attention? I'm twenty-seven, not seventeen. Looking back, even though it accomplished what I'd set out to do, I'm pretty mortified."

I shook my head. "I think sometimes we're all so busy looking for what's out there that we miss something amazing right in front of us. Does it matter if jealousy or whatever makes us wake up, as long as it does?"

She shrugged. "I don't know. I guess. Maybe that's just the way life is—but it seems silly."

It hit me that although Molly was talking about Will, she could have been talking about what went down with her mother and father. And it wasn't lost on me that Will had the same occupation as her old man, and Molly and her stepmother were both nurses. I was no psychiatrist, but I sensed there might be some deep-rooted correlation.

I got up to put my plate in the sink. "When's the next time you work with Dr. Hyperopia."

Her nose scrunched up. "Hyperopia?"

"As opposed to myopia. It's what you call someone who can see long distance, but not up close."

"Oh." She smiled. "I get it." Molly took her plate to the sink and rinsed it. "He's the on-call OB this Friday night. So if anyone goes into labor, I'll probably see him then. It's rare we go a night without the OB having to come in to deliver."

"Why don't I come pick you up for lunch, then?"

"Uh...because I work seven at night to seven in the morning. My lunch hour is at midnight."

I shrugged. "So?"

"I'm not going to ask you to come to the hospital at that hour."

"You didn't ask. I offered."

"I know...but..."

"It's a date, Mollz."

She sighed. "Okay, thank you. Let's see if he's even there."

We cleaned up the rest of the kitchen together in silence, and then Molly said, "I think I'm going to call my mom back. If I don't, she'll worry all night about how upset I was when I hung up. I should probably also get in touch with my sister, though it's pretty late in London now. Maybe I'll wait until morning to call her."

"That sounds like a good idea."

"By the way, I haven't had Belgian waffles and ice cream since I was a kid. It was delicious. Thanks for making me breakfast for dinner."

"No problem. I'm going to go do some reading in my room for work. But if you want to talk after you hang up with your mom, you know where to find me."

"Thank you."

Molly poured herself another glass of wine and said goodnight before heading down the hallway to her room. She turned back as she got to her bedroom door, only to catch my eyes glued to her ass. I'd thought she was going to be pissed off, but instead she smirked.

"I guess you're not afflicted with hyperopia?"

My lips curved to a grin. "Twenty-twenty vision. Thank God."

"Goodnight, Dec. Thanks for everything. And I don't just mean making me dinner."

"Anytime. 'Night, Mollz."

CHAPTER SIX

Molly

"Holy crap. Some woman who just pushed out a watermelon is going to be pregnant again too soon."

Daisy and I were sitting at the nurses' station next to each other, but I had no idea what she was talking about. I looked up from the computer screen and traced her line of sight.

Oh my. A man was strutting down the hall carrying an enormous bouquet of flowers. He had on a well-fitted, three-piece suit with the knot of the tie slightly loosened, and a five o'clock shadow peppered his carved jawline. Not just any carved jawline—*Declan's* carved jawline. Spotting me, he flashed a million-dollar smile and two cavernous dimples.

"Actually..." Daisy whispered. "I think he just got *me* pregnant."

I'd had no idea he was coming since he was supposed to call first. So between the surprise of seeing him and how amazing he looked, I seemed to be incapable of speaking. Instead, I sat and stared until he walked right up to me.

"Hey, gorgeous."

Daisy's eyes widened as I stood.

"Declan...what are you doing here?"

He held up a bag I hadn't even noticed in his hand. "I made you dinner...or I guess it would be your lunch." He extended the flowers to me. "And brought you these."

"They're beautiful. But...you didn't have to do that. I didn't realize you were coming."

"I wanted to surprise you. Did you take your break yet?"

I shook my head. "No. But I can go in, like, fifteen minutes. I just need to finish up a few things here."

Daisy, whom I'd forgotten was still sitting next to me, stood up and plucked the patient's chart from my hands.

"I'll finish for you."

"Oh...okay. Thanks, Daisy."

Declan's ears perked up hearing the name. "Daisy, huh?" he said. "I'm Declan, Molly's date for dinner this evening."

"Nice to meet you, Declan."

"You, too. I appreciate you covering for my girl so I can eat with her. I work days, and she works nights, so I miss seeing her face."

Daisy seemed unable to stop smiling. "That's so sweet. Take as long as you want. It's pretty quiet tonight, so I can handle things on my own."

Declan held out his hand for me to take over the counter and led me to his side. "Lead the way, beautiful."

As soon as we were out of earshot, he leaned to me. "So that's Ivy, huh? She doesn't hold a candle to you. If

Dr. Dickalicious picks that over you, he's not only blind, he's a moron."

For some odd reason, my heart was racing. I wasn't sure if it was the surprise visit, the act we were putting on at work, or the fact that I'd actually sort of swooned when Declan walked in the way he had. The man had such a big presence.

"That's very sweet of you to say, even if you're full of shit," I said. "But I hate to tell you, we seem to be having one of those rare nights where none of our patients are in labor, so Will isn't even here. I wish you would've called first so I could've saved you the trip."

Declan shrugged. "It's okay. I wanted to check in on you, anyway. Today was your dad's first day of chemo, right? You mentioned he was going to call you afterward. I figured you might want to talk about it."

I led Declan into the break room. Technically, it was supposed to be for employees only, but no one really cared, especially on the overnight shift. He began his food prep, just like he did in the kitchen at home. Taking a Tupperware out of the bag, he popped it into the microwave and pulled out a chair for me to sit in while he warmed up whatever he'd brought.

"Did you get to talk to him?" he asked.

"I did. We talked for almost a half hour, which is honestly the longest conversation I can remember us having in a decade. Mostly we discussed his treatment plan, and which doctors we liked and didn't like. It was sort of more like a doctor and a nurse going over a patient's medical records than a father and daughter talking, but I guess it's a start."

He nodded. "It's good that you have common ground to ease into things." The microwave dinged, and he removed the dish and set it down in front of me. "Homemade gnocchi in cream sauce."

"Wow. Homemade? Like, you made the pasta, too?"

"Yup. Told you I'm the perfect roomie."

I forked two pasta dumplings and slipped them into my mouth. If Declan hadn't been standing there to watch my reaction, I might've let my eyes roll into the back of my head and moaned a little. It was *that good.*

"This is absolutely delicious."

He sat down across from me and smiled. "Good. Eat up."

I forked more pasta. "You want to share?"

"Nah. You eat. I already had some. But tell me how you left things with your father. Did you make a plan to visit him in person?"

I sighed. "He invited me to come over for dinner."

"That's good. When?"

"Tuesday."

Declan scratched his chin. "I have a meeting, but I can probably reschedule it."

"No, you don't have to do that. I can go on my own."

He took out his cell and started to type. When he was done, he tossed it on the table. "Done. I emailed the guy and asked him if we can do it Friday instead. I'm sure it won't be a problem."

I shoveled more gnocchi into my mouth. "You're really a good friend, Declan." Even though we'd only known each other a couple of weeks, I somehow knew I could count on him.

A few minutes later, I had nearly emptied the container. I scooped up a few more gnocchi and lifted the fork halfway to my lips. "I want to eat the rest of this, but I'm stuffed."

"You sure you're full?" Declan asked.

"Positive."

"Good." He leaned across the table and closed his lips around the fork. "Because I lied. I haven't eaten anything yet. I worked really late, and those damn dumplings take a while to make. I rushed out because I didn't want to miss your break." He chewed and kept his face in front of me, leaning over the table. "So feed me the last of that, will ya?"

I laughed, but shoved two more heaping bites of gnocchi into his mouth. We were both so busy with the food and enjoying each other's company that neither of us heard someone walk into the break room.

Not until a man's deep voice interrupted. "Hey, Molly..."

I turned to find Will Daniels holding a coffee mug. His eyes moved back and forth between Declan and me.

I cleared my throat. "Hi, Will."

Declan's eyes went wide as he realized what was happening, a smug look of "mission accomplished" written all over his face.

Will extended his hand to Declan. "Will Daniels."

"Declan Tate. Nice to meet you."

"You're a friend of Molly's?"

"We're dating, actually," Declan answered without missing a beat.

Will looked over at me, understandably confused. We'd just had coffee last week, and I'd mentioned my roommate, but not that I was dating anyone. I hadn't mentioned Declan's name, so he had no way of figuring out that my new "love interest" was the same guy I'd spoken about.

Not knowing what to say, I stammered, "Uh, it's... new."

Will forced a smile. "I guess a lot can change in a week."

"Yeah."

He turned to Declan. "Whatever you guys nuked in the microwave smells amazing."

Declan grinned. "Thank you. Gnocchi. I made it."

"Ah. A chef." Will walked over to the coffee pot and filled his mug for what felt like ten awkward seconds. He put the top on and said, "Well, I'll let you two get back to your dinner."

Then he was gone.

After Will was safely out of earshot, Declan spoke low. "Okay...you want my assessment on Dickalicious?"

"Yeah."

He continued to whisper. "Doc was definitely jealous. That whole thing was awkward. It was great. He was clearly disappointed and surprised to find you with me."

Hope filled me. "You think?"

"I don't *think*, I *know*. So this was good. Definitely not a wasted trip."

"What now?" I asked. "I mean, could this backfire? Now that he thinks I'm taken?"

"I didn't say we were dating exclusively, just that we were dating. Trust me, next time he gets you alone, he's going to ask about me. That will be your opportunity to let him know we're not that serious. I'll just be present enough to make him realize he needs to hurry, or he'll lose the opportunity."

Blowing a breath up into my hair, I said, "Well, this is far simpler than exposing my nipples. And I don't even have to be disgusted with myself."

"It'll be fun, Mollz." Declan replaced the lid on the gnocchi container. "Speaking of the fun we're having, I was hoping maybe you wouldn't mind being home next Wednesday night? That's a night off for you, right? I was thinking of asking Julia to come over to brainstorm on the campaign at our place. Might be a good opportunity for you and me to...flirt."

I couldn't exactly say no; he'd helped me out a lot tonight.

"Oh...yeah. Of course. I can do that. It's only fair. You just did me a huge favor."

He smiled wide. "Cool."

He did look especially handsome in the suit tonight.

Declan stayed until my break was over, and then I went back to work.

Later that night, sure enough, Will caught me at the nurses' station.

He shuffled through some folders and said, "Declan, was it? He seemed nice."

My heart pounded. "Yeah. He is. Like I said...it's new. Nothing serious or anything."

"He seems pretty serious, though, if he's bringing you food at midnight..."

"I thought that was nice of him, yes. But it's not exclusive."

He put a folder back in its rightful spot, then turned to me and said, "Good to know." He winked before heading back down the hall.

That thrilled me, but at the same time, I had to wonder what the hell was taking him so long to ask me out. He could have easily done so by now.

A few minutes later, Daisy appeared. "Holy shit, Molly. Spill on your new guy."

I gave her the same story I'd just given Will—that it was new and the verdict was still out.

"Well, if it doesn't work out, send him my way, because a man who looks like that *and* brings you food and flowers is gold."

I felt like saying, *yeah, men like that don't exist.*

But then again, what about Declan was really fake? He *does* look the way he does, and he *is* an amazing cook. While tonight's dinner might have been for show, the Belgian waffles he made me the other night weren't. And neither was his offer to accompany me to visit my dad, or the fact that he was a really good listener.

My sights were set on Will, but for some reason, as the night wore on, it was Declan I couldn't stop thinking about.

CHAPTER SEVEN

Molly

Declan found a parking spot around the corner from my father's house in Lincoln Park.

"So I'll just be here doing some work if you need me."

I felt bad making him wait in the car. He'd said he had work to do, but I couldn't imagine he would have chosen to be stuck in his vehicle if he weren't doing me a favor. And if I admitted that I felt bad asking him to wait here for me, he'd insist on doing it anyway. So instead, I made it seem like I needed his support at dinner. It wasn't a total lie.

"Do you...think we could change the plan? I'd love it if you could come inside with me."

His forehead wrinkled. "You want me to have dinner with you and your dad?"

"I know it's kind of random for me to bring you along, but I'd prefer not to be alone."

"Well, that's all you had to say." Declan removed his seatbelt. "But what's the story?"

"What do you mean?"

"Who am I supposed to be?"

I punched his shoulder gently. "How about my roommate, Declan?"

"Now there's a novel idea." He chuckled.

"Just be yourself."

He winked. "I can do that."

We exited the car and made our way up my father's front steps. He lived in a three-million-dollar, single-family home on a posh, tree-lined street in one of the nicest neighborhoods in Chicago.

My "stepmother" Kayla answered the door. "Molly, it's so good to see you."

She patted me on the back as we did the obligatory hug.

"You, too."

"And who's this?" she asked.

"This is my friend Declan. Hope you don't mind me bringing him along."

"Of course not! We have plenty of food."

"Good to meet you," Declan said.

I could've sworn Kayla gave Declan a once-over. That wouldn't have surprised me. Anyone who could steal a man from his family has no shame.

"Where's Siobhan?" I asked.

"Your sister is at her friend's house. She wanted to see you, but she was invited to a sleepover that started at four. She was torn."

"Ah," I said. "Hopefully I'll catch her next time."

As much as I would have liked to see my nine-year-old half-sister, I was kind of happy to have my father all to myself tonight. Siobhan was so talkative that no one would have gotten a word in edgewise.

"Your father is in the living room," Kayla said.

We followed her through the foyer into the house. Dad had been looking out a window and turned when he heard us enter.

He opened his arms. "There's my beautiful daughter."

"Hey, Dad."

As we embraced, I could feel how thin he'd become. His head was bald, but I knew that was because he'd proactively shaved it. But it was still shocking to see.

His eyes moved to my right. "Who's the guy?"

Declan extended his hand. "Hey, Dr. Corrigan. I'm Declan, Molly's roommate."

My father nodded in recognition. "Oh...this is the funny guy you told me about."

Declan's eyes widened.

"Shh..." I smiled. "Declan can't know I talk nice about him."

"I'm glad he could join us."

"Me, too, Dr. Corrigan."

"Please call me Robert, Declan. Can I offer you something to drink?"

"That'd be great."

We followed Dad into the dining room. The room was adorned with gorgeous crown molding. The old-school architecture of my father's house was striking. He opened the liquor cabinet, which was a built-in hutch in the corner.

"I've got almost anything to suit your fancy. What do you like?"

"A scotch will be great," Declan said.

"Coming right up." He turned to me. "And my Molly? What does she want?"

"I'll just have a white wine."

He hollered into the kitchen. "Kayla, can you pour Molly some of the white you opened last night?"

"Of course," I heard her say.

Over a dinner of pasta carbonara that was surprisingly good, considering it was made by a juvenile, my father told stories from my childhood while Declan seemed to enjoy every minute. Kayla just nodded most of the time, which was fine by me. I didn't want to have to pretend to be enjoying a conversation with her. With my dad, on the other hand, as much as we'd had our troubles, I genuinely enjoyed his company. I'd missed him.

Kayla got up to do the dishes. Declan and I offered to help, but she insisted we stay and talk to my father. With just the three of us in the room again, the tone of the entire evening changed, as if someone had flipped a switch.

"Why did you really come along, Declan?" my father asked. "Is it because my daughter didn't want to face me alone?"

The room went silent for a few seconds.

My roomie, who never lacked for something to say, looked at me before stumbling over his words. "No, I..."

"Yes," I interrupted. "I needed his support. I was nervous for so many reasons—scared mainly, because I didn't want to see you sick. I have a lot of regrets about our relationship, but in the end, you're still my daddy. I was just afraid, afraid to be afraid."

"I know," my father said. After a few moments of silence, he turned to Declan. "Thank you for accompanying her."

"It's my pleasure."

"How did you two come to live together?"

Declan grinned mischievously. "She couldn't resist my charms."

"Well, that's not exactly the story," I said.

"Actually, I got in by default. Everyone else was so godawful, she had no choice but to give in—that and I made her cupcakes."

"Very resourceful idea." My father laughed. "How bad could a guy who makes cupcakes be?"

"That was exactly my thinking, Robert."

"How is my daughter to live with?"

Declan glanced over at me and smiled. "She's fun, which you wouldn't immediately know from her rigid organization and rules."

My father turned to me. "Rigid, huh?"

"She likes everything very neat and organized," Declan clarified. "But there's nothing wrong with that. It's who she is."

My father's gaze permeated mine. "That's not who she always was. When I lived with Molly, I remember her being quite messy and carefree." He paused. "After I left home, my ex-wife would tell me Molly had become a bit obsessed with neatness and having everything in order." He looked down at his plate and sighed. "And all I could think was...that's not Molly at all." Dad shook his head. "I wondered if her becoming that way had something to do with my leaving."

I didn't know what to say. That hadn't occurred to me, but then I'd never analyzed my behavior.

My father continued, looking straight at me. "My therapist thinks we do certain things to create a sense of order or stability in our life, because those are things we can control. When I left, I turned your entire life upside down."

I was surprised to learn my father *knew* about my quirks, but apparently my mother had let him in on more than I realized. I was also surprised to hear he saw a therapist.

"You see a shrink?"

"Yes. I have for some time now. I have a lot of regrets, Molly—about how I handled things with your mother and you girls. And I'm sorry."

My chest tightened. He should not be beating himself up right now. I tried to reassure him. "We all make mistakes."

"Mine was quite a mistake."

It broke my heart that my father was focused on his regrets while battling this illness. He could very well have limited time; he needed to focus on the positive.

"Dad, please don't worry about the past right now."

The tension in the air was thick, and I felt Declan's hand cover mine—not sure how he knew I really needed it.

He squeezed my hand. "If I may say something, Dr. Corrigan..."

My father took a sip of his drink. "Of course."

"I know you left home when Molly was sixteen, and most of us are who we are as people by that age. You were there for her formative years. That fact shouldn't be discounted. Sure, you made some mistakes, but your daughter is an amazing, well-adjusted person with a good head on her shoulders and a great career. She's happy, loves the simple pleasures in life—loves food especially." He looked at me, and I rolled my eyes. "She's going to be just fine. And I, for one, am happy to call her my friend."

Whether Declan's words were the truth didn't matter. He knew *exactly* what my father needed to hear.

And I wanted to kiss him right now. *Jesus, where did that come from?*

"You should go into advertising," my father joked, knowing full well from our dinner conversation that Declan's career *was* in advertising. "But thank you. I'm happy my daughter has someone like you looking after her."

After a minute, Declan went to use the bathroom.

My father took me into the living room and said, "He's gay, right?"

I nearly spit out my wine. "What? No! What makes you say that?"

"You're kidding. He's not?"

"No. He's totally hetero."

"You mean to tell me he talks about you like that and looks at you that way, yet there's nothing going on *and* he's heterosexual?"

I swallowed. "Yes."

"Well, he sure had me fooled."

I took a long sip. "He's infatuated with another woman."

Dad took a moment to ponder that. "I don't even know that person, but there's no way she holds a candle to you. I'm sure it's only a matter of time before he sees that."

"Well, he's leaving in a matter of months, so..."

My father's eyes narrowed. "I didn't realize that."

"Yeah. He'll be heading back to California, where he's from. He's only here on a temporary, six-month assignment for work."

Wow. Somehow thinking about Declan leaving had a much greater effect on me than it had when he'd first moved in. That was really going to suck when the time came.

We stayed for about a half hour more before I went to the kitchen to thank Kayla for dinner and hugged my dad goodbye. All in all, the visit went better than I ever could have anticipated. I made plans with Dad to visit again next week on my own. This would hopefully be the beginning of a fresh start to our relationship.

Once Declan and I got back in the car, I turned to him. "I have a funny story for you."

"Whatcha got?"

"That whole time, my dad thought you were gay."

He'd just been about to start the ignition but paused. "Say what?"

"Yes."

A perplexed look crossed his face. "Do I seem gay to you? You'd tell me, right? Do I give off vibes?"

"No." I laughed. "He thought you were gay because he couldn't understand how you and I get along so well, how you could say all those nice things about me, how we could be living together, but not *be together*. So, he just assumed."

"Well, damn," Declan said as he started the car. "No wonder he was so nice to me. He didn't see me as a threat. Did you tell him I'm not gay?"

"Of course. I told him you were infatuated with someone else."

He scrunched his face as if I'd somehow offended him. "Infatuated? I don't think that's the right word exactly. I mean, I really like Julia. A lot. But *infatuation* is a bit much. That makes it sound creepy."

"When I first met you, you told me you were in love with her. You're not even with her, and she has a boyfriend. If that's not infatuation, I don't know what is."

"I might've exaggerated a little. I was also trying to weasel my way into your apartment and would've said anything to peg myself as someone who wouldn't be interested in sex with you. I should have just told you I was gay."

I winked. "Apparently my father would have believed it."

CHAPTER EIGHT

Declan

The following night, Julia and I were working together in my living room. Once again we'd taken position together on the floor, using the coffee table as a makeshift desk. Wasn't sure if it was my imagination, but she seemed to be sitting closer to me than usual.

The plan was for Molly to come out at some point and flirt with me. It wasn't going to be anything too crazy, just something to ruffle Julia's feathers.

But the plan hadn't been going according to schedule because Molly was taking her sweet-ass time. I didn't know what the fuck she was doing in her room— masturbating to her Hulu show or what—but she hadn't made an appearance yet.

I looked up from typing on my laptop to notice Julia looking at me. Caught in the act, she turned away. *Perfect.* Now if only Molly could get her act together so we could stir the pot.

"You said your roommate is home, right?"

"Yeah. You wouldn't know it though, would ya? She's pretty quiet."

"True. I don't hear a peep. You think she's not happy that I'm here? Are we disturbing her?"

"No. I don't think so. I think she might have fallen asleep."

That was the only explanation that made sense.

I pretended to need something from the fridge, and instead texted Molly on the down-low.

Declan: Are you coming out sometime tonight?

The three dots moved around as she typed.

Molly: I'm having some technical difficulties.

Declan: What are you talking about?

Molly: I was trying out these new lashes, and I got glue stuck in my left eye. I can hardly open it.

Declan: What made you decide to do that tonight?

Molly: I wanted to sex it up...for our performance.

Declan: So you glued your eye shut? The one-eyed look is so damn sexy, Mollz. Truly.

Molly: Shut up. This is all your fault.

The funniest visual of Molly walking out of her room with a patch covering one eye popped into my head. But that quickly morphed into her wearing a wench's costume—with one of those cinched-waist things that laced up and covered her rib cage. It would stop just below the swell of her breasts, making her tits practically spill over from her top.

I'd been staring at my phone, lost in some ridiculous fantasy, and hadn't heard Julia walk into the kitchen.

"Who are you texting over there?" she asked. "You have the dirtiest smirk on your face."

Shit. "I, uh, my sister." I closed my eyes, silently cursing myself and my dumbass answer. *Great, now she probably thinks I'm freaking creepy.* "She was, uh..." I attempted to iron out the wrinkles. "She's trying to fix me up with one of her friends."

"Oh?"

"Yeah, with four sisters, it's a pretty common occurrence."

"Are you...going to go out with the woman?"

I shook my head. "I learned my lesson a long time ago. Keep your love life as far away from your sisters as possible. The last time I let one of them set me up, I wound up on a date with a woman who loved cats."

"So? Are you allergic or something?"

"No. But she picked me up in her car, and when I got in, I realized just how much she loved her cats. Six of them were in the backseat."

"She brought her cats on your date?"

I nodded. "Said they got lonely at home, liked to go for car rides, and were a good judge of character."

"That's a little bizarre. Did the cats approve of your character, at least?"

"One leaped into the front seat while we were on our way to the restaurant and threw up all over my pants."

Julia laughed. "Oh my God. You mean they weren't even in carrying cages? What did you do?"

"She drove me back home so I could get changed, and I feigned a headache. But that's not even the worst part."

"It's not?"

I shook my head. "My sister didn't talk to me for a month because her friend told her I wasn't nice to her cats. She was convinced I'd made them nervous, and that's why one threw up on me."

My phone buzzed in my hand. Julia looked down at it. "I'll let you finish letting your sister down easy. I was just coming to ask if you had any wine."

"I think Molly does. I'm sure she wouldn't mind if we had some. I'll pour you a glass and be right in."

After Julia went back to the living room, I texted Molly again.

Declan: Are you okay? Do you need me to get you an eyewash or something?

Molly: No, I'll be fine. I just need a few minutes for the stinging to subside so I can try to glue these on again.

Declan: Forget the eyelashes. You don't need 'em. Your eyes are pretty without any makeup at all.

Molly: That's sweet. But I don't have a choice at this point. I have one on, and I can't get the damn thing off! I'll be out soon.

I chuckled as I typed.

Declan: Aye, aye, Captain.

I didn't think she'd get my humor, but she texted back right away.

Molly: Ha ha. I'll be out to see ye wench shortly.

Ten minutes later, Molly finally emerged from her room. I'd decided to join Julia in a glass of wine and was mid-sip when I caught sight of my roomie. Unfortunately, I hadn't been prepared for what she was going to look like. I swallowed down the wrong pipe and started coughing, and I inadvertently sprayed wine all over Julia.

"Shit. I'm sorry." I grabbed the napkin from under my glass and started to blot the mess I'd made on her face.

Smooth, Declan...really smooth tonight.

Molly walked over to where Julia and I were seated on the floor next to the coffee table. She looked smoking hot in a short, black mini dress and sky-high silver strappy heels that wrapped around her ankles. Her hair was blown out into a mass of soft waves, and she had on way more makeup than she usually wore, including super long, thick, dark eyelashes. Damn, those things were worth a little glue in the eye. They really made the light blue color of her eyes pop.

"Hey, Moll." I cleared my throat and tried to come off nonchalant, as if she walked around the apartment looking like that every day. I held up my wine glass. "I hope you don't mind, we had some of your wine. I'll replace the bottle for you tomorrow."

Molly batted her lashes and smiled. Her lips were painted bright red and covered in a thick layer of gloss. I didn't know where to look first—at her seductive eyes, full, shiny lips, or the mile of legs on display.

"No problem," she said. "I don't mind at all. Plus, I'm off tomorrow night, so maybe we can share the replacement bottle." She held my eyes for a few extra seconds and then pretended to have just noticed Julia.

"Oh, hi...Jessica."

Julia pursed her lips. "It's Julia."

Molly twirled her hair. "Sorry. Right. Julia..." She turned her attention back to me. "Are you almost done working, Dec?"

"Almost," I said. "Why? Are we disturbing you?"

"No, not at all." She lifted her hand and rubbed the back of her neck. "But that knot is back, and I was hoping you could work your magic fingers into it again— like you did the other night."

"Uh, yeah. Sure...no problem."

Molly looked over at Julia and practically cooed, "He's got the strongest hands."

Julia smiled, but I knew from watching her with difficult clients that it wasn't her real smile. This one was more plastic and forced. The muscle in her jaw tightened. I watched as her eyes swept up and down Molly's body for the second time. In all honesty, I couldn't blame her... Mollz looked fucking amazing.

"Were you on a date tonight?" Julia asked. "You're so dressed up."

Molly laughed and waved off Julia's comment. "No, I just threw this on because it was the only thing clean."

Julia frowned. "Uh-huh."

"Alright, well, I'll let you two get back to work. I'm just going to get a glass of wine myself so I can relax a little before you help me with that massage. Let yourself into my bedroom whenever you're done, Dec." Molly blinked, and one of her eyes got stuck closed.

I almost lost it when she turned her head to try to hide it and had to use her fingers to pry it open. I guess she hadn't figured out the glue situation after all.

Once Molly returned to her room, Julia downed the rest of her wine in one gulp. Her cheeks were a little flushed. "Could she be any more obvious?"

I pretended to have no clue what she meant, but a person would have to be blind and deaf to have missed Molly's over-the-top flirting. "What do you mean?"

Julia snort laughed. "That dress, the full face of makeup—not to mention that she was winking at you when talking about her *massage*. She doesn't even have a sore neck, Declan."

Winking? Not exactly. But close! She thought Molly's glued eyeball was a come-on.

I cleared my throat. "What do you mean, she doesn't have a sore neck?"

Julia rolled her eyes. "She's into you and wants your hands on her."

"Oh, well... Is that a bad thing? I mean, we're both single..."

"It would definitely be a mistake, Declan."

My brows furrowed. For some inexplicable reason, I felt defensive. "Why is that? Molly's really cool."

"Well, for starters, she's your roommate."

"That seems like it would go on the plus side of the pros-and-cons analysis." I shrugged. "Convenience."

Julia's face reddened. "Look, I just don't think it's a good idea for you to get into something you might not be able to come back from. I know from personal experience that once you go down that road, it's difficult to go back to simpler times. Take Bryant and me, for example. We went into an exclusive relationship right away. At the time, I didn't give any thought to the idea that it might not be a good idea since I travel so much for work. Recently, we've been having some difficulties, so I suggested we pull things back a little—keep our relationship more on the casual side."

"I take it that conversation didn't go too well, since you're using your own situation to warn me off anything happening between me and my roommate."

She shook her head. "No, it didn't. Bryant doesn't like the idea of a non-exclusive relationship because it's hard to go backward once you've moved forward. That's why I think you might want to give some serious thought to anything happening with your roommate. Once you go there, it would probably be hard to rewind."

She'd said a whole lot of words, but the only part I heard was *non-exclusive.*

"So, where are things with you and Bryant now, if you don't want the same thing?"

Julia sighed. "He told me to give what I really want some thought—basically an ultimatum. Either I'm with him and him alone, or I'm not with him at all."

I nodded. "Wow. Okay. Sounds like you have a big decision to make."

She surprised me by reaching out to touch my hand. I looked up, and our eyes met. "I do. I care about you, Declan. So maybe we should both take some time to think about what we really want, rather than making any rash decisions."

Well, well, well. My eyes dropped to her lips, then raised to meet her eyes again. "Yeah. That sounds like a good idea."

A half hour later, Julia hugged me goodbye—something we rarely did. As I shut the door behind her, I probably should have been elated at how shit had gone tonight, but instead, I felt a weird turmoil in the pit of my stomach.

Molly must've heard the front door, because she came out of her room a minute later.

"How did it go?"

She still had on that little black dress, and I couldn't help but notice how much more shapely Molly was than Julia. Julia's body type was more waif, whereas Molly had feminine curves. And tonight, in that dress, it was impossible not to notice how dangerous those curves were.

I forced my eyes to meet hers, though it wasn't an easy feat.

"It went well. She said she told her boyfriend she wants to be in an open relationship."

"Oh wow! Like our fake relationship!"

I chuckled. "Apparently Bryant gave her an ultimatum. It's either exclusive or nothing. So she's thinking about how to proceed."

"Well, if she's even considering that she wants to see other men, clearly the current guy isn't *the one.*"

"Yeah."

"So our diabolical plan seems to have worked."

"Thanks to you. I can't imagine any woman who wouldn't be jealous of the way you look tonight. You went all out."

Molly blushed. "Are you going to bed?"

"Nah, not yet. I'm not tired."

"Would you want to take a walk and get some ice cream? I have such a craving for strawberry right now. There's a place two blocks away that I love."

"Sure. That sounds good."

"Okay! I'll throw on some jeans real quick and be right back."

I felt a little disappointed that she was going to lose the sexy dress, but it only made sense. Plus, it wasn't easy to keep my eyes off of her in that getup, and I didn't want to get caught ogling.

She came back out wearing a pair of ripped jeans and a T-shirt, but honestly, she looked just as beautiful as she had all done up. I didn't realize I was staring until she called me on it.

"What?" She wiped at her cheek. "Did my eyelashes come off again?"

I chuckled. "No. I was just looking at you. You don't usually wear that much makeup."

She pointed to her eye. "Yeah, now you know why. I'm not exactly a wizard with this type of stuff. Gluing my eye shut wasn't the first complication I've had with cosmetics."

"You don't need all that crap anyway."

She arched a brow. "Really? So you're saying you didn't notice me a little more with all the work I put in tonight?"

"Of course I did. I'm a man, and you made it hard not to notice. But sparkle only gets a person's attention. It doesn't keep it."

Molly smirked and bumped shoulders with me. "I made it *hard*, did I?"

I opened the front door and extended my hand for her to walk through first. *Damn...her ass looks fantastic in those jeans, too.* Shaking my head, I blew out a deep breath.

My roommate was most definitely making things *hard* on me.

• • •

The next morning, I smiled, seeing my sister Catherine's name flash on my cell phone. She was my favorite person to screw with, so I leaned back into my chair and tossed my pen on my desk before answering.

"Satan's house of sins. We got porn, gambling, and prostitution. What can I do you for?"

"Ha ha. You know, when I became a nun, you were supposed to start being extra nice to me."

"Who says?"

"It's in the rule book."

"What rule book?"

"The nun one."

"I'm going to call BS on that, Sister-Sister. I'd like to see this rule book you constantly claim exists."

"Well, you can't. It's strictly for nun eyes only."

I chuckled. "How've you been, Cat? What's new out in sunny California?"

"Well, I started taking a yoga class, so that's new. I love it. Have you ever tried yoga?"

I pictured my sister in full nun garb reaching up into warrior position; even though I knew she actually rarely wore the whole outfit. "I gave it a whirl once," I said. "But I found it hard to concentrate during the class."

"Really? It does just the opposite for me. I find it completely conducive to focusing. Maybe you didn't have a good instructor."

"Nah. The instructor was fine. I probably just needed to be in the first row."

"Oh, you mean you couldn't see her from the back?"

"No. I could see her just fine. But how the heck was I supposed to concentrate with a room full of women bending over wearing those tight yoga pants?"

My sister laughed. "I should have known that's what you meant, you horn dog."

"Horn dog? Isn't that a bad word you're not supposed to use?"

"I don't know. I'll have to check my nun manual."

I chuckled. I really missed Catherine. She might be a nun, but she was funny as shit and had the best sense of humor out of all of my sisters. "So what else is going on out there in sunshine land? Have you been to see Mom and Dad lately?"

The tone of her voice changed. "Yeah, I saw them last week."

"Not good?"

She sighed. "The usual."

I knew what that meant, so I didn't press. For the next fifteen minutes, we made small talk about the weather in Chicago, she told me about a quilting class she was teaching, and I told her a little about my new roommate and how things were going at work.

"So...how have you been?" she finally asked. "Are the medications still working?"

"I'm fine, Cat."

"Have you talked to Dr. Spellman?"

"No, because I'm not supposed to talk to him unless I need to."

"But *you're sure* you're feeling okay?"

I'd been waiting for these questions. My sister meant well, but she worried too much.

"Would I lie to a nun?"

She chuckled. "You absolutely would. But that's beside the point. Seriously, Declan. I'm concerned about you. Six months is a long time to be away from the doctor."

I didn't mention that Dr. Spellman had expressed the same concern and given me some numbers for local people I could see here in Chicago. "Listen, if anything changes, I promise you'll be the first to know. Okay?"

"Do you promise?"

"You can't see me right now, but I'm crossing my heart."

She sighed. "Okay. But do me a favor and keep in touch more."

"Yes, ma'am."

"Love you."

"Love you, too, Sister-Sister."

After I hung up, I thought about what I'd told her. I hadn't been lying when I said I'd felt really good lately. Coming to Chicago had turned out to be good for me on so many levels. The job gave me a lot of visibility with the higher-ups, and edged me closer to the promotion I'd been gunning for. Plus, things with Molly were going great.

Julia.

I meant Julia.

Things with *Julia* were going great.

Weren't they?

CHAPTER NINE

Molly

"**S**omeone's in a good mood at 2AM."

Will's voice caught me off guard. It was Sunday night, and I hadn't seen him in the last few days. I didn't think he was even on call tonight. Daisy and I were sitting at the nurses' station. She was busy entering notes into a patient's electronic chart, and I was busy goofing off on my phone—texting with Declan about the ironing he had for me to do in exchange for the leftovers I'd stolen today.

"She smiles all the time lately," Daisy said. "Can't say I blame her after getting a look at her new guy."

Oh...Will had been referring to me with his comment? I hadn't realized I'd been smiling while texting.

Will glanced down at my phone and frowned. "Do you have a minute, Molly?"

I tucked my cell into the pocket of my scrubs and stood. "Sure, of course."

As we walked down the hall together, Will filled me in on a patient who was on her way in. The woman was pregnant with triplets, and her labor had started too early. So he'd come in on his day off to try to stop the labor. Together we prepped an exam room, making sure we had the medications he would need, and then we reviewed the patient's history together. When we were done, Will looked at his watch.

"Mrs. Michaels was about an hour out when I spoke to her, so we have another twenty minutes or so until she gets here. It's probably going to be a very long night. Do you want to grab some coffee?"

"Sure."

In the break room, the coffee pot was empty.

"I'll make us a fresh batch," I said.

Will leaned a hip against the counter while I rinsed the glass pot and measured the grounds and water to make the new one.

"So..." he said. "How are things going?"

His question was vague, but I got the feeling he was asking about something specific.

"Good. How about you?"

"Pretty good." He paused for a few awkward seconds. "So...things with the new guy... I guess they're going well if you're smiling all the time."

I shrugged. "I guess. It's still pretty new, and we want to keep it casual."

He scratched his chin. "It's funny; I wouldn't have taken you for an open-relationship type of person."

"No? How come?"

"I don't know. You're just a very loyal, levelheaded person. More serious, I guess."

"Well, I like to keep my options open."

He was quiet while I poured us each a mug of coffee. I knew Will took his with cream and sugar, so I prepped it before handing it to him. "Here you go."

"Thanks." He sipped his coffee and continued to watch me over the brim. "Have you tried that new Greek place over on Amsterdam Ave?"

I shook my head. "I haven't. But I pass it on my way home, and it seems to be packed all the time."

"Would you want to go Friday night?"

For some reason, I assumed he meant with the group—before happy hour. "That sounds great. Who else is going?"

Will smiled sheepishly. "Just me..."

"Oh..." I shook my head. "I thought you meant with the happy-hour crew."

He dragged a hand through his hair. "And here I was thinking I was being so smooth."

"You were... I mean, I think you were. Are you asking me to go to dinner, like on a date?"

He chuckled. "I guess I'm so slippery smooth that my intentions just sailed right by you. Yes, Molly, I'm asking you on a date."

"Oh." My pulse sped up, and my palms grew sweaty.

"Do you want to change your mind now that that's clear?"

I shook my head. "No, definitely not. I'd love to go out with you, Will."

Of course Daisy had to walk into the break room at that exact moment. From the disappointed look on her face, I knew she'd heard what I said.

Will's phone chimed. Looking at the screen, he said, "It's the admitting department. Mrs. Michaels has arrived. If she made it here this fast, I'm guessing they had their foot on the gas for a reason. I better run down to make sure they don't hold her up filling out fifty-seven HIPAA forms. I'll see you in a bit."

I smiled. "Okay."

The minute Will walked out of the break room, Daisy put her hands on her hips.

"Oh my God. Will, too? You already have that other sexy beast of a man. Now you're going to go out with Dr. McHottie?"

I chuckled. "I guess so."

"Are you going to keep both of them?"

"I'm not sure that's my decision, considering they're humans, and I don't own them."

Daisy rolled her eyes. "Okay, well, if you dump the first guy... Can I have his number?"

I shook my head and walked to the break room door. "Goodbye, Daisy."

She grumbled under her breath. "Greedy."

Declan had been up late working on a project for his client. Since we'd been texting less than a half hour ago, I figured he'd still be up.

Molly: I have big news!

The response came almost immediately.

Declan: You stole someone's Tupperware from the break room at work and got caught. Now I have to come bail you out of jail, don't I?

Always the wiseass. I chuckled as I typed.

Molly: Nope, bigger! Will asked me out!

The little dots started to jump around, then stopped. Then started again. Then stopped yet again. It was a solid five minutes before I received another message.

And this one made it clear we were done chatting for the evening.

Declan: That's great. I'm glad you got what you wanted. Goodnight, Molly.

It was definitely odd for him to cut off a text exchange like that. For a split second, I wondered if maybe something about that announcement upset him. But that was ludicrous, right? God, it was the freaking middle of the night, and he'd been working late. He was probably tired. That had to have been why he said goodnight so suddenly.

• • •

The following evening, Declan was at the office, and I was home alone when there was a knock at the door.

A woman in a Yankees cap held a large white box. "Hi. Cake delivery for Scooter?"

I squinted. "Scooter? We don't have anyone here by the name of Scooter."

"Well, this is the right address, so I'm gonna leave it here with you."

"Uh...okay." I took the cake and shut the door with my foot.

There was a note on the top of the box. I opened it.

Scooter,

Happy Birthday! Wish we could be there with you!

Love,
Your sisters, Samantha, Meagan, Catherine, and Jane

Birthday? It was Declan's birthday? Furthermore, his sisters called him Scooter?

I took out my phone and immediately texted him.

Molly: How come you didn't tell me it was your birthday?

Declan: How did you find out?

Molly: Your sisters sent you a cake.

Declan: Uh-oh. What does it have on it?

Molly: I haven't opened the box. The note is addressed to Scooter!

Declan: Great. Don't open it yet. I'll be home in half an hour.

• • •

When Declan walked in, I greeted him with a glare. "I can't believe you didn't tell me."

He threw his jacket on a chair. "It's no big deal. It's just another day. My sisters always make a fuss. If I were home in California, they'd be bombarding my apartment and making a big deal out of nothing. They do it every year." He undid his tie. "Did you take a peek at the cake?"

"No. You said not to."

Declan went to the fridge and took out the box. I leaned against the counter, eagerly awaiting my view of the cake. He opened the lid and shook his head before facing the cake toward me.

I covered my mouth in laughter. It featured a photo of the most awkward-looking little boy with crooked teeth and a bowl cut. It vaguely looked like a young Declan. *Happy Birthday, Scooter* was written on top.

"Oh my goodness! That's you?"

"They always get a cake made with the worst photos of me. Last year, it was just my fat baby butt. This year, my first-grade class picture takes the cake. Pun intended."

It was funny to think such a goofy-looking boy had turned into such an Adonis.

"Wow. You look so...different."

"That's putting it lightly."

He opened the drawer and grabbed two forks, handing me one. Declan dug into the center of his face on the cake and took a bite. "At least it's good," he said with his mouth full. "Try it."

"Not as good as your cupcakes, but yeah," I said after sampling. "So where does the name Scooter come from?"

"I was waiting for you to ask that." He wiped some frosting off his bottom lip. "Well, you know I'm the youngest and the only boy. I used to follow my sisters around the neighborhood on my scooter, like a little pet. So, all the neighborhood kids would call me Scooter. It stuck, and my sisters started using the nickname, too."

"It must have been something being the only boy in that house, huh?"

Declan nodded. "They gave me a lot of shit growing up, but I wouldn't trade it. I think having sisters makes me a better man. I don't think I could relate to women in the same way if I hadn't had sisters. I've witnessed a lot—their hurt over guys, the challenges they've had to face in being seen as equals in things like competitive sports. Even though I'm the little brother, I'm very protective of them."

That squeezed my heart. "That's so sweet."

"At the same time, I'm pretty sure any one of them, especially Sister Catherine, could still kick my ass any day."

"*Still* being the operative word. Meaning it's happened multiple times?"

"Yup." He sighed.

"I would so pay to see that." I laughed.

Declan swiped a chunk of frosting off of his bowl cut and smeared it on the tip of my nose. We both started cracking up. I was relieved. Despite him ending our texts abruptly last night, it seemed things were all good between us.

CHAPTER TEN

Declan

My birthday turned out better than I'd expected. I hadn't planned to say anything about it, but thanks to my sisters, Molly and I devoured half that cake. Then she insisted on taking me out, so we went to the Italian place on the corner. We had a great time, but then again, I always did with Molly. It had been not quite a month since I'd moved in, but she'd become a good friend. Molly was funny, bright, and easy to talk to.

The following day at work, Julia was acting a little odd. She seemed spacey and not really attentive to the presentation one of our managers had flown in to give.

As we exited a conference room that afternoon, I asked her about it.

"Everything okay with you?"

She hesitated then said, "Bryant and I broke up."

Her announcement stopped me in my tracks.

"What happened?"

Julia blew out a breath. "I decided to just nip it in the bud. If I didn't want to be with him exclusively, there was something wrong, right? Even if I couldn't pinpoint it?"

Still trying to process, I nodded. "Yeah. I'd have to agree. You shouldn't feel trapped in a relationship. You should want to be there. That person should be all you think about. You shouldn't want to be with anyone else."

"Exactly. So...that was my revelation last night. I decided to call him early this morning and tell him. If I've been a little out of it today, it's because I feel sad that I hurt him, even though it's a huge weight off my chest."

"I bet."

This was a weird feeling. I'd waited for Julia to break up with her boyfriend for the longest time. But now I didn't know how to react.

"What now?" I asked.

She batted her lashes. "I don't know. You tell me. How should I mark this occasion?"

"I think we should have a drink. Or two."

Always the opportunist, Declan.

She smiled. "That sounds awesome. I want to go home and change first, though, if that's okay. It's been a long day."

"Yeah. That's cool. I'll do the same. I can pick you up at seven at your place?"

"Perfect."

For someone who'd just broken up with her boyfriend, Julia seemed to perk up pretty fast.

• • •

Molly was getting ready for her date with Dr. Small Willy when I got back to the apartment. My reaction the other night when she told me he'd asked her out had been a surprise. There had definitely been a vibe between us since the night she'd dressed up in that fuck-hot outfit to make Julia jealous. But I don't think I realized the shift had to do with *my* feelings for her until that text.

But it didn't matter if her date made me jealous. Nothing could happen between Molly and me. She was getting what she wanted with Will, and soon enough, we'd be living on different coasts.

I stood in the doorway as Molly applied her makeup. Once again she had on those long lashes. The red dress she wore tonight was even sexier than the black one she'd had on last time.

"Will is going to freak when he sees you."

She jumped. "You scared me."

"Sorry." I took a few steps into her room.

"I didn't think you'd be home so early," she said.

"Well, our meeting ended early, so Julia and I skipped out of work. I'm picking her up later to get drinks."

She puckered her lips as she applied lipstick. "God, her boyfriend can't be too happy that she spends so much time with you."

"Well, funny you say that..."

She closed the lipstick tube and turned around. "What?"

"She broke up with him."

Molly's eyes widened. "She did?"

"Yup."

She paused. "Holy crap."

"I know, right? It's strange that you and I both got what we wanted at almost the same time."

Molly's eyes widened. "Yeah, I mean... Jeez. What are the chances, right?" She blew out a breath. "You must be happy."

I lay back on her bed and put my hands behind my head as I stared up at the ceiling. "I don't know. It's kind of weird."

"How so?"

"I've wanted her for so long, and now that the biggest obstacle is out of the way...it just kind of... doesn't feel the way I thought it would."

"I get what you mean. Same thing happened when Will asked me out. It wasn't as climactic as I might have imagined."

I turned to look at her, and my gaze traveled down to the sexy shoes she wore. Clearing my throat, I said, "Anyway... It's all good, right?"

Our eyes locked for a few seconds.

"Yup." She smiled. "All good."

I changed the subject. "How's your dad?"

Her expression darkened as she sat at the edge of the bed. "I spoke to him today. He didn't sound too great, to be honest. His voice was really hoarse. I'm getting scared."

Shit. "Try to think positive. I know it's hard, but an optimistic outlook is better for everyone. Your dad will feel a lot better if he doesn't think you're down about him."

"I know. It's just so hard." Tears began to form in her eyes. "Losing him is a real possibility. And I don't think I've fully grasped that."

This was my fault; I'd brought up the subject.

Sitting up, I moved in closer, wiping the tears from her eyes with my thumb. "I'm sorry, Mollz. I wish I could do something. I'd take the pain away if I could."

"Thank you." She wiped her eyes. "I started seeing a therapist."

"Really? You didn't tell me you were thinking of that. Good for you."

"Well, strangely, it was the knowledge that my father had been going to therapy that gave me the courage to do it."

"I'm proud of you. When did you start?"

"Just this week. I told her what Dad's therapist said about my need for perfection. She agreed that the fact that those behaviors started after my dad left could mean there's a correlation. She wants me to practice letting go gradually of some of those habits as a way of accepting that there's no real control in life. She says that will also help my acceptance of his illness."

"Like, what is she asking you to do?"

"That's the thing—she didn't suggest anything specific. I have to identify where I'm being controlling or seeking perfection and create my own exercises." She tilted her head. "You got any ideas?"

"I'm sure I could come up with something." I went with my first instinct, getting up off the bed and opening her top drawer.

"What are you doing?"

"Helping you."

Without looking at the contents, I grabbed the clothes inside and tossed them into the air. Unfortunately, something that wasn't clothing landed on the ground with the rest of the stuff—a fucking vibrator.

I lifted it off the ground. "Oh shit. I'm sorry. I never—"

She held out her hand. "Give me that, please."

"I obviously didn't—"

"I *know* you didn't know. Just give it to me."

Brushing off my hands, I announced, "I think that was enough of an exercise for this week."

"Yeah. I'd have to agree." She turned pink. "This one is good for a month!"

I wondered if I'd be able to think about anything else tonight besides Molly massaging her clit with that rubber dick.

CHAPTER ELEVEN

Molly

Will stood up from his seat as I entered Mykonos restaurant. "You look amazing, Molly."

"Thank you," I said, leaning in and accepting a kiss on the cheek.

Will looked great in a blue, collared shirt and khaki pants. It was always nice to see him out of his scrubs.

Sitting down, I took the napkin in front of me and placed it on my lap. "I've always wanted to try this place."

He took a whiff of the air. "You can smell that the food is going to be amazing, can't you?"

"Yeah, my stomach is growling."

"You know..." he said. "I'm actually a quarter Greek."

"No way!" I smiled.

The crowded restaurant was bustling. A band got ready to play in the corner, and the smell of garlic, mint, and other spices saturated the air. It was a delight for the senses. But mostly my eyes and ears were focused on the handsome doctor across from me.

Will ordered the moussaka, and I got a Greek salad with grilled chicken. We made easy conversation over the next hour. He shared some of his craziest labor stories, and we compared notes on our experiences working with certain colleagues. There was definitely no shortage of things to talk about, and I started to think there could definitely be a future for Will and me if every night were like tonight.

From time to time, my mind would drift to Declan, though. Knowing he was out with Julia for the first time since her breakup was definitely on my mind. I wondered if they were truly compatible, or if it was mainly about "the get" for him. I supposed only time would tell.

At one point, Will changed the subject, and it transformed the mood of the entire night.

"So, confession…" he said, wiping his mouth with the blue cloth napkin.

Fidgeting in my seat, I said, "Okay…"

"I've had a massive crush on you for some time."

Feeling my cheeks heat, I said, "Wow. Well, thank you. I've definitely admired you as well."

"As you probably know, I just got out of a relationship," he added.

"Yup. I'm aware."

"Part of the reason that relationship ended is because she wanted something I couldn't give her right now."

I swallowed. "What was that?"

"Well, she wanted a bigger commitment sooner rather than later, ultimately marriage and kids."

"Oh." A knot began to form in my stomach. "You… don't want those things?"

"Not any time in the near future. But besides that, she just wasn't right for me."

Even though the restaurant was noisy, somehow everything seemed drowned out in that moment.

"I see..."

He continued, "One of the things that attracted me to you was your carefree philosophy on dating. You know, you don't seem to want anything too serious right away. I need time to breathe after that relationship. So it felt safe to ask you out."

Safe? I nodded, needing a moment to let this sink in.

What attracted him to me was the fact that I was dating someone else? That was the reason he asked me out?

Not my personality.

Not our common interests.

But the fact that I would let him date other people?

Trying to keep my cool, I finally said, "Ah, I see."

"I hope you don't mind me being honest. I realize it's only our first date, but I believe in full disclosure."

Forcing a smile, I said, "Yeah...well... I do appreciate your honesty."

"Thank you. And I appreciate you being honest with *me*. That was what finally made me take the plunge and do something I'd wanted to do for a long time."

The food turned in my stomach. It felt like this was over before it even began. To say I was disappointed wouldn't even cover half of what I felt.

Then again, this was my fault, right? I had given him the impression that I didn't want anything serious.

After we left the restaurant, I was just about to head over to my Uber when Will wrapped his hands around my cheeks and pulled me in for a kiss. As he slipped his tongue inside my mouth, I could only think how different it felt than I'd imagined. It felt good, but nothing like it might have if he hadn't squelched my hopes tonight. It made me realize more than ever that I truly did want to find a partner—my person. The question was, would I casually date Will in the hopes that his attitude might change as we got to know each other? I felt like I needed Declan's take on this.

When I got back to the apartment, though, my roommate wasn't there. That was no surprise. I knew he had plans with Julia. I just wished his night had also ended early, so I could talk to him.

It was almost 2AM when the door finally latched open.

I got up from the couch. "Hey."

Immediately, I noticed it. Declan's hair was all messed up, and he had lipstick on his mouth. I was unprepared for the level of jealousy that hit me.

"Hey." He flashed a crooked smile.

"Looks like you had a good evening."

"It was alright. Why do you say that?"

"Go look at yourself in the mirror."

Declan walked over to the mirror in the hallway. "Oh shit. Yeah."

"I take it Julia needed consoling because of her breakup?" I huffed.

He wiped his lips. "We got a little drunk and made out in the cab."

Feeling hot, I cracked, "Wow. She moves fast, huh?"

Rather than address that, he asked, "How was your date?"

Somehow, I felt weird complaining now. Not that this was a competition, but I didn't want to stress how lame my date had been compared to his—which had clearly gone well.

So, I downplayed my disappointment. "It was okay. We went to that new Greek place, Mykonos."

"Was it good?"

"Yeah. The food was delicious."

"Cool." He paused to look at me, then narrowed his eyes. "You okay?"

Apparently I wasn't doing a good job of seeming nonchalant. My emotions were all over the place, and I needed to go to bed, call this day over.

"Yeah. I'm fine."

"You sure?"

"Yup." I forced a smile. "Gonna hit the sack. Super tired."

Declan didn't move from his spot as he watched me move toward my room.

"'Night, Mollz," he called after me.

I turned one last time and smiled. "Goodnight."

• • •

Over the next couple of days, I didn't cross paths much with Declan. He'd been spending more time out— probably with Julia. Due to a scheduling change, I'd worked the past two days but had Friday off.

I woke up to find a note:

TGIF! Happy day off, roomie. I made this pasta last night but ended up going out to dinner last minute. Have it for lunch "penalty free" on me. ;-)

xo Declan

For some reason, this simple note made my chest tight. It had been the longest week, and I missed him. It was fucked up how much.

Deep down, I knew it was good to have these periods of time where I didn't see him, because I was going to have to get used to it anyway once he left. It just sucked.

• • •

Friday night, I met my co-workers for happy hour downtown. Will sat across from me, but you'd never have known we'd been out on a date recently. He hadn't initiated going out again. And tonight, while he stole some flirtatious glances at me, he hadn't come over to even kiss me on the cheek. Clearly he was keeping his options open.

I wasn't sure I would take him up on it if he asked me out again. Casual sex with Will Daniels wouldn't be the worst thing in the world, but I didn't want to waste time with someone who'd already written off the possibility of a relationship. So, if he asked me to hang out again, I'd have to see how I felt.

My phone vibrated.

Declan: I was hoping to catch you tonight. I feel like I haven't seen you in forever.

My heart fluttered.

Molly: I'm at happy hour.

Declan: With Will?

Molly: Well, he's here, but we're not really together. It's a bunch of people.

Declan: What's up with that?

My first inclination was to be honest and tell him about the date. But the selfish part of me wanted an excuse to see Declan tonight and stick it to Will at the same time.

Molly: I'm thinking I could use your presence here, if you don't mind showing up.

Declan: You mean as your "date"?

Molly: I know you're seeing Julia now, so no worries if you don't feel comfortable with our previous agreement.

The dots moved around as he typed.

Declan: Julia is not my girlfriend. She's not ready for that. We're just having fun right now.

Molly: So she won't mind if I borrow you? ;-)

My heart thundered in my chest as I waited for his response.

Declan: I'll be there in twenty.

"Act surprised to see me," Declan whispered in my ear as he wrapped his arm around my waist from behind. He moved his mouth to my cheek and planted a soft kiss.

I turned in his arms. "Uh...Declan. You're here. This is...a nice surprise."

He brushed a lock of hair from my face and smiled. "Is it? I hope you don't mind me dropping by like this. You'd mentioned the other day you were coming here for happy hour. I was only a few blocks away and thought I'd surprise you."

"No, it's fine. I'm glad you did."

I'd been standing next to my friend Emma, and I caught her mouth hanging open in my peripheral vision. It made sense, since I'd just finished catching her up about the date I'd had with Will, and now another man had his hands on me in an intimate way—another gorgeous man.

"Umm. Declan...this is my friend Emma. We work together at the hospital."

Declan flashed his dazzling smile and extended his hand. "Good to meet you, Emma. I'm sorry if I'm interrupting."

"You're not at all. Molly and I just finished catching up. I was on vacation the last two weeks." She gave me the stink eye. "It's amazing how much you can miss in just fourteen days."

"I bet." Declan motioned to my almost-empty glass. "I'm going to order a drink. Is that your usual pinot?"

"It is."

He pointed to Emma. "What can I get you, Emma?"

"Oh, you don't have to do that."

Declan grinned. "Of course I do. Rule number one: make sure you keep the friends of the woman you're crushing on liquored up and happy."

Emma laughed. "I like that rule. I'll take a vodka cranberry. Thank you."

While Declan spoke to the bartender, Emma whispered to me, "Umm...is there something you forgot to mention?"

Emma was a good friend, but I didn't think this was the time or place to explain the truth about my relationship with Declan. Plus, I was a little embarrassed that I'd resorted to these childish games. "It's...new. We're keeping things casual and just having fun."

"Fun, huh?"

I nodded.

Emma brought her drink to her lips and spoke. "Well, you know who *doesn't* look like he's having fun at this moment?"

"Who?"

Her eyes shifted to look over my shoulder. "Dr. Dandy. And he's heading this way."

CHAPTER TWELVE

Declan

Well, that certainly didn't take long.

By the time I turned around, with the drinks I'd ordered in my hands, Dr. Dickface had already walked over ready to piss on Molly like she was a fire hydrant. God, I didn't like this guy.

"It's Declan, right?" he said as I approached.

I passed Emma her drink and gave Will my hand. Shaking extra firmly, I smiled. "It is. How you doing, Bill?"

He frowned. "It's Will."

"Will...right, okay. Sorry about that." I shifted to Molly and held her glass of wine out to her. "Here you go, babe."

Molly's eyes widened. She looked like she might shit her pants. So while I wanted to put my free hand on her ass in front of this guy, I refrained for her sake.

The four of us stared at each other as I sipped my drink. *Well, this is uncomfortable.*

"So, Declan, are you from the downtown area?"

"I live on the west side."

"Ah...Molly's side of town."

My eyes slanted to meet Molly's. "Yeah. We live *very* close."

"Is that how you two met?"

Good ol' Will was definitely nosy, wasn't he?

"Actually, yes." I looked at Molly. "I'll probably embarrass her if I tell the story, won't I, Mollz?"

Molly's eyes flared yet wider. "Maybe you shouldn't tell it, Declan."

I couldn't resist. "I was on the L on my way home one night. Molly here was sitting across from me reading a book. I couldn't keep my eyes off her. The corners of her lips kept twitching as she read, like she really wanted to smile. Like a dumbass, I let her get off the train without trying to talk to her. But that night, I couldn't stop thinking about her. So the next day I took the train at the same time, hoping to run into her again. She wasn't on it—and not the next day or the day after that, either. Then, one night a week later, I was walking to my train at a totally different time. On my way, I passed a bookstore, and the book she'd been reading happened to be in the window, so I went in to pick it up. The clerk told me the second book in the series had just come in, so I grabbed a copy of that, too. When I got on my train twenty minutes later, there she was." I looked at Molly adoringly. "I sat next to her, gave her book two, and asked her out for drinks."

Emma had dreamy hearts in her eyes. "That's the most romantic thing I've ever heard."

I winked at Molly. "I'm just glad she didn't think I was a stalker."

I had to sip my drink to keep myself from cracking up at the look on Dr. Dick's face. I'd heard the term *green with envy* before, but I'd never actually seen it on another human being. His skin looked a little sallow.

Some guy walked over. "Hey, Will. Do you have a minute? Mark and I are thinking about doing a stint volunteering with Doctors Without Borders. We wanted to get your take on which area we should go to since you've volunteered a few times before."

"Yeah, sure."

I'd been feeling pretty smug about myself the last few minutes, but hearing that Dr. Dick volunteered his time took some of the wind out of my sail. The closest I'd come to helping save lives was the time I'd yelled, "Watch out" when a baseball was flying toward my sister's head. How the hell could I compete with that shit? Better yet, why was I feeling like I had to? Maybe I was getting myself a little too into character.

After Will walked away, Emma excused herself to go to the ladies' room, which gave Molly and me some alone time.

"You saw me on the train and fell madly in love?" She chuckled. "Could you lay it on any thicker, Romeo?"

I shrugged. "Hey. I'm a helpless romantic. You're a very lucky girl."

Molly sighed. "We haven't had a chance to catch up lately, but things with Will didn't go exactly as I'd hoped on our date."

"What happened?"

"Well, it's my own fault, really. I'd stressed how you and I were in a non-committed relationship, so Will took that to mean I was into doing casual."

My heart sped up. "You mean he wants to be fuck buddies?"

She shrugged. "He didn't say that point-blank. But he told me he'd never asked me out before because he didn't think I was the type of woman to do a casual relationship. Basically, he decided to ask me out once he found out I was open to that type of thing. But the problem is, I'm really *not* a casual dater. The thought of being with someone who might also be sleeping with other women, especially Will, doesn't appeal to me at all. Don't get me wrong, I don't need a man to propose marriage or anything, but once I have feelings for someone, I've only ever been monogamous."

My palms were sweaty. "So you two are..."

"No, we didn't have sex on our first date."

I felt a giant wave of relief. "I'm sorry, Moll. What are you going to do? Will you tell him how you feel?"

"I'm not sure I'll actually need to say anything since he hasn't asked me out a second time. I don't think he's interested in casually dating me, much less anything more."

Was she blind? I shook my head. "Oh, he's interested, alright. The dude practically had smoke puffing from his nose when he saw me standing next to you."

"I don't know about that..."

"Trust me, Moll. I know."

Molly bit down on her lip. "I guess only time will tell."

Yeah, but I'd bet my last dime it was going to come sooner rather than later. There was no way that guy wasn't going to try to lock her down. He felt threatened.

I sucked back the remnants of my drink in one gulp, feeling like I needed a few more to take the edge off. "You want another wine?"

"I usually limit myself to two when I go out. But since you're here with me, and I won't be traveling home in the dark by myself, sure. Why not?"

After I got us another round, Emma came back from the ladies' room. Molly introduced me to a few more of her friends, and we had some laughs. But throughout the evening, I caught Dr. Dick with his eyes on Molly at least a dozen times. At one point, he was talking to her co-worker Daisy. The woman was blatantly flirting with him, making as much body contact as she could and tossing her blond hair around. Molly looked over and saw it, too, and my heart clenched at the disappointment on her face. So I put my arm around her shoulder and pulled her close. Apparently, Mr. Casual didn't like that too much, because within a few minutes he was again by our side.

"I'm going to head out," he said. "Do you have a minute, Molly?"

I had to give him credit; the guy had balls walking up and asking her to talk in private when I had my arm around her shoulder.

Molly looked over at me. I had the strongest urge to squeeze her closer and tell the jerk to take a hike, but instead I let her decide how to handle things.

"Umm...sure. Excuse me for a minute, will you, Declan?"

My heart sank. "Yeah...of course." Reluctantly, I let go of her.

The two of them spent about fifteen minutes talking in the corner alone. During that time, I had two more drinks. Even though I talked with some of her co-workers, my eyes never wandered too far from Molly.

When she came back, she had a smile on her face. My smile wilted.

"So that was an interesting turn of events..." she said.

"What happened?"

"Will admitted that he was jealous seeing us together. He asked me to have dinner tomorrow night to talk."

What a dick.

Yes, the plan had been to use jealousy to make our crushes notice that they might lose their chance. But something about this guy made me think it was less about losing his chance with Molly and more about winning a competition. But Molly seemed happy, so I didn't want to piss on her parade.

"That's great." I looked around and didn't see Dr. Dick. "Is he gone?"

"Yeah. He has an early morning tomorrow, so he left."

"You don't have to work tomorrow, right?"

"Nope. I'm off for three glorious days."

I'd had a fair amount of drinks already, but I suddenly had the urge to get shitfaced. "What do you say we have a celebratory shot?"

"Oh boy... I'm sort of a lightweight."

I winked. "That's okay. I'm strong. I can carry your ass."

• • •

"Do you have any rattoos?"

I dropped the key to our apartment on the floor a second time as we stood in front of the door. "Rattoos?"

Molly drunk snorted. "You said rattoos!"

I laughed. "I'm just repeating what you said. *You* said rattoos."

"I didn't say rattoos. I said rattoos." She hiccupped. "Oh my God! I did say rattoos. Why can't I say rattoos?"

I scooped the key off the floor and squinted as I tried for the third time to get it in the lock. "Got it!" I pushed the door open to let Molly walk inside ahead of me.

In the doorway, she turned to face me. Her mouth overexaggerated every syllable as she slowly formed each sound. "Tat-tooo. Do you have any tat-toos?"

"Ah. *Tat*toos. Yes, I do. But I don't have any rattoos yet."

Molly kicked off her shoes just inside the front door and went straight to the kitchen. "What do you have in here today? I'm starving."

"I think there's some leftover penne alla vodka."

She ripped open the refrigerator door and grabbed the Tupperware. "Let's eat it cold."

I chuckled and plucked the container from her hands. "How about I heat it up for us. It'll only take five minutes."

Molly pouted. "That's four-and-a-half minutes too long."

I dumped the pasta into a small pot and turned on the stove. We'd both had way too much to drink, but Molly was leaning on the kitchen counter, and it looked like she might need it to keep herself upright.

"Why don't you go get comfy in the living room?"

"I want to watch you cook. It's sexy having a man make me food."

"Oh yeah?"

I turned to look at her just as her elbow on the counter slipped and she almost toppled over. "Whoa there. Be careful." I caught her waist and lifted her up onto the counter. "How about you sit up here then?"

Molly grabbed the glass jar of pink M&Ms next to her. She pulled out a handful and popped some into her mouth before holding out her hand to me. "Want some?"

"No, thanks. I can handle the five-minute wait."

She stuck her tongue out, which made me smile.

"So, where is it?" she asked with her mouth full.

"Where's what?"

"Your tat-too."

"Ah. It's a secret. If you want to know, I'll need to know something personal about you. A secret for a secret."

"Okay!" Her face lit up. "You go first."

"Alright. I actually have two tattoos: one on my left shoulder blade and the other on my side, on my rib cage."

"Oh wow. What are they?"

I wagged a finger at her. "Not so fast, Miss Nosypants. That's a second secret. You have to share a secret first."

Molly tapped her pointer finger to her lip. "Oh! I know! I have a tattoo, too!"

My brows jumped. "You do?"

She nodded. "I do."

"Where is it?"

She grinned. "Not so fast, Mr. Nosypants. That's a second secret. You'll have to share a second secret first."

I smiled. "Nice. Okay. The tattoo on my back is a compass. Don't ask why a compass, because I have no goddamn clue. I was eighteen when I got it and just liked it. The one on my ribs is a cross with the words *Dimittas tua consilia*—it's Latin. It translates to *Let go of your plans*. I got it the night my sister became a nun. They had a nice ceremony the afternoon she took her vows. Before that, I couldn't understand how someone could wake up one morning and just decide to become a nun. But the priest who officiated the ceremony talked a lot about how one of the biggest obstacles we have in life is overcoming our perceived plans for our future. He said if we can let go of our plans, we can do anything." I shook my head. "It helped me figure out that not everyone's plans in life need to be the same. I was so proud of Catherine that day. I wanted to honor her in some way."

"That's beautiful."

"Thanks. But let's get to the good shit." I lifted my chin. "Where's your tattoo?"

She laughed. "It's on my hip. It's three small blackbirds. I got it after my grandmother died. We were really close, and she was a huge Beatles fan. 'Blackbird' was her favorite song. They played it at her wake. I knew all the words, but I never understood them until that afternoon. I got it a few days later."

"That's really cool."

The sauce in the pot started to bubble, so I lowered the flame and stirred.

"Can I see yours?" Molly asked.

I set the spoon down on top of a paper towel next to the stove, making a mental note for the tenth time that I needed to pick her up one of those spoon-rest things, and turned around. "You can... But you know what that means? If I show you mine, you'll have to show me yours."

Molly bit her bottom lip and debated that for a moment. The thought of her unzipping her pants and showing me her hip bone had my pulse speeding up. It was probably best we didn't start undressing.

Though, just as I accepted that wisdom, Molly said, "You go first."

Shit. Alright. Whatever you say...

I unbuttoned my dress shirt and shrugged it off. Underneath, I had on a T-shirt, so I reached behind me and tugged it over my head. The tattoo on my rib cage wasn't visible when my arm was down, so I lifted it and twisted my body so she could get a closer look.

Unexpectedly, Molly reached out and ran her finger along my skin. She traced the cross with her nail, and my skin broke out in goose bumps.

God, that felt good. I found myself wishing she would dig in a little deeper, maybe leave some marks.

"It's really beautiful, Declan."

"Uh...thanks."

Our eyes met, and if I didn't know she was drunk, I would've thought she was turned on. Her lids were hooded, and the light blue of her eyes had darkened to almost all black pupils. When my eyes fell to her lips, I knew it was time to turn around. Showing her my left shoulder, I bent at the knees so she could get a look at the compass. I wasn't sure if I was glad or disappointed that she didn't trace that one. Her nails scraping my back might've been more than I could take.

When I turned around, Molly's eyes roamed over my chest. She spent a solid minute checking me out in complete silence. Then she reached for her jeans and started to undo her pants. For a half second, I'd forgotten she had to reciprocate and show me her tattoo. My sex-deprived brain got carried away and thought she was undressing for me.

I swallowed hard when she pulled back the denim and showed me her creamy skin. Maybe it was the alcohol loosening my inhibitions, or maybe I just wasn't strong enough to stop myself, but I reached out and did exactly what she'd done to me. I gently traced with my finger, outlining the three tiny birds. Her skin was so soft and warm, and I had the craziest urge to bury my hand down her pants and feel the rest of her *soft and warm.*

Not good.

I watched her face as I traced the skin. Molly's eyes closed, and her jaw went slack.

Fuck.

She was gorgeous.

Absolutely fucking gorgeous.

And I wanted to kiss her more than anything.

Just one little kiss...a little taste of her tongue.

I knew it was dumb.

I knew we were both drunk.

I knew there was a distinct possibility that once I pressed my lips to hers, I'd never be able to stop.

Not to mention...

I had no shirt on.

Her pants were wide open...

My chest heaved up and down as I tried to talk myself out of doing anything other than putting my shirt back on and stuffing both our mouths full of food.

But when Molly's eyes fluttered open and dropped to stare at my lips, I knew I was about five seconds away from losing my battle. Her pink tongue peeked out and ran along her full bottom lip, wetting it.

Fuck.

I wanted her *so goddamned badly.*

Molly's eyes lifted to meet mine. Her voice was breathy. "Declan..."

I took a step closer and put my hand on her hip. "Molly...."

Her eyes lifted, but something caught her attention over my shoulder, and her eyes grew wide. "Oh my God, Declan—turn around! The paper towel caught on fire!"

CHAPTER THIRTEEN

Molly

Blinking my eyes open the next morning, I was surprised to remember last night pretty clearly, given how drunk I'd gotten.

My head pounded, and my stomach churned.

I remembered that we'd almost burned the building down. But Declan had acted fast and put the flames out.

I also remembered Will asking me to go out with him again.

Oh my God. I have a date with Will tonight.

What stuck out the most about last night was being more turned on than I'd been in a while when I touched Declan's skin, tracing his ink. It was a simple touch, but it had been erotic as hell.

I cringed as I also remembered pulling my pants down slightly to show Declan my tattoo.

Ugh.

What would've happened if that fire hadn't interrupted our little show-me-yours-I'll-show-you-mine game? Would we have kissed? That might have been inevitable. Clearly the gods above thought that was a terrible idea.

What time is it?

The clock showed 11AM.

When I walked out to the kitchen, Declan was nowhere to be found.

There was a note on the counter.

Hey, roomie,

I went to meet Julia for brunch. Didn't want to wake you, but the coffeemaker is all set up. Just press start. Figured you'd need it stat. We both drank too much last night. In case you don't remember, we almost starred in an episode of Chicago Fire, *and you created a new word: rattoo.*

xo Declan

He always knew how to make me laugh, even when I felt like I'd been hit by a truck.

I checked my phone and saw a text from Emma.

Emma: We didn't have nearly enough chance to catch up last night. I want to hear all about what happened after you left with Declan!

Taking a deep breath in, I pondered how to handle this. I didn't want to lie to her. Emma was my closest friend at work. And I did trust her. It was bad enough that I hadn't been honest with Will.

After I poured my coffee, I thought about it some more and decided to ask Emma to meet me for lunch so I could properly explain everything. It would also be nice to have someone to vent to about this whole situation.

An hour later, Emma and I met at a spot halfway between my apartment and hers.

After the waitress brought our food, Emma wasted no time trying to get me to spill.

"Okay, so tell me everything. What's the deal with that hottie Declan? Are you sleeping with him?"

Playing with one of my French fries, I shook my head. "The story is a bit crazy. But you have to promise you won't utter a single word about this to anyone."

Emma's eyes narrowed. "Now I'm really intrigued. But of course." She leaned in. "What the hell is going on?"

Over the next several minutes, I told her the entire story of how Declan came to live with me and the agreement we'd conjured up.

She shook her head in disbelief as she stirred sugar into her iced tea. "So let me get this straight. You and he had this agreement, and now you don't really know who you're trying to make jealous—Declan or Will? You fell for your fake boyfriend?"

Taking a huge bite of my burger, I spoke with my mouth full. "I didn't mean for things to get complicated. My attraction to Declan has been gradually growing. And he certainly doesn't have a clue how I feel. It wasn't until he started seeing Julia that I even realized the extent of my feelings." I stared off. "We just get along so well. He's a really good friend. But last night—before we were interrupted by the fire—I'm pretty sure something was about to happen."

She nodded. "So you're juggling feelings for two different men. You're going out with Dr. Dandy tonight, though. Maybe that will steer things to his corner."

"We'll have to see what happens." I sighed. "Like I said, Declan is leaving in a few months anyway. So this is a temporary situation."

"Then you have your answer. Just focus on Will. Obviously, his admission that he was jealous last night means you stand a bigger chance than you thought."

"Yeah, but what if it's just about the competition? I don't know whether I can trust that his interest is genuine. I guess I won't know unless I continue to see where things go."

She chuckled. "There are definitely worse problems to have. You're living with a gorgeous man and dating another."

I smiled, though neither scenario was what I wanted. I didn't want to live with a man or just date one. I wanted to be someone's ride or die.

I want love.

• • •

Declan and I never crossed paths that day. He wasn't home when I returned to get ready for my date with Will.

Later that evening, when I got there, Will had already arrived at the Italian bistro we'd agreed on. He stood and pulled out my chair for me as I approached the table.

Looking me up and down, he said, "You look absolutely gorgeous, Molly. Thank you for agreeing to a date on such short notice."

He leaned in and placed a firm kiss on my cheek. The contact sent chills down my spine.

The bluntness of my response shocked me a little. "I wasn't expecting you to ask me out again, to be honest."

He seemed perplexed as he sat back down and slid his chair closer to the table. "Why is that?"

"Well, you hadn't mentioned anything about going out again until Declan showed up last night."

He blew out a long breath and nodded. "I had an amazing time with you earlier this week. In fact, I couldn't stop thinking about you and that kiss. So if you think my lack of contact meant anything, it didn't. It was a crazy week—stressful, many more-complicated births than usual. That was all." He paused. "But...as I admitted to you at the bar last night, seeing you with him gave me a push. It made me realize that my feelings for you are even stronger than I was willing to admit."

His behavior still confused me. I felt the need to lay everything on the line while I had his attention. But the waitress interrupted when she arrived to take our order. I hadn't had a chance to look at the menu yet, so she gave us a few minutes to peruse it.

When she returned, Will ordered the lasagna, while I pondered the choices and ultimately opted for the pasta primavera. She brought two glasses of wine soon after.

Once she left, I took a long sip of my pinot and decided to take up where the conversation had left off.

"Will... The truth is...even though I'm dating Declan, it's not my intention to date more than one man forever. I'm looking for stability in the long run. I'm sorry if I gave you the impression I wasn't. You already told me you're not interested in a serious relationship.

I respect your honesty, and that's why I'm also being honest right now. I don't want to waste your time if you don't ever want anything serious. I—"

"Molly..." He held out his palm. "I think I need to clarify something. It's true I didn't want to get into anything serious *right now*, but I also think maybe I didn't communicate properly on our first date. It seems you think the *only* reason I wanted to date you is because you were open to a casual relationship. That's not true. I think you're absolutely amazing, smart, beautiful— that's why I'm drawn to you." His eyes lingered on mine.

Feeling my pulse race, I said, "I appreciate you saying that, but I'm not sure we should continue things beyond tonight if you don't think you want a serious relationship down the line."

He stared off toward the entrance for a bit before meeting my eyes again. "How about this... I don't want to stop seeing you. Not in the least. I think we should take this slow and with the goal of keeping an open mind. If we're both feeling things are going well between us, I would love the option to date you exclusively. I suppose you would have to figure out your feelings for this other guy, though."

I blinked, trying to process his words. "I would love to take it day by day. But you also said you didn't want marriage and kids. I know it's very premature to be talking about this, but those are things I definitely want someday. So if you're sure you don't want that kind of a future, that would be a hard limit for me."

Will reached for my hand and looked deeper into my eyes. "Let me explain. Marriage and kids are not something I want in the near future. I'd like some time to travel and enjoy my life. My last girlfriend very urgently wanted those things. That was the main reason we broke up. That said, if I fall in love with the right person, I wouldn't deny her the opportunity to be a mother. I would be open to having a child as long as it was the right time and the right woman."

His contradictory statements between the last date and now definitely left me feeling confused. But nevertheless, tonight he'd given me a little hope back.

"I know it seems silly to be discussing such things on a second date," I said. "But I don't want to waste my time with someone who would completely close the door on a future from the get-go, and honestly, that was the impression you gave me."

"Understood." He smiled. "I hope I've eased some of your concerns about continuing to date me."

"You did. Thank you." I let out a long exhale before taking another sip of wine. "Well, that was a serious conversation for so early on in the evening."

He laughed. "Yes, but see, now we've gotten it out of the way and can take the rest of the time to enjoy each other."

Soon after, our food arrived. It was the perfect buffer to transition to a lighter vibe. Will and I had a fantastic, stress-free meal.

After dinner, we decided we didn't want the night to end. Since his apartment was closer to the restaurant (and since mine was off-limits due to the fact that I lived with my supposed other man), we went to Will's place to hang out.

He popped open a bottle of wine and played jazz music from his impressive collection of vinyl albums.

We enjoyed some heavy kissing, but things didn't go further than that. Will was the perfect gentleman, but whether he was the perfect man for me remained to be seen.

• • •

Over the next few days I returned to my night shifts. Will was off, so I didn't cross paths with him at work nor Declan at home. And I rather enjoyed the reprieve from obsessing over my feelings for each of them.

On my first day off, though, I arrived home from running errands to find Declan shirtless, cooking at the stove.

"Be careful you don't start a fire," I cracked over the music he played.

He turned to me and winked. "Because I'm hot?" He set the spatula down and startled me when he ran over and drew me in for a hug, his hard chest pressing against me, making me all too aware of my attraction to him.

He pulled back to look at me. "I feel like I haven't seen you in forever, roomie."

I knew he'd spent at least one night at Julia's this week, so I assumed they were having sex. That made me uneasy, but at least he didn't insist on her sleeping over at our place.

"You hungry?" he asked.

The smell of French toast wafted through the air. So did the smell of Declan, his delicious, musky scent.

I swallowed. "I could eat." *Gosh*. It felt different around him after the other night, like the volume on the sexual-tension meter had been turned from low to full blast.

"Well, I just so happen to be making your favorite: breakfast for dinner," Declan announced before running to his room.

He returned wearing a shirt and resumed his position at the stove. It was like he knew his being shirtless had made me uneasy.

Declan flipped the French toast and sprinkled cinnamon over it. I spent the next several minutes watching him cook. That had become one of my favorite pastimes.

I vented to him about a staff shortage at work, while he opened up about one of his sisters having marital problems. It seemed some of our sexual tension dissipated once we got into a good conversation.

After he plated two big pieces of toast for each of us, we sat down and began devouring it together.

"This is the best French toast I've ever had." My eyes wandered over to the jars on the counter. I stopped chewing. "What did you do?"

I couldn't believe I was just now noticing it, but I'd been a little distracted when I walked in. My pastel, color-coordinated M&Ms had been replaced by a mish-mash of primary rainbow colors, all mixed together in each jar. I was about to break out in hives.

"Just helping you out," he said. "You mentioned your therapist wanted you to become accustomed to things in disarray. I thought of this idea when I walked by the bulk candy store."

"So thoughtful of you to nearly give me a heart attack."

As ballsy as this was, I knew he'd done it with good intentions. And I had been slacking on my exercises lately. In fact, I hadn't challenged myself at all.

"What did you do with the other M&Ms?"

"Don't worry. I stored them away for safe keeping. You'll get them back when you've earned them." He winked.

"Oh boy. Great."

"Needless to say, Julia wasn't too thrilled when I made her stop into the candy store for a five-pound bag. But I think it was because of who I was buying them for."

The bread caught a little in my throat. "She's still jealous of me?"

"Well, I told her you're dating Will now. But she still seems insecure about us living together."

My heart raced and several seconds of silence passed.

"Should she be?" I muttered.

You could've heard a pin drop. I regretted my question but couldn't take it back.

His eyes bore into mine.

Flashbacks from the other night ran through my mind—my fingers grazing his hard body, the goose bumps on his skin. I remembered every second of those moments.

Instead of answering my question, he set his fork down with a hard clank. "I never had a chance to ask you about your date with Will."

I cleared my throat. "It went really well. We had dinner and then he took me to his apartment and showed me his vinyl record collection."

He laughed, but it held an air of insincerity. "And you had to pretend to be interested?"

I shrugged. "I...appreciated it. He has eclectic musical taste."

136

Declan nodded. "Did he show you more than just his collection?"

That question was a little brazen. But I suppose I'd been a bit brazen myself tonight. I told the truth.

"No. I showed him nothing. It's too soon."

"Good." He let out a breath. "I'm not sure I trust the guy. I don't like the one-eighty he pulled just because he saw me show up at the bar. He changed his tune awfully fucking fast."

I felt the need to come to Will's defense. "I don't fault him for his honesty or his jealousy. I respect his admitting that he isn't interested in anything serious right now. He could've just led me on. But last night he clarified some things. He said he might be open to something serious in the future. He wants to take things slow."

"How noble of him," he huffed. "Fuck that. You deserve someone who's not so wishy-washy, Molly. I mean, the guy says one thing one day and another the next? What does that tell you?"

Deep down, I'd felt those warning signals loud and clear myself. But while I appreciated Declan sticking up for me, his words struck a bitter chord.

"And Julia isn't wishy-washy? She flirted with you for weeks while she had a boyfriend. That's the opposite of honesty and sounds pretty wishy-washy to me."

"I didn't say she was perfect, either."

"You used to think so. You made her sound like she walked on water when you first described her to me." I rolled my eyes.

He raised his brow. "Did that bother you?"

Blood rushed to my face. "No. Why do you think that?"

"I don't know. You seemed irritated when you said that just now—that I used to think Julia was perfect. Do my feelings for her upset you?"

"No. Get over yourself. Why would that upset me?"

"I don't know. You tell me."

Feeling defensive, I blurted, "Why would I care how you feel about someone? I don't like you that way."

Big. Mistake. But it was too late to take it back. My words almost immediately bit me in the ass.

"You seem to like me *a fuck of a lot* when you're drunk," he quipped.

Shit. I don't like where this conversation is going. "We were *both* drunk, Declan. If I remember correctly, you were the one who suggested I show you my tattoo in return for you showing me yours."

He didn't say anything for a few seconds. Then he leaned in so I could feel his breath on my face. "Funny how we were both supposedly *so drunk*, yet we remember our actions clearly."

My phone rang, interrupting the tense exchange. Relief washed over me—until my heart sank.

It's Kayla, my dad's wife. She never called.

CHAPTER
FOURTEEN

Declan

"**H**ow is everything?" I jumped out of my seat in the waiting room the minute Molly walked through the double doors.

She sighed. "He's okay. They think he passed out because he's become anemic. It's a common side effect of the chemotherapy. The initial bloodwork is back, but they're going to admit him so they can run some more tests. He also has a pretty bad bump on his head from when he hit the table as he went down. So they're treating him with concussion protocol, to be safe."

I raked a hand through my hair. "Okay. That all sounds treatable, right?"

Molly nodded. "Yeah. The anemia is treatable. They're starting a blood transfusion now, and he'll go on a regimen of iron pills for a while." She shook her head. "He just looks so fragile already. It's only been a little over a month since his diagnosis, and a couple of weeks since I last saw him, yet I can see how fast things are progressing. He's lost a lot of weight, his skin is sallow, and he looks exhausted. Kayla said he's been talking about stopping the chemo already."

"Because of this? Can't he start again once they get him better?"

Molly was silent for a moment. I watched her face as she swallowed, trying to fight back tears. "He has small-cell carcinoma. It's metastasized to other organs already, so the survival rate is..." She again tried to swallow and keep the threatening tears at bay. But one giant drop spilled over and ran down her cheek. "His quality of life from the chemo..."

"Come here." I pulled her against my chest and wrapped her in my arms. Stroking her hair, I wanted to say something, but the sound of her falling apart clogged the words in my throat. Her shoulders shook as she succumbed to her emotions with an aching wail. I hated that all I could do was squeeze her tighter and wish I could take away her pain.

After about ten minutes of standing in the middle of the waiting room, Molly pulled back, wiping her eyes and sniffling.

"Thank you, Declan."

"For nothing. I'm happy to be here for you." I leaned down and kissed her forehead. "What happens now? If they're admitting him, he'll need some clothes, right? There's a twenty-four-hour Walmart about fifteen minutes from here. I can run over and get him some pajamas and toiletries and stuff."

"That's very sweet of you to offer. But I told Kayla I'd go to their house and get some of his things so he can be more comfortable. It'll be at least an hour or two before they move him into a room, and they don't like more than one person at a time in the emergency room with a patient, anyway. No one said anything because I'm friends with a few of the nurses, but I don't want to take advantage since I work here. I'll run to his house while they're admitting him, now that I know he's stable. But it's late. I can drop you off at home on my way."

Like hell was I letting her drive around the city alone in her current state. "I'm coming with you."

"I'm probably going to be here all night after I go get his clothes."

I winked, trying to lighten things up a bit. "It's okay. Going all night is my specialty."

She rolled her eyes, but I saw the smile in them. A few minutes later, we were back in the car. Molly's father's house was a forty-minute drive from the hospital. He'd been at a restaurant when he'd passed out on his way back from the men's room. I'd been to his house for dinner a few weeks ago, but I'd only seen the downstairs, not the bedrooms, which were tucked away on the second floor. When we arrived, I offered to wait in the living room while Molly went up to pack him a bag, but she asked me to come with her. Apparently, she'd only ever been in his bedroom once, years ago, when he'd first bought the place.

I waited near the door to the master bedroom while Molly walked over to a tall dresser and opened the top drawer. A bunch of framed photos on display seemed to catch her attention. She reached out and took one into her hands.

"Oh my God. I can't believe he has this in a frame. I'm going to kill him."

I walked in to peek over her shoulder. "What is it?"

"It's an old photo of me and my sister. I think I was about six, and she was seven."

The photo was adorable. It was clear from the big blue eyes which one of the little girls was Molly. Her head was thrown back in laughter, her hair was tied up in lopsided pigtails, and she wore the biggest, toothiest smile I'd ever seen. Just looking at it made my lips curve upward.

"Why are you going to kill your father? I think you look cute."

"Uh...because my pants are wet?"

I'd been staring at her giant smile and hadn't even noticed her clothes. But sure enough, when I looked down, the shorts she had on were indeed wet. And not like she'd spilled something. "Did you pee your pants?" I asked.

She covered her face. "Yes! He has a framed picture of me with soiled shorts on! Why the heck would he display this?"

I chuckled. "Was this a frequent occurrence for you? You look a little old to be pissing your pants here."

"My father and sister had just tickled me. I warned them to stop, but they didn't. I cannot believe he still has this, let alone framed it."

It *was* a little strange to show off a picture of your school-age daughter who'd wet herself, but I understood why he did it. "He loves your smile in the photo, and it reminds him of good times."

She sighed. "Yeah...I guess so."

Setting the photo back on top of the dresser, she shook her head, looking through the others on display. She picked up one of her wearing scrubs and a stethoscope.

"This is my nursing-school graduation picture. I didn't give him this. My mother must have sent it to him."

"Well, it looks like he's proud of you, if he framed it."

Molly's face became solemn as she ran her finger along the edge of the frame. "I didn't even invite him. My mother told me it was the right thing to do, but I felt like inviting him was some sort of disrespect to her. He's missed so many things in my and my sister's lives because we couldn't forgive him for leaving us."

"Don't do that, Moll. Don't put that on yourself. You were hurt and had your reasons. We can't change the past, but we can learn from it. You're here for him now, and I'm sure that means a lot to him."

She smiled halfheartedly. "Thanks."

After she packed a bag and collected some toiletries, we headed down the hall to the stairs. But as she took the first step, she stopped and backed up. "Hang on a second. I want to see something."

I followed as she walked back to a door we'd just passed. She opened it and flicked the lights on. The bedroom was decked out in a pink comforter and had pink-and-white-striped window treatments. It was neat, but sort of barren.

"Is this your half-sister's room?"

She shook her head. "Her room is down the hall. This was supposed to be my room. I was sixteen when he bought this place. He brought me over to show it to me, and this room had been all set up, just like this. I never stayed in it, but it looks like he hasn't changed anything over the years."

"Wow. I guess he never stopped hoping you might come spend time here."

"Yeah." She sighed, flicked off the light, and shut the door. But she held onto the handle with her head down. "I'm glad I came here tonight."

I put my hand on her shoulder and squeezed. "I'm glad I came, too...Molly P. Corrigan."

She turned around with her face all wrinkled. "P? My middle name is Caroline."

I wiggled my eyebrows. "Not anymore. From now on, it's Molly Pee-Pee Pants Corrigan."

She rolled her eyes, but smirked. "God, you're such a two-year-old."

"Maybe. But at least I'm potty-trained."

• • •

It was four in the morning by the time Molly came back to the waiting room this time. Her dad had been admitted to the intensive care unit, and I'd dozed off in the waiting room down the hall.

"I'm sorry. I didn't mean to wake you." She pointed to the snack machines lined up along the far side of the room. "I'm so thirsty and wanted to get a water."

I rubbed my eyes. "I wasn't really sleeping. Just resting my eyes."

She smiled. Taking two bills out of her wallet, she fed them into the vending machine and bought herself a bottle of Poland Spring. "You want something?"

"No, thanks. I already ate two bags of hot fries, some Twizzlers, and a peanut chew that I'm pretty sure took out one of my fillings."

Molly sat down in the chair next to me. "They're helping him get changed. I figured I'd give him some privacy and let him sleep for a while. Rounds in ICU usually start about seven o'clock. It's so late already; there's almost no point in going home now. I want to be here to talk to the doctors when they come through."

"So we'll stay. These seats are pretty comfy."

"You should go, Declan. You have to work in a few hours. I can Uber home when I'm ready to go."

I shrugged. "Nah. I can juggle around my schedule. I don't need to be anywhere at a certain time."

Molly's eyes stopped on the end table next to me and widened. "What did you do?"

I'd forgotten all about my project. Lifting the large Styrofoam cup I'd gotten from a nearby nurses' station, I handed her the snack I'd prepared for her. "Only the reds for my little pee-pee girl."

She looked inside the cup. "Where did you get these?"

I lifted my chin toward the snack machine, which I'd drained of every last bag of M&Ms. "They sold them in the machine."

"There had to be ten bags of M&Ms to get this many reds. And where did the other colors go?"

"Thirteen, actually." I rubbed my stomach. "And don't worry, no unacceptable colors were harmed during the process. I put them all to good use—though my stomach might disagree right about now. You know, it's a good thing these machines take credit cards. A buck seventy-five for one bag of candy? What a rip-off."

Molly just kept looking at me.

"What?" I wiped at my face. "Did I drool on myself during my cat nap?"

She shook her head. "No. You're fine. It's just... Why exactly did you buy all these and do this?"

I didn't understand the question. "What do you mean? Because you like to eat one color. Why else would I do it?"

"But you had to know I wasn't going to eat this entire giant cup of M&Ms right now."

I actually hadn't thought about that. "I wasn't suggesting you had to eat them all."

"I know. I realize that. You didn't spend more than twenty dollars and sit here separating the colors because I might eat them as a meal."

I wasn't following. "Okay…"

"You did it because you knew I was feeling down, and I'd get a kick out of it."

I shrugged. "So?"

Molly reached over and took my hand. She laced her fingers with mine. "You're a good friend to me, Declan."

I knew she'd meant it as a compliment, but her saying I was *a friend* didn't sit quite right. Our conversation earlier this evening felt like a lifetime ago now. But my feelings for Molly had changed sometime over the last few weeks. At first I'd thought it was just a natural sexual attraction. I mean, there was no denying she was a beautiful woman. But lately I'd been wanting to spend all of my free time with her, and I'd been questioning the feelings I'd thought I had for Julia.

Of course, this wasn't the time or place to continue our discussion, but nevertheless, hearing her call me *a good friend* kinda made my gut feel like it had taken a punch.

Still, I squeezed her hand in mine. "Just doing what you'd do for me, if the shoe was on the other foot."

She leaned her head on my shoulder. "I would. I absolutely would be here for you."

• • •

"Molly?"

I woke to the sound of a man's voice about 6AM. Opening my eyes, I found the last thing I wanted to see: Dr. Dickalicious standing in the waiting room. Luckily, Molly was out cold. We'd both fallen asleep an hour or two ago. I'd been sitting up, but Molly had spread out across three chairs, and her head rested on my lap. Since the asshole didn't seem to care that he might wake her, I managed to gently lift her head off me and set it down on the chair so I could get up.

Nodding my head toward the door, I whispered, "Let her sleep. We can talk outside."

In the hall, I dragged a hand through my hair and stretched my arms over my head. "Her father passed out at a restaurant a few blocks away. She was up all night."

Dr. Dick planted his hands on his hips. "I just heard. She should have called me."

Considering the problem wasn't her father's vagina, I disagreed. "For what?"

Will's jaw tightened. "Well, for one thing, I'm a doctor."

I folded my arms across my chest. "You're never going to believe this, but this big building? It's *filled* with them."

Will rolled his eyes. "I could have kept her company."

"I had that covered. You weren't needed."

He sighed. "Listen, I'm not going to get into a pissing contest with you. Molly and I have a lot in common. There's been something brewing between us for years. I realize it probably hurts your ego that we started dating after you started seeing her. But the truth is, she wouldn't be dating me if you did it for her."

My hands balled into fists. "Listen, asshole, I don't like you. But that's not important right now. What is important is Molly. She's going through some tough shit. It's not about who gets to hold her hand, but that someone does. So when she wakes up, don't go giving her a hard time."

The sound of the waiting room door creaking open caused both of us to change our focus. At the sight of a groggy Molly, Will immediately stepped around me. "Hey. Daisy told me you were here and what happened to your dad. I just sent a false labor home, so I figured I'd come find you."

Molly glanced over at me, then back to Will. "His hemoglobin was three when they brought him in."

Will frowned. "Who's the attending?"

"Dr. Marks. I don't know him that well. But he's been very nice."

"I golf with him occasionally. I assume they scanned him?"

Molly nodded. "His head because of the fall, and his chest."

"Why don't we go talk to Dr. Marks together and then take a walk over to diagnostic imaging? We can pull his scans up and see for ourselves where things stand."

Molly's shoulders relaxed. "That would be great, Will."

While I was happy to hear Molly would have help getting information, I freaking hated the source of that help. But I did my best to hide it.

"Declan, I'm going to go see if we can get any new information, if you don't mind?"

I shook my head. "Of course not. Do what you need to do. I'll be right here."

Will put his hand on Molly's back, and I suddenly felt like the odd man out.

"Actually, Declan," he said, "I got it from here. Thank you for keeping Molly company. I'm sure she'll want to stick around for rounds soon. Since I'm off now, I can drop her at home afterward. You look like you could use some sleep."

Molly looked over at me and frowned. "He's right, Dec. Why don't you go home? I'm going to be here a few more hours, at least, and you've been here all night with me."

I didn't want to leave, especially not with Dr. Dickalicious trying to pick her up like she was some sort of fumbled ball. But I also realized he could give her access to things I couldn't. Not to mention, if I made a scene, the only one I'd hurt was Molly.

So I reluctantly nodded. "Okay. I'll go. Call me if you need anything, Moll."

She stepped forward and kissed my cheek. "Thanks for everything, Declan."

My eyes caught with Dr. Dick's, and his sparkled with victory. *God, I don't like this guy.*

"Thanks, Declan." He extended the hand that wasn't wrapped around my girl's back. "Take care."

I watched as the two of them strode off together, an empty feeling churning in my stomach. At the double doors to the intensive care unit, Molly looked back and gave me a conciliatory smile. I waved and pretended everything was fine.

But it wasn't.

After the doors closed, I realized what was fucking with my head more than anything. It wasn't the fact that Dr. Dick had offered her help I couldn't give. I cared about Molly enough to put her needs first and accept what was best for her. It also wasn't the fact that he'd put his hand on her back as they walked down the hall. What freaked me the fuck out was that I'd been upset because he'd put his hand on *my girl's* back.

My girl.

That's how I'd thought of her.

But she wasn't, was she?

Either way, I was leaving her in the hands of the guy who was supposed to get the girl all along.

CHAPTER FIFTEEN

Molly

I'd missed my apartment so much.

After a few days, Dad had been released from the hospital, and I'd decided to take some time off from work and spent a week with him at his house. I knew if something happened to him, and I didn't make more of an effort to spend time there, I'd regret it. So, I'd slept in the formerly forbidden pink bedroom.

Luckily, his condition had stabilized, and he was now back where he'd been before the fall happened. Today I was finally returning home after nearly seven days away, with the promise that I would spend the night at Dad's again soon.

I hadn't told Declan I was returning tonight. He was standing in the kitchen when I opened the door. I expected him to greet me with his usual cheery smile, especially given how long I'd been gone. But he didn't even look up when I entered.

"Hey!" I said. "I wasn't sure you'd be home."

"Hey. Welcome back." His smile seemed forced.

"Yeah. I'm here. Wasn't really feeling up to going out tonight."

My stomach sank. "Is everything okay?"

He hesitated. "Yeah, everything is fine."

I reached out to hug him, taking a deep breath of his delicious scent. The warmth of his arms felt so good, although his body was noticeably more rigid than usual. Something didn't seem right.

"I'm glad you're here," I said as I pulled away. "I'm definitely better off not being alone with my thoughts at this point."

He nodded but didn't say anything. I'd hoped he'd tell me how glad he was that we could hang out tonight, but right now I felt more like I'd disturbed his peace by coming back. In all the weeks I'd known him, Declan had never given me the impression he wasn't happy to see me, until now.

"How was your time at your dad's?" he asked after a moment.

I shrugged. "It was okay. Definitely glad I did it. He's doing a little better. I know he liked having me there. Better late than never, right?"

"Absolutely."

"I spent every waking hour with him, and when he napped, I'd go to my room and read. I didn't really force myself to make small talk with Kayla. I did get to take my sister Siobhan out for lunch one day, and we bonded a little. She's scared, too. I think the only thing worse than the fear of losing your dad in your twenties would be losing him as a child."

"She's lucky to have you for a big sister."

"Yeah, I suppose." I plopped down on the couch and stared at the ceiling.

"What are you thinking about?" he asked.

"I have so many regrets when it comes to my father, Declan."

He took a seat next to me.

"We all have regrets in life. No one is perfect." His expression grew somber.

"Are you okay?"

"Yeah. I'm fine."

Does he not realize I can see through him? "You seem...down or something."

He shook his head. "It's nothing. Don't worry about me."

"Did something happen at work?"

"No. Nothing happened." His tone was a bit short. He let out a long breath. "I'm the last person you should be worrying about right now, okay?" Then came another forced smile that didn't reach his eyes. "Tell me about what you were saying. What specific regrets are you referring to?" He seemed intent on moving the conversation off of this issue and back to me.

I paused to examine his face again before I answered his question. "Well, I guess what I mean is, I was so young when my father left home. I didn't understand how complicated relationships could be. I faulted him for leaving us when it was really more about his marriage to my mother not working out than him wanting to abandon his kids. He wasn't happy. What—did I need him to stay in a loveless marriage for my sake? I don't agree with how he handled things. But to have shut him out all these years for making the decision to put his own happiness first? In retrospect, that seems very harsh."

Declan shook his head. "Okay, but like you said, you were young, you were hurt—we can't help how we feel." He placed his arm along the top of the couch and scooted a few inches toward me. "And you know what? You're *still* young. You're figuring these things out while your dad is still here. It's never too late to make amends, as long as the person is still with us."

Nodding, I wiped my eyes. "I feel like I've really tried over the past few weeks."

"You have. And your dad loves you no matter what. He's proven that—from the room he kept for you, to the way he looks at you. You can always tell someone's true feelings by the way they look at someone. He's not holding anything against you."

It was ironic that Declan had said that. Because one of the only things that made me wonder about *his* feelings for me was the way he occasionally looked at me. I loved the way he didn't seem to notice anyone else in the room but me. He was always fully engaged with our conversation—like whatever we were talking about was super important, even if we were just discussing the weather. But that look was nowhere to be found right now. Instead, his eyes were vacant and distant.

"Are you sure you're okay?" I prodded.

"I am," he said and again pushed the subject back to me. "Tell me what else has been on your mind."

I was tempted to continue prying about why he seemed melancholy. But I knew he'd just brush me off again. So I exhaled and answered his question. "This whole thing with my father has caused me to reflect on myself. My dad is too young to be facing death. He hasn't had time to accomplish everything he would want to. And it makes me feel like I'm not doing enough with my own life."

He nodded. "Yeah, sometimes it takes something like this to get us thinking about stuff like that." He stared down a moment before looking back at me. "I can tell you right now, if I died tomorrow, I wouldn't feel like my life had been enough. I mean, I work in advertising, shoving products down people's throats with exaggerated claims. How is that helping the world, you know? It's not. It's helping put money in the pockets of already-overpaid executives. My sister Catherine is on the other end of the spectrum, living her entire life doing good deeds. But I try to make small differences where I can. The hope is that they add up in the overall scheme of things."

I smiled. "They always say what people remember most about someone is how that person made them feel. You definitely make those around you feel like you're truly invested in them. That's how you make *me* feel. You're a good friend."

"And to think, you almost let me walk away because I have a penis." He winked.

I laughed, relieved to see his first genuine smile of the night. "That would've sucked."

"In all seriousness, being a good friend is one way people can make an impact. It's never too late to call that friend you've been meaning to call, or to do small things that add up. Stop the homeless person on the sidewalk and offer him lunch. You don't have to carry the weight of the world on your shoulders to contribute to change. You can do it little by little."

"How did you get so insightful?" I smiled, clutching one of the throw pillows to my chest. "Hey, I never got to properly thank you for being there for me the night my dad was rushed to the hospital."

"Anytime."

I hesitated a moment. "Will seemed freaked out to see you with me, but I guess I can't blame him considering what he thinks of my relationship with you."

"Did he tell you we got into a pissing match outside the waiting room before you woke up?"

"No, but I sensed something when I saw you two talking." I paused. "I know why he must hate you. He thinks you're his competition. But...why do you hate *him*?"

Declan's jaw tightened. "I've already told you. The verdict is still out on Dr. Dickalicious. I don't like how fast he changed his tune on things." He shrugged. "But look, I just want you to be happy. If he ends up making you happy, that's what matters."

You make me happy. Those words were at the tip of my tongue as the tension in the air grew thick.

Declan jumped up off the couch and clapped his hands, seeming to forcibly shake himself out of his funk. "You know what this night is missing?"

"What?"

"Breakfast for dinner. You hungry?"

Rubbing my stomach, I grinned. "I'm starving, actually."

"Go relax. I'm gonna head to the store because we're out of eggs. I'll be back in twenty."

"Sounds good."

After spending so much time at my dad's house, I was glad to be back in my happy place. A casual night in with Declan was exactly what I needed right now. The only thing dampening the evening was Declan's strange mood. Maybe I was overreacting. Everyone has the right to feel crappy and not have to explain themselves. Maybe I'd just been spoiled by his happy-go-lucky demeanor up until this point.

While waiting for him to come back, I took a nice, hot shower. Closing my eyes as the water rained down on me, I reflected on our conversation, pondering some of the small things I could do moving forward: be a better daughter to my parents, a better big sister to Siobhan, volunteer my nursing services somewhere once a week on one of my days off. Declan was totally right. There were lots of small ways I could make my life more meaningful—in honor of my dad.

I exited the shower feeling refreshed and hoped Declan would be in a better mood when he returned. I'd just wrung out my hair when the doorbell rang. I thought it was a little strange that he was using the bell, but perhaps he'd forgotten his key.

Wrapped in my towel, I walked over to the door and opened it with a huge smile on my face. It faded when I realized it wasn't Declan returning with the groceries. It was Julia.

I clutched my towel closer to my body. "Oh...hey. I thought you were Declan."

Her eyes wandered from my head to my toes. "You thought I was Declan, so you answered the door in your towel?"

Is she seriously judging me in my own damn house?

"No. I answered the door in my towel because I live here, and the bell rang when I'd just gotten out of the shower."

"Of course." She nodded and made her way into the apartment without being invited. "Where is Declan?" she asked, looking around suspiciously.

"He went grocery shopping."

"Ah." She ran her finger along the granite countertop. "You mind if I hang out until he gets back?"

What the hell am I supposed to say?

"Sure."

I went to my room to change. God, this sucked. I did not want to deal with her tonight.

As soon as I returned to the living area, the front door opened, and my and Julia's heads turned in unison.

Declan's eyes widened. "Julia, what are you doing here?"

"I was heading home from a late spa appointment. Since your apartment was closer than mine, I figured I'd stop by. I know you said you were just going to chill at home tonight, but I missed you."

He feigned a smile, but I could tell it wasn't genuine. "How come you didn't text me to tell me you were coming?"

"I guess I wanted to surprise you?"

He looked over at me, and I could tell he was uncomfortable.

"I was just getting out of the shower when the doorbell rang," I explained. "She hung out and waited for you while I got dressed."

He smiled sympathetically at me, and turned to her. "Okay. I just wish I'd known you were coming. I would've bought extra bread. I only bought eggs."

She looked between us. "Oh, I didn't realize I was interrupting...dinner?"

Shit. I actually felt bad for Declan. She was definitely suspicious when this was just a platonic dinner between roommates. He was trying to do something nice for me, and she was probably going to give him shit about it.

"Declan was just going to make breakfast for dinner. Nothing fancy," I said.

"Molly had a tough week, and it's her favorite."

"But..." I looked at him. "There should definitely be enough for everyone, right?"

Julia pretended not to care. "I haven't been eating carbs anyway."

Figures. Skinny bitch.

"I can make you a nice omelet," Declan offered. "We have some veggies in the crisper. You like spinach, tomato, and a little feta?"

"I would love that. You're so sweet."

He's being sweet right now because he has no choice. You forced him into it by showing up unannounced.

Declan smacked his hands together. "Okay, veggie omelet coming up." He turned to me. "French toast for us, okay?"

"You know it. Of course." I excused myself. "I'll be right back. I'm going to dry my hair."

After I disappeared into my room, my phone chimed.

Declan: I'm sorry she showed up unannounced.

Molly: It's okay.

Declan: No, it's really not. I know you wanted a chill evening.

Molly: Well, she's here. And I would never expect you to tell her to leave. I'm really okay. This is your apartment, too. And you've been more respectful than you need to be. You barely bring her over. It's fine.

Declan: I owe you one.

I sighed and turned on the blow dryer.

After I finished with my hair, I returned to the kitchen. "As always, that cinnamon French toast smells so good."

Julia took a deep breath in. "God, you're right. I wish I didn't care what I looked like."

Is that an insult?

Declan waved the spatula. "You're assuming men don't like a little meat on a woman's bones."

Thank you, Declan.

"Last I checked, you seemed to like *these* bones just fine," Julia quipped.

Ugh. Barf.

Declan didn't respond and resumed flipping the toast and tending to Julia's annoying veggie omelet on the opposite burner.

He plated everything, and the three of us sat at the kitchen table together. Declan had bought my favorite orange juice with heavy pulp and poured it into wine glasses for me and him. Julia opted for water, since the orange juice apparently had too much sugar.

With his mouth full, Declan turned to me and asked, "How's the toast?"

"Delicious. Thank you."

He smiled in a way that looked like a silent apology.

"So, Declan tells me you're dating a doctor from work?" Julia asked.

I wiped syrup off the side of my mouth. "Yes. It's still new."

"That's exciting."

I shrugged. "I don't get excited about anything so early. It would be dumb to do so. I'm looking for more than just someone to screw."

"But you're young. Why do you need to settle down?" she asked, seeming confused.

"It's not so much about settling down as it is being with someone who only has eyes for me. That's important to me."

Declan's eyes snagged with mine for a moment before he returned to his French toast.

After several minutes of eating in silence, Julia broke the ice again.

She rubbed her belly. "That omelet was so good. It reminded me of something I'd get at home. I miss all my healthy food places in California. I can't wait to get back."

Declan's eyes narrowed. "You can get healthy food here."

"Yeah, but it's not the same. You can't find a smoothie place on every corner here. It's a challenge to find an all-organic restaurant. It's not just that, either. I guess I just miss home, in general. The sunshine. The fresh air. The Pacific Ocean. And obviously my family."

Declan nodded. "I miss my family, too. But I *love* Chicago." He glanced at me. "There's a lot I appreciate about this city."

"It's not bad, I guess," she said. "I'm just ready to go."

She's ready to go and take Declan with her.

"I want to get a dog, too," Julia added. "I was just about to get one before we got this assignment. So, the first thing I'm gonna do when I get home is get a dog."

"And what if you get another out-of-town assignment?" I asked.

She shrugged. "My sister can watch it."

I lifted an eyebrow. "Your sister would be down with that?"

"I know she'll do it."

Julia was an entitled brat. Or maybe it just seemed that way since I generally hated her for getting to fool around with the man I was crushing on hard.

"My sister loves animals as much as I do."

I looked down at her designer boots, which I happened to know had real fur.

"If you love animals, you should consider not wearing fur. An animal died for those boots."

She looked down at her feet. "I suppose you're right. Hadn't really thought about it."

"Yeah, just something to consider," I said, shoveling another bite of toast into my mouth.

Declan smirked and attempted to change the slightly hostile tone of the night.

"Anyone up for a post-dinner cocktail? I bought this margarita mix the other day I want to try."

I could definitely go for a little alcohol right about now.

Julia licked her lips. "Mmmm... That sounds delicious."

This from the girl who's sworn off carbs? Yeah, that made sense. I guess margaritas don't count.

The next part of the night was perhaps the worst. Julia was all over Declan as he stood at the counter making our drinks. She wrapped her arms around his waist and just hung on him.

He managed to break free long enough to hand me my drink. "Here you go, Mollz. Just how you like it, with extra salt."

"Thank you."

I took a sip of the slushy, frozen margarita. It had the perfect amount of sweetness to complement the lime. But as much as this drink rocked, I was done being an audience to Julia rubbing herself all over my man.

Shit.

What?

My man?

That was such a random and inappropriate thought. But yet I'd had it.

Yeah, definitely time for you to be out, Molly.

I lifted my glass in a salute. "You know what? I think I'm gonna take this to my room, if that's okay. I'm feeling kind of tired. Hopefully the alcohol will just knock me out altogether."

Declan's expression dampened. "Okay. If you want another one, let me know. There's plenty still in the blender."

"Will do. Thanks." I smiled. "'Night, Julia."

"'Night, Molly."

I flashed Declan one more smile before I walked to my room.

Letting out a long sigh of relief as my bedroom door closed, I turned on some Hulu and downed the rest of my drink.

I dozed off a few times, in and out of sleep. The final time I woke up, I noticed I no longer heard the muffled sounds of their talking.

I'd also missed a text about fifteen minutes ago from Declan.

Declan: You still awake?

I typed.

Molly: Yeah.

Declan: Are you decent?

Molly: Yes.

A few seconds later, he knocked on my door. "Come in."

CHAPTER SIXTEEN

Declan

"**H**ey." Molly sat up in bed, leaning her back against the headboard. "Julia leave?"

I nodded. "Is it okay if I sit down?"

Molly pulled up her legs and wrapped her arms around her knees to make room for me.

"Yeah, of course."

Sitting at the bottom of her bed, I was tempted to tell her why I'd seemed off when she walked in earlier tonight. The last week had been tough—so much so that I'd given in and called Dr. Spellman back home. Molly had clearly picked up on the fact that I wasn't myself, and I didn't want her to think it had anything to do with her. But she'd just returned from a difficult time away dealing with her dad. I didn't want to burden her. I needed to snap the fuck out of it.

"I just wanted to say sorry again about Julia coming over like that."

"It's fine. You don't have to apologize for your girlfriend stopping over."

I ran my hand through my hair. "She's not my girlfriend."

Molly tilted her head. "She's not? Does she know that?"

Blowing out a deep breath, I felt my shoulders slump. "I don't know what I'm doing, Moll."

"What do you mean?"

I decided to go back to the beginning. "For the last year, I've had a giant crush on Julia. We've been traveling together more over the last few months, spending a lot of time alone together, and as you know, I'd hoped our chemistry would make her second-guess things with the guy she was dating. It finally did, and now she seems totally into me. And yet I'm the one keeping things moving slowly now."

Molly bit down on her bottom lip. "It doesn't look like you're going slow, the way she's hanging all over you and how much she says you like her *bones*."

I shook my head. "We haven't... You know..."

A look of surprise crossed Molly's face. "Are you saying you haven't slept together?"

I shook my head again.

"I'm surprised," she said. "You seem pretty cozy."

"I don't know what happened. I was so into her, and then...I guess it fizzled out."

That wasn't an entirely true statement. I knew exactly what had happened. *Molly* happened. The fucked up part was that I'd had no problem being with other women while I crushed on Julia. I hadn't been celibate for the last year while I was biding my time with her. Maybe that was a shitty thing to admit, but it was the truth. Yet my crush on Molly seemed to make me incapable of sealing the deal with Julia. I'd slept at her place once, but only because I'd fallen asleep while we were watching a movie. Though lately, Julia had been asking me to stay over and had also made it her business to let me know she was on the pill. I had zero doubt that if I hadn't been reining things in, I would've fucked her already.

"Perhaps you only wanted her because you couldn't have her," Molly suggested. "It's human nature to want things that are off-limits."

I looked down for a long time, giving it some real thought. When I raised my head, my eyes locked with Molly's. "I'm pretty sure that's not it."

Molly's lips parted, and my eyes fell to stare at them. Her breathing seemed to speed up and become shallower, and I became acutely aware that I was sitting on her bed. *Has her room always been this small?* The longer I sat there, looking at her luscious lips, the more the walls felt like they were closing in around me.

The talk we'd been about to have when her father ended up in the hospital *really* needed to happen. And I *really* needed it to happen in a safer room.

I stood. "Do you think we could talk...in the living room?"

Molly looked confused but lowered her knees and began to get up off the bed. That's when I noticed she'd taken off her bra.

I cleared my throat. "Hey, Moll?"

"Yeah?"

"Could we talk in the living room *and* can you put a bra on?"

The corner of her lips twitched. "Yeah, sure. I'll be right out."

"You want another margarita?" I asked.

"Are you having one?"

I'd already had one and knew it wasn't a smart thing to do since I'd just had a medication adjustment. "I shouldn't. I have to get up early tomorrow."

Molly pouted. "Have one with me."

She was pretty much impossible to resist. What the hell? I was determined to get out of the funk I'd been in all night anyway—well, the funk I'd been in for over a week now.

"Alright. One more."

While I went to the kitchen to whip up a fresh batch, Molly got herself settled in on one corner of the couch. After I finished, I walked over to the sofa and handed her one of the drinks in a salt-rimmed glass. "For you."

"Thank you."

I went to sit beside her, then thought better of it. The chair adjacent to the couch was probably a smarter idea, mostly because it was as far away from her as I could sit without leaving the room.

She sipped her drink and spoke with it still at her lips. "Are you sure you don't want to sit in the kitchen? I think that would put another four feet between us."

I squinted at her with a smirk. "Wiseass."

Molly took a gulp of her drink and set the glass on the coffee table.

"Can I ask you something, Declan?"

"Of course. Whatever you want."

"What's going on between us?"

Shit. Okay. We were having *this* conversation. Maybe I should've taken a shot of tequila in the kitchen instead of sipping this margarita.

"That's a pretty big question."

"I know. And I can't believe I just came right out and asked it. But I'm so confused lately."

I let out a deep breath. "When you were a kid, did you ever play the fill-in-the-blank game?"

Molly's forehead wrinkled. "I don't think so. How do you play?"

"It's easy. One person starts a sentence, and then you go around the room and each person has to fill in the blank for the rest of the sentence. Sometimes they use it as an icebreaker at corporate events for people to get to know each other. Like, someone will say, 'When I was little, I wanted to be a *blank*, and then everyone fills in the missing word by saying *fireman* or whatever."

Molly nodded. "Sounds easy enough."

"It's usually played with a group, but it'll work with just two people."

"I take it you want to play now?"

I nodded. "With a few caveats: we tell the absolute truth, neither one of us gets to avoid any questions, and in fifteen minutes, we both go to our rooms. *Alone.*"

"Wow. Okay. Hang on a second. I think I need to prep for this." Molly took a big swig of her margarita, placed it on the table again, and sat up a little straighter. "I have a feeling I'm going to regret this, but I'm ready. Let's play."

"I'll start with some softballs."

"That would be good."

"Let me set the timer on my phone first." I set it for fifteen minutes and gave some thought to a nice, easy first question. After a moment I said, "My favorite color is *blank*."

"So now I just finish the sentence?"

"Yup."

"That's easy. My favorite color is pink."

"Perfect. Your turn."

I could see the wheels in Molly's head turning. "If I could have one superpower, it would be to *blank*."

I didn't hesitate at all. "Telepathy with animals."

Molly laughed. "Totally not what I expected."

I shrugged. "What can I tell you? I was obsessed with those *Dr. Dolittle* movies when I was younger."

"Figures. Your turn."

I could do this all night with Molly, but I needed some real information, so I steered things in another direction.

"Tonight when I saw Julia touching Declan, I felt..."

Molly bit her bottom lip.

I knew she was debating filtering her response, which defeated the entire purpose. I gave her a little nudge. "Just say what belongs in that sentence, Moll. Don't overthink it. There's no right or wrong answer."

I'd assumed she might say *jealous*, but I found her answer a hell of a lot more amusing.

"Stabby," she said. "Tonight when I saw Julia touching Declan, I felt stabby."

I smiled and nodded. "Nice."

She lifted her margarita and knocked back half of what remained. "My turn. I asked Molly to come out to the living room for our talk because *blank*."

It was me who now gulped from my glass. I'd started to consider what I could say, but Molly caught on real fast.

"Uhhh...no filtering," she said. "Just say it, remember?"

"I'm not so sure that's a good idea."

"It's your game. I agreed to play by the rules, so you have to, too. Spit it out, Mr. Tate."

"Okay. Don't say I didn't warn you, though." My eyes found hers. "I asked Molly to come out to the living room for our talk because when I was sitting on the bed so close, I couldn't stop imagining myself inside her."

Molly laughed nervously. "Oh...wow."

I finished off my margarita and set down my glass. My meds definitely intensified how it affected me. A few drinks and I felt damn drunk, which was why I seemed to have lost my filter. "I'm just going to say it, Molly. Forget the game. I'm extremely attracted to you. I have been since the first time I laid eyes on you. But lately... It's getting harder to fight." I shook my head. "In my experience, things often happen in the other direction. I'm physically attracted to a person, and once I get to know them, that wanes a bit. But with you it's the opposite. The more I get to know you, the stronger my physical attraction becomes."

Molly looked down and then back up at me. "What about Julia?"

I shook my head. "I don't know. I'm attracted to her. I'm not going to lie about that. But it's different."

"Different how?"

"She's pretty and all—without being disrespectful, it wouldn't be a hardship to be with her. But I don't feel like a caveman when I look at her, like I want to conquer every part of her body and make it mine."

Molly blinked. "You feel that way about me?"

I nodded. "Yeah, I do. Are you attracted to me, Molly?"

"Very."

"Maybe I shouldn't admit this, but if you were any other person in the world, I wouldn't be fighting it anymore. I wouldn't be sitting all the way over here." I shoved a hand into my hair. "Christ, I wouldn't even have left your bedroom to come out in the living room... I'd be in your bedroom *for days*."

Molly swallowed. "But yet here we are, and you're all the way over there..."

"Do you remember what you said to Julia earlier when she asked about Will?"

Her brows drew together. "No. What did I say?"

I remembered her words verbatim, not that they were news to me. I'd pretty much known all along the woman Molly was. "You said, '*I'm looking for more than just someone to screw.*' I'm only here for a few more months, Molly. I live and work in California. Your life is here in Chicago. Do I think the two of us could enjoy the hell out of each other during the time I have left? *Absofuckinglutely.* But I can't promise you anything long term, and as much as it makes me feel...*stabby* to think of you with Will, I also don't want to come between you and a guy you've liked for a long time. What if I ruin your chances at a good, long-term thing for just a couple of phenomenal months?"

Molly was quiet for a long time. "If you'd never met me, and things with Julia had evolved to where they are now, would you two be...together?"

We both knew the answer to that question, so I tossed it back to her. "If you'd never met me, and things between you and Will had evolved to where they are now, would you be happy with him?"

Molly frowned. We stared at each other until the timer on my phone went off.

"I could stay out here and talk to you all night, Moll. I don't think either of us is surprised by the things we've just admitted. But now that we've said what we needed to say, we need some time to think things through—alone. That's the reason I set the timer."

Molly smiled sadly. "You're a smart cookie."

I winked. "Don't tell anyone. I prefer to be underestimated and let people think I'm just a pretty face." I paused. "Why don't you go get some sleep? I think we could use a few days to think about everything."

She nodded. "Yeah. That's probably a good idea."

Molly stood. For a few awkward seconds, she looked unsure how to say goodnight to me. Eventually, she walked over and gave me a hug. "Goodnight, Declan."

God, she smelled so damn good. Where the hell was a caveman's club when I needed it?

Molly walked toward her bedroom. When she got to the door, she stopped and spoke without looking back.

"Hey, Dec?"

"Yeah?"

"Maybe you should lock your door tonight. That margarita really went to my head."

I smiled. "You too, babe. You too."

CHAPTER
SEVENTEEN

Molly

"So what's going on in the adventures of Molly these days?" Emma twirled her fork in a container filled with spaghetti and shoveled it into her mouth.

"Not much. The usual. I'm supposed to go out with Will Friday night, and last night Declan and I admitted that if there were no Will for me or Julia for him, we'd be banging all over the apartment."

Emma's eyes bulged, and she started to cough. "Oh my God. You just made pasta go down the wrong pipe." Her eyes watered as she reached for her bottle of water.

I chuckled. "Sorry, but you asked."

Since we worked the same shift in different departments, we sometimes managed to schedule our dinner break together. If it hadn't worked out for us tonight, I probably would've asked her to go for coffee after our shifts ended, because I needed to talk to someone.

"Last week you said you were attracted to him, but he had no idea how you felt."

I sighed. "Yeah, I was wrong."

Emma shook her head. "So the feeling is mutual?"

"Apparently..."

"And you guys talked about this, but nothing physical happened?"

I nodded. "We're taking a few days to think about things."

"What are you going to do?"

"I have no damn idea."

"Well, you've been head over heels for Will for years."

"I know I have. And honestly, if it weren't for Declan, I'd probably be super excited about where things are going with Will and me. At first he said he wanted to keep things casual, but he's since told me he could see things progressing with us, and that *someday* he wants a wife and kids and stuff."

"Isn't that exactly what you want? A guy you're crazy about who's looking to settle down with the right woman?"

"It is, but..." I shook my head. "I don't know. I'm confused."

"Well, let's look at the pros and cons of each relationship. Tell me what you like about Will."

"We have a lot in common. He's an obstetrician, and I'm a labor and delivery nurse. He's handsome and levelheaded. I love the way he's always so good under pressure, and how much passion he has for his work. He's smart, yet he never tries to show off, like a lot of other doctors do."

"Okay. That all sounds awesome. Now tell me the cons."

I couldn't think of much. "If we were to go into a serious relationship and then split up, it might be awkward at work."

"That's fair. What about Declan? Tell me what you like about him."

"I like how thoughtful he is. When I first found out about my dad's illness, Declan had just moved in. Yet he always asked how Dad was and made sure he was around when he thought I might be upset and needed to talk. He just seems to know when I need support, and he makes himself available and never makes me feel like it's a burden. He's very funny and makes me laugh all the time, and..." I pointed to the eggplant rollatini I had in front of me. "He's also a great cook. And, of course, let's not forget that he's ridiculously hot."

"And what about the cons?"

Unlike Will, there were some glaring cons related to Declan. "Well, for starters, he lives two-thousand miles away in California. He also travels all the time for his job, and he travels with Julia—the woman he's currently fooling around with that he's been pining over for almost as long as I've been dreaming of a relationship with Will. We don't have that much in common—he's kind of a *leave the clean dishes in the dishwasher because you're just gonna use them anyway* kind of person, whereas I like things put where they belong."

Emma nodded. "Well, they both have a lot of pros, but Declan has a lot more cons. And one of them seems pretty major—he lives in California, Molly. How much longer is he even here?"

I frowned. "A little over four months."

"Is that where his family lives? Where his job will be when his work here is done?"

I nodded. "He has four sisters and both his parents there, plus nieces and nephews. Chicago was just a temporary assignment. He's hoping to get promoted once he goes back to the corporate office in California."

"So, say you pick Declan. What happens when his time here is up? Does he uproot his life and move here? Or do you leave your mom and sister and your sick dad?"

I sighed. Neither sounded ideal. Not to mention, we hadn't even kissed. So thinking about any of this was putting the cart long before the horse. "I know what you're saying." The choice should've been simple. Yet it wasn't.

"Do you want to know what I think?"

I had a feeling I already did. But I nodded anyway.

"If you pick Declan, you're going to wind up very hurt in four months. And you're going to be kicking yourself in the ass over the one who got away."

After dinner, Emma and I both went back to work, but I couldn't stop thinking about our conversation. Making a list of pros and cons was right up my alley—a way of organizing my thoughts to make the right decision. So later, when things were quiet on the floor, I took out a notepad and again listed all the pluses and minuses for each man. Declan's were pretty much the same as I'd rattled off to my friend. But when I listed Will's cons again, I realized I'd failed to admit the biggest obstacle currently standing in my way.

He's not Declan.

• • •

That Friday night, Will and I were in the back of a cab, on the way to our date.

177

"Where are we going?" I asked.

With a glimmer in his eye, he placed his hand on my knee. "It's a surprise."

"Well, now I'm intrigued."

A half hour later, Will took me up to an exclusive rooftop restaurant—except there were no other people. There was just one table amidst a gorgeous setup of lanterns and little white lights around the space.

"Will, what did you do?"

He held out his hands. "It's all ours for the night."

My mouth hung open. "How did you manage this?"

"Let's just say the owner has felt like he owed me one since I delivered his breech daughter."

"Wow. Who was that?"

"Richard Steinberg—he owns Steinberg Financial and this restaurant. That delivery was actually a couple of years ago, and I never thought to take him up on it until I met someone special enough to bring here. The rooftop is reserved for private parties. And this is ours."

My heart fluttered. "Wow. I don't know what to say."

"You don't have to say anything, beautiful. Let's just enjoy tonight."

I beamed as we settled into our seats at the candlelit table.

After our waiter came by with waters, Will unfolded his napkin and placed it on his lap. "How's your father doing?"

I frowned. "He could be better. I've been keeping tabs on him every day. Right now, he's stable. But it's mentally hard on him. As a fellow physician, I'm sure you can understand. He's always felt like his job is to take care of other people, and now that he's unable to

178

do that—unable to even take care of himself—you can imagine how tough it is."

Will closed his eyes momentarily and shook his head. "I absolutely can, Molly, and you know, it's very important that everyone rally around him right now. Distraction from his own mind is probably the best medicine. The last thing he should be feeling is inadequate. He needs all the strength he can get."

"I agree."

Will reached across the table to take my hand. "If there's anything I can do for him, please let me know. If you're not getting the answers you need, I know a lot of people."

"Thank you, Will. I appreciate that more than you know."

A short time later, the waiter brought the most delectable seafood I'd ever smelled to our table: king crab legs and lobster that had been taken out of the shell. From previous conversations, Will knew I loved seafood, so he must have preplanned the menu, considering we hadn't even ordered.

"This is the most romantic dinner I've ever had," I told him as we dug in. "I can't thank you enough."

His response was pretty abrupt. "Are you still seeing Declan?"

Well, don't beat around the bush. I had to make a split-second decision, and what felt best was relieving myself of the lie I'd created. "No. Actually, I'm not."

He exhaled. "That's the answer I was hoping for."

"Really?" I broke open a crab leg.

"Yes. Seeing you with him at the hospital got to me in a way I didn't expect. It made me wonder why the hell I was wasting time and not telling you how I really feel."

I put down my crab and wiped my mouth. "Well, this is good timing, because I've been needing some guidance when it comes to me and you."

He came right out with it. "I don't want to just *date* you anymore, Molly. I want to be exclusive."

Oh. Wow. "Where is this coming from all of a sudden?"

"It's not that sudden. I've had feelings for you for quite some time, long before we started seeing each other. I've realized my fears about commitment were entirely about me not having found the right person. The more time I spend with you, the more I'm certain I don't want to share you."

After taking a long sip of water, I said, "I have to admit, I'm surprised this is what you want so soon."

"I get that. I told you early on that I didn't want anything serious—"

"Right. I guess I'm still not quite sure about your change of heart."

He nodded. "There's nothing like the threat of losing someone to push your heart in the right direction. If it's not this Declan guy, it will be someone else. I know a good thing when I see it. You deserve to be cherished. I want to be that man. I don't want you to have any hesitation about being with me because you think I'm interested in dating other people. I'm not. I'm only interested in you." He paused. "Will you be with me exclusively?"

Needing a moment, I looked up at the gorgeous lanterns hanging above us. This was something I'd been waiting for, yet I wanted time to process before committing to him.

"This is a lot to take in. I really like you, Will. I think we have a lot in common, and I'm very attracted to you. I'm just a little surprised."

"I understand."

"I know this is probably not the answer you were hoping for, but can I have a little time to mull it over?"

"Of course. I've had several days to think about it, so it's only fair that you should have the same."

CHAPTER EIGHTEEN

Declan

I loved messing with my sister when I called her at the convent. "How's the sex, drugs, and rock and roll?"

"Oh you know, the usual..."

"When I get home, the first thing I'm gonna do is come see you," I said.

"As long as you don't try to taint Sister Mary Jane like you did last time."

"Come on. That was fun, and you know it."

She sighed. "What's going on? Something's up. You don't normally call me in the middle of the day."

"You know me so well, Sister-Sister."

"Talk to me."

Sitting on the couch, I kicked my legs up. "Okay. I told you about the girl I'm living with last time we spoke, right?"

"Yeah. Molly, is it? You guys still getting along?"

Where do I begin? I spent the next several minutes telling Catherine about my complicated relationship with Molly and the games we'd played with Will and

Julia. I wrapped up the story with the half-drunk conversation we'd had a week ago.

"So you were honest with each other about your feelings," she said. "Why is that a bad thing?"

"Well, I didn't tell you about the week she was away."

"Okay..."

"Long story short, she went to stay at her dad's for a week after he got out of the hospital. While she was gone I...had a hard time."

"You mean you missed her?"

"No, I mean... I sort of had a new episode."

"Oh no, Declan. What happened?"

"Nothing. I just spent a couple of days in bed. I had to call out of work and stuff. But eventually I called Dr. Spellman."

"Okay, good. Did that help?"

"He adjusted my meds, and I think it did."

"Alright, well, that's good. I'm sorry it happened, but I'm glad you recognized it and dealt with it. It sounds like you handled things well. How did Molly take coming home and seeing you like that?"

"She didn't... Well, not really, anyway. I did my best to pull myself together. I'd been starting to feel a little better by then, anyway, and I knew she needed to talk to me about her dad, who's really sick. But she could definitely tell something was off, because she kept asking me what was wrong."

"Are you afraid to tell her, Declan?"

"It wasn't the right time to get into it. I ended up drinking a little, and it didn't mix well with my medications, which lowered my inhibitions, and that's when we had the conversation about sex."

"Oh my." She laughed. "Well, you shouldn't be drinking alcohol. You know that."

I sighed. "The thing is, Cat, I know turning a blind eye to these feelings for Molly is the right thing to do. The distance thing—me living in California and her being here in Chicago—is definitely an issue, but I made it seem like distance was the main reason we couldn't be together. Deep down, I know that's not it. It's more the fact that I haven't told her anything about the messed-up stuff that sometimes goes on in my head."

Her voice grew louder. "You're not messed up, okay? So get that terminology out of your mind. You have some dark patches periodically that you need to get through. And you also worry way too much about what it could mean in the future, how it relates to Mom. And that cripples you. You're not our mom. Please don't let your fears derail things if you really like this girl."

"After my conversation with her, the minute I got back to my room, all I wanted was to talk myself out of my fears. Like, what if I could somehow make it work? Why does it have to be so hard?"

"It sounds like you *want* to make it work. But let me ask you something, Declan. You had a thing for the woman you worked with, and you've had girlfriends over the last few years. Did you avoid relationships with them because of your situation?"

"No, but that was different."

"And why was it different?"

"Because... This is Molly. I don't want her to get hurt."

"Exactly. I think that says a lot about how you must feel about her. You want what's best for *her* over what's best for you."

"Yes, so that's why I need you to talk some sense into me. I need you to say, 'Declan, this girl is going through a rough time. She doesn't need your mental baggage on top of everything. Not to mention, you're dating the girl you've been chasing for a year who doesn't seem to require a commitment. Don't turn everyone's lives upside down by messing around with your roommate.'"

Catherine sighed. "But she's more than just a roommate, isn't she?"

I thought for a moment. "More than anything, she's a good friend. And that's the other part of this that's so hard. I care about her so much and don't want to cause her complications by pursuing this. But I just—"

"You can't help how you feel."

"Apparently not."

"How would you feel if your boss told you that you had to return to California immediately—like, this second? Leave everything in Chicago behind and never return."

That was easy. "It would really suck. I'd be devastated."

"Do you think you're gonna feel any different when you leave in a few months?"

Letting out a long breath, I said, "Probably not."

"Then maybe you need to reassess. If you have real feelings for this girl, you need to listen to them. And you need to tell her about your fears, about all the things you *think* she can't handle."

Catherine wasn't helping. She was usually a very reasonable person. That's why I'd called her and not one of my other sisters. But today she'd gone all listen-to-your-feelings on me.

"I guess I don't trust myself, Cat. Maybe she'd be better off with that jerk doctor. I'm a loose cannon and certainly not good at serious relationships. That's what she wants."

"How would you know you're not good at them if you've never had one?"

"Why do you ask tough questions?"

"That's my job! To make you think when your head seems stuck in your ass."

"Are nuns supposed to say *ass*?"

"Every time you call me, I nearly get myself kicked out of this place."

"Well, your little brother will always take you in, even when the Big Man won't have you anymore."

She laughed. "Remember that game we used to play where I'd throw out a single word, and you'd have to answer with the first word that came to mind?"

"Yeah?"

"That's a good way to assess your true feelings on things. A one-word association tells a lot. Let's play right now. Ready?"

I was never one to refuse a game. "Okay. Ready."

Catherine started. "Chicago."

"Pizza."

"Dad."

"Old Spice."

"That's two words," she said.

"Sue me." I laughed.

Catherine continued. "Advertising."

That was easy. "Lies."

"Beer."

"Buzzed."

"Nun."

"Catherine."

"Declan."

"Screwed." I chuckled.

"Ocean."

"Home."

"Julia."

"Pretty."

"Mom."

"Belt."

Catherine paused. "Belt?"

"That one time I ran away, she whooped my ass. Never forgot it. So yeah, belt."

"Coffee."

"Life."

"Sister."

"Scooter."

"Chocolate."

"Lick."

"I don't even want to know what you've been up to that triggered that association."

"Something you *haven't* been up to, dear sister."

She laughed and said, "Molly."

"Mine."

Shit. Mine? That was the first thing that came to mind for Molly?

"Hmmm..." Catherine chuckled.

"Alright. Alright. I know what you're thinking."

"You do, huh?"

"You're thinking I'm an idiot for even needing to have this discussion."

"Look," she said, "I'm the last person to be giving advice on romantic relationships. But this does seem obvious to me. You care for her. That should trump everything else."

Then, of course, there was Julia. I sighed. "I care for Julia, too, but in a different way, I guess. I don't want to hurt her, either."

"You didn't call me to talk about Julia," Catherine noted. "That says it all, my brother."

• • •

Molly and I had managed to avoid talking about anything for over a week. I knew she had to work Sunday night, so I was hoping to catch her before she left for her shift. That way if anything we said or did was awkward, she'd be away for twelve hours soon after.

When I woke up Sunday morning, Molly was sleeping. Despite my nerves, I felt mentally better than I had in a while. I'd come out of the fog, and my energy was back, so I spent the day at the gym and running errands.

When I returned to the apartment late in the afternoon, Molly wasn't there. I wondered if she'd be coming home at all before she had to go to work. I took a shower, then not-so-patiently waited to find out.

I still didn't know what I was going to say to her, and I certainly didn't know where she stood. I decided I'd respond to her based on the vibe she gave me. Maybe she would give me a signal. I'd let her talk first, and if she expressed any doubt about things, game over.

I took advantage of the alone time and started writing down some of what I wanted to say on a notepad. I must have scratched out a hundred different things.

Fuck it. Let's just try.

Scratch.

I can't stop thinking about what it would be like to fuck you, Molly. But it's so much more than that.

Scratch.

Maybe we should take it day by day and see where it goes.

Scratch.

I'm crazy about you, Molly. So let's just do this.

Scratch.

The door opened, and I shoved the notepad under my bed.

I strolled out into the living room as if I hadn't just been jotting down sweet nothings like a damn high schooler.

"Hey! Long time no see."

"Yeah. It seems like it's been forever," Molly said. "Were you waiting for me?"

Apparently, I wasn't as casual as I thought. Who brought the fucking cool guy?

"Yeah. I figured we could finish the talk we were having the other day."

She looked around, seeming nervous. "Okay. I'm just gonna take a quick shower and get into my scrubs. Then we'll talk?"

"Sounds good. Want me to brew some coffee? I know you like to drink it on the way to work."

"That would be great."

For the next several minutes, I sat in the kitchen, taking in the smell of freshly brewed coffee and hoping it would calm me down. But nothing could. When Molly walked out wearing her dark purple scrubs, I was no more ready to have this conversation than I'd been before.

I bit the bullet. "You want to go first or shall I?"

"I can go first," she said, taking a seat across from me. "So, I think everything you said the other night made a lot of sense."

Uh-oh. The other night I'd pointed out all the reasons we were *wrong* for each other. *Why did I do that?*

"You mentioned that you didn't think you could give me anything long term and expressed concern about interfering in my relationship with Will."

I blew out a shaky breath. "I did say that, didn't I?"

What she said next jarred me. "Last week at dinner, Will asked me to be exclusive."

My heart sank. "He did?"

"Yeah. It came as a shock, to be honest."

Feeling like the walls were caving in, I nodded in silence as she continued.

"I told him I needed to think about it. But the more I think about what you said, the more I realize I should be realistic. Will is a good guy. I know you have your reservations about him. But that's only because you care about me."

"Right," I muttered.

"Anyway... I've done a lot of thinking over the past several days. And I'm...gonna tell him yes. I think I might not have been able to make a decision if you hadn't been so real with me. Whatever was happening between us would have held me back if we hadn't had that conversation. So thank you for giving me what I needed to move on."

I was speechless.

Utterly fucking speechless.

Everything I'd planned to say clogged in my throat, ready to choke me. How could I put all that on her now? Jesus, this fucking sucked.

Molly exhaled, as if getting all that out had been a relief. "What were you gonna say to me?"

You could've heard a pin drop, and I could somehow hear my brain ticking in my head. I could be honest and throw her a curveball right now, or I could lie and give her the peace she deserved. I chose the latter, even though I knew I might regret it for the rest of my life.

"I can't tell you how happy I am that we're on the same page. I won't take back what I said about how I feel about you, but I think it's best if we acknowledge it and move on. So, as much as I rag on Will, I'm happy for you. I truly am."

"Thank you, Declan." Molly smiled as she got up from her seat and wrapped her arms around me.

Then things went quiet again as she walked over to the coffeemaker and poured some into a travel mug. She looked back at me, and even though we'd just supposedly resolved things, nothing felt resolved.

I leaned against the counter and tried to be nonchalant. "So you haven't answered him yet about being exclusive?"

She shook her head. "No. We're supposed to go out again in the middle of the week. Our shifts don't overlap the next few days, so I'll see him on Wednesday. I figured I'd wait till we see each other in person." She winked. "Plus, I don't want it to seem like it was too easy a decision."

"Right."

She looked deeper into my eyes. "Are you okay?"

"Yeah." I looked away for a moment. "I am. Just relieved we got this conversation out of the way."

• • •

When Molly and I crossed paths again the following

night, I'd just gotten home from work, and she was already in her scrubs, getting ready to leave for her shift.

"Hey, roomie."

She smiled. "Hey."

I'd hoped to feel different by the next time I saw her, but it was even harder to look at her now than it had been before. Adding fuel to the fire, the thin material of her scrubs was oddly revealing. I often stiffened at the sight of Molly's ass in her scrub pants.

I felt jealous and angry—angry at myself, mostly. But I still knew I was making the right decision. Despite that, I was still feeling a little greedy. I deserved some sort of parting gift.

Molly was preparing her lunch bag when I opened the cabinet next to her and pretended to be getting a glass for water.

"So I assume you still haven't spoken to Will about his proposition?"

"No. Remember I told you I won't see him until our date on Wednesday night."

I crossed my arms. "So technically, you're still single."

"Yeah." She smiled. "I guess for another couple days." She must have noticed the way I was looking at her, because she laughed nervously as her cheeks turned pink. "What?"

"Since you're still single..." I swallowed and forced the words out. "I want to kiss you. Just once."

Molly's mouth fell open. Instead of taking her shock as a hint to stand down, I went into full-on staring at her lips. They were so full and inviting, so pink and supple. I had the strongest urge to take the bottom one between my teeth and bite, yanking it in a good, firm tug.

Her breathing sped up, and I was mesmerized by the rise and fall of her chest. Watching her get worked up right before my eyes was the sexiest thing I'd ever seen, and it made me feel a thousand-feet tall.

I stepped around to stand before her, face to face. Taking a hold of the counter on either side of her hips, I boxed her in. More than anything, I wanted to push her up against the cabinets and take the taste I'd been dying for since the day I moved in. But this was Molly, whom I respected and adored, so I needed her to give me something—anything—to let me know she wanted it, too.

"Talk to me, Molly." My voice was strained and gritty. I moved a half step closer, slipping two fingers under her chin and gently lifting so our eyes met. "Tell me it's okay, that you want me to kiss you."

She swallowed. "I do."

My heart raced. I closed the tiny gap still remaining between us. Her warm, soft breasts pressed against my chest. "Do what, Molly? Say it. Tell me what you want."

"I...I want you to kiss me."

My mouth curved to a wicked grin. "Oh yeah?"

Molly's hair was in a ponytail, the way she often wore it to work. I reached up with one hand and slowly wrapped the entire length of it around my fist. Dipping my face so our noses brushed, I groaned. "Say it again."

Up until now, she'd seemed pensive, but I guess she was growing as impatient as I was. She wet her lips and looked straight into my eyes. "Goddamn it, Declan. Kiss me already. I have to leave for work in a few minutes, and that's already going to be too soon."

My eyebrows jumped. But she was so right; I needed to stop wasting precious time. Plus, I could get lost staring into those big baby blues. I smiled. "Yes, ma'am."

Leaning in, I cupped her cheek and tilted her head with the hand wrapped in her hair before I planted my lips over hers. The moment we connected, my entire body lit up like a goddamned Christmas tree. *Jesus Christ*. However good I thought we'd be together, the reality had exceeded my imagination already. Usually with a first kiss, there's a certain feeling-each-other-out period where you get to know the other's style—the logistics take a bit to fall into place. But not with Molly. We were completely in sync from the get-go.

I slid my hands down to her ass, readying to nudge her to wrap her legs around me and let me take her weight. But by the time I got there, she was already climbing me like a fucking tree. Molly dug her nails into my shoulders as she hoisted herself up. Needing some leverage so I could press her even closer, I walked with her wrapped around my waist until her back hit the refrigerator with a thud. Our lips never parted as my body smashed against hers, and I grinded my hips between her legs to show her exactly what she was doing to me.

Molly gasped into our joined mouths, and I almost lost my mind.

I had so much frustration, desire, and anger pent up that I couldn't be gentle. With a firm yank of her ponytail, I forced her neck back so I could suck my way down from her lips. My teeth scraped over her chin, and I used my tongue to trace her pulse from her jaw down to her collarbone.

"Declan..." Molly whimpered.

PENELOPE WARD & VI KEELAND

God, I wished I'd had the foresight to record this audio. The sound of her moaning my name would come in handy when she wasn't around much anymore.

When she isn't around much anymore.

That thought—the thought of her not being around because she was with some other guy—sliced through me. It made me feel possessive and angry. But if this moment was all we were ever going to have, I refused to let Dr. Dickalicious ruin it. So I tamped down the negative thoughts and let my need for her flow into our kiss.

I had no idea how long it lasted; time seemed to stand still. When we finally came up for air, we were both panting. I held her cheeks in my palms as my thumb wiped at the wetness on her lips.

"Wow..." she whispered, looking a bit stunned. "That was..."

I smiled. "Yeah, it was."

Molly blinked a few times, as if trying to snap out of a daze. "Was that... Are you... Is that just how you kiss, or was that something special?"

I was a man after all, so of course I wanted to take credit and tell her it was all my doing—I was just that good of a kisser. But it would've been bullshit. "That was definitely special. It wasn't me—it was us."

She swallowed. "Yeah."

Too soon, reality crept in. Molly's eyes lifted above my shoulder, and she must've caught the time on the microwave. "Shoot." She frowned. "I have to go. I'm going to be late for work. That was... It took longer than I thought."

Her legs were still wrapped around my waist, and I dreaded the thought of letting go. Especially because I knew this was it. I was going to be letting her go in more ways than one after this.

"I'll drive you."

Molly shook her head. "No, it's okay. I think I need a few minutes alone to clear my head."

I wanted every last possible second with her, yet I reluctantly set her down on her feet.

Molly stared at the floor. "Okay, well... I guess I'll be going."

I couldn't resist one more little kiss. So I cupped her chin and nudged her head up until our eyes met again. Leaning in slowly, I pressed my lips to hers and kept them there for a long time. It felt like my heart leapt into my throat when I pulled back. "Bye, Molly."

She looked at me funny. "You sound like you're going to be gone when I get home in the morning."

I forced a smile. "No, I'll be here." *Licking my wounds and mending a broken heart.*

"Okay. Well, have a good night."

"You, too, Mollz. You, too."

CHAPTER
NINETEEN

Molly

"I was going to ask how things were going with you and Dr. Daniels." Daisy lifted her chin, pointing to my neck. "But I can see they're going pretty well." She chuckled.

We'd been making up a bed together for an incoming patient, and my scrub top had pulled to the side. I looked down but couldn't see what she was referring to.

"What?"

She laughed. "You have a red mark—a hickey right on your collarbone."

My eyes widened, and I ran to the en suite bathroom to look in the mirror. Sure enough, I had a love bite. Declan must have done it earlier, and I'd had no idea. I straightened my top, and thankfully, it covered the mark again. But then it hit me that Will could have noticed it, rather than Daisy, and that made me feel sick.

What the hell was I doing? I'd been crazy about Will for a long time, yet I'd struggled to make the decision to be exclusive with him. And then I finally made the choice to go for it, and less than forty-eight hours before I'm going to commit to him, I'm sucking face with Declan and getting a hickey.

Why would I have done that if the choice I'd made was the right one? I felt more confused than ever.

Overwhelmed, my emotions got the best of me, and tears welled in my eyes. *Great. Just great. Now I'm going to have swollen eyes, a red nose, and another man's mouth marks on my body.* I felt like a horrible person—as if I'd done something traitorous, even though I hadn't yet told Will we could be exclusive. I tried to sniffle back the tears, but a crushing sadness seeped into my chest, and apparently crying was the way it needed to come out. Fat tears rolled down my face, no matter how hard I tried to stop them.

Since I hadn't shut the bathroom door, Daisy thought nothing of walking in.

"Molly, do you know where the—"

She took one look at my face and froze. Clearly, she had no idea what to do. We were friendly, but it wasn't like I told her my problems. She seemed torn between coddling me and running out of the bathroom to get as far away from me as she could. "Are you...okay?"

I sniffled. "I just need a few minutes."

"Sure, of course. Do you...want me to stay? Is there something you want to talk about?"

I shook my head. "No, I'm sorry. It's just been a long day. I'll be out in five."

"Don't be silly. Take all the time you need. I'll cover the desk for as long as it takes. It's quiet right now, anyway."

"Thanks, Daisy."

The next morning, I wasn't ready to go home after my shift ended. I hadn't been to see my dad in a few days, so after texting Kayla to make sure it was okay, I picked up some bagels and headed to their house.

"Hey, Dad." I leaned down and kissed his cheek when I arrived. He had a home oxygen system set up now, but the plastic face mask was hanging on the back of the kitchen chair he sat in. I fingered it. "Umm... This works best when it's on, believe it or not."

Dad shook his head. "Wiseass. You sound like Kayla. I'm drinking my coffee. I feel fine."

Every time I came to see him, he looked a little worse. Being a nurse, I was used to seeing sick patients deteriorate, but Dad's decline was not the norm. The difference between small cell and non-small cell cancers was really staggering. It was almost as if we were watching the rapid spread on the inside happen on the outside, too.

I put the bag of bagels on the table. "I brought your favorite."

He smiled. "Oh yeah? You remember my favorite?"

"Of course I do. Salt—the more of it, the better. Probably not the best thing to bring you, considering what it can do to your blood pressure."

My father waved me off. "That's the least of my worries."

I dug into the bag. "I'll make it for you. Cream cheese or butter?"

"Butter, please."

Kayla came down from upstairs while I was making Dad's breakfast. We said hello, and she walked over to

Dad and kissed him on the forehead. "I'm going to run some errands."

"Okay, dear."

"I'll be back in about an hour. Can you stay that long, Molly?"

My father answered for me with a grumble. "I don't need a babysitter."

She rolled her eyes. Clearly this wasn't the first time he'd given her a hard time about this. "Of course you don't. But the doctor said you need rest, at least until your blood count is back to normal. So it makes me feel better to know someone is around in case you feel dizzy again."

"Doctors just cover their asses."

I chuckled. "I guess you should know."

After Kayla left, my father and I ate breakfast. We made small talk, and I'd thought I was doing a good job hiding the turmoil I felt inside. But after he finished eating, he leaned back in his chair and squinted at me.

"Are you worried about me, or is something else going on?"

My brows furrowed. "What do you mean?"

He looked down at my hands. "You pick at the cuticle on your thumbs when you're nervous."

I totally did, but I didn't realize my dad knew that. I tucked my thumb into a fist to stop myself and sighed. "It was just a long night."

"A delivery gone wrong?"

I shook my head. "No, nothing like that."

"Okay..."

Dad waited. I didn't want him to think my issue was because of him. I mean, of course that was always in the back of my mind, but that wasn't what he was seeing on my face today. So I thought it might be best to put his mind at ease.

"It's a...a man problem."

Dad sipped his coffee. "Okay. Well, believe it or not, I am one of those, so lay it on me."

It was hard to explain, and I wasn't sure my situation was something I wanted to get into with my dad. We'd never discussed my dating life or anything like that. "I'm just struggling with what I think is the right choice for me."

Dad nodded. "That happens to be a subject I'm an expert on."

At first I was confused, but then I realized he was referring to my mom and Kayla. I'd only ever looked at what happened from an abandoned child's side, not from the point of view of a man in a relationship.

"What happened between you and Mom, Dad? I've only ever heard it from her."

My father sighed. "How much time do you have? I think that story could take a while."

I smiled. "Tell me the abbreviated version."

"Alright. Well, as you know, your mom and I were college sweethearts. We got married at twenty-one. People told us we were too young, but we didn't listen." He looked away for a moment, and a wistful smile grew on his face. "She was the most beautiful girl on campus." He shook his head. "Anyway, this is supposed to be the abbreviated version, so I'll jump forward a few years. Your mom worked a lot while I was in med school. Then when I graduated and you girls came along, she stayed home, and I worked a lot. Over the years, we sort of drifted apart. At first, we had you girls to bind us together. I'd come home, and your mom would catch me up on the happenings of you and your sister. But as the years passed, that became the only thing we discussed. So when you guys got a little bit older and started to spend time with your friends at sleepovers and whatnot, we felt like strangers. Sometimes we'd sit at the kitchen table for dinner, just the two of us, and have nothing to say, even though we'd spent the entire day apart. That led to frustration, and frustration led to arguing. I'm sure you remember the argument part. It was almost like we'd grown up together, yet never learned how to communicate."

"What about Kayla?"

Dad sighed again. "I know you think Kayla was the cause of my breakup with your mom, but she really wasn't—nothing on her part, anyway. I swear, God as my witness, I never cheated on your mother—at least not in the physical sense. I'd be lying if I said I didn't grow too close to other women during those tough years in a non-physical way. Looking back, I think I was seeking the emotional connection your mom and I were missing. I should have worked on that with her instead of finding it with others. And I own that. In a relationship, cheating isn't just a physical connection. I developed feelings for Kayla. At the time, they weren't reciprocated. She had no idea. She was just so easy to talk to at work. And once that happened, I realized things weren't right with your mom and me. I had a lot of guilt, but I was also a selfish asshole. So rather than invest the time to try to fix what had gone wrong with your mother, I took the easy way out."

Wow. I don't know what I'd expected him to say, but that wasn't it. Though it did feel like the truth.

Dad shook his head, and his eyes filled with emotion. "I'm sorry I let you down. I should have been a better man."

I took his hand in mine. "You're human. And when you left, I don't think I understood that. In my eyes, you were my father, not an actual person, if that makes any sense. I was sixteen and didn't understand boys yet, so I couldn't have possibly understood the complexities of making a marriage work or your heart falling out of love. I just wanted someone to blame because my father was gone and my mother was sad, and it was easiest to blame you."

We were both quiet for a long time, but eventually, I asked, "What if there was no Kayla? Would you have stayed with Mom?"

Dad shook his head. "That's obviously not a simple question to answer, since there *is* a Kayla. But I'm pretty sure the answer is no. If it wasn't her, it would've been someone else eventually. The problem wasn't me falling for a specific woman, Molly. The problem was *me*. Can I ask you something?"

"Yes."

"Do your man problems have to do with Declan and Will?"

I nodded.

"I know I'm probably the last person who should give advice on relationships. But sometimes hindsight is a lot clearer than when you're in the thick of things. So if I can offer any advice, it would be not to make a commitment unless you're certain and ready to work at it."

CHAPTER TWENTY

Declan

"**H**ow are things going over there?" Ken's voice boomed through the speakerphone.

Julia and I had a standing conference call with our boss once a week, almost always on Fridays. But earlier today he'd emailed us both to ask if we could speak at four this afternoon, even though it was only Tuesday.

"Good," I said. "We're still a bit ahead of schedule, so we've started working on the media plan."

"Wonderful. Good to hear it. That makes this much easier."

I looked across the table at Julia to see if she knew what he was talking about, but her forehead was just as wrinkled as mine.

She shrugged, so I spoke up. "Makes *what* easier, Ken?"

"You know Jim Townsend?"

We both nodded. "Sure. Is everything okay with him?" I asked.

"Yes, but he gave his notice this morning—only gave me one week. Apparently he got an offer he couldn't refuse that doesn't require traveling, and since he and his wife just had a baby, he couldn't pass it up. They needed him right away."

"Oh wow," Julia said. "He's been working on that big dairy campaign, right?"

"Yep. Over in Wisconsin. He has two team members with him, but they're both too junior to put in charge of an account the size of Border's Dairy. So I'm afraid I need one of you to take the reins over there for a while."

I dragged a hand through my hair. "For how long?"

"Campaign is set to launch in a little less than nine weeks. So I'd say right around two or three months."

Shit.

"What about here?" I asked. "It's too much work for one person to handle."

"I'll send a replacement out to Chicago—two juniors, if you think it's necessary. When Wisconsin wraps up, if there's still work to be done in Chicago, whoever goes can go back to lend a hand. I know you two have created the vision for your campaign, and there's a certain amount of satisfaction in bringing it to fruition. So I'm sorry about this. But one of you needs to pick up some bulky sweaters and head to Wisconsin."

My eyes caught with Julia's. We both were thinking the same thing, but it was she who asked, "Which one of us is going?"

"Welp, Declan is the more senior marketing director, even though you two have the same title. So I'm going to leave it up to him to decide who goes where."

My sister, Catherine, seemed surprised to hear from me again. "Calling again so soon? To what do I owe this honor, dear brother?"

"Sister-Sister, I need your help big time."

"Uh-oh, is this about the Molly situation?"

"I wish it were just about that."

"What happened now?"

I told her about the bomb my boss had dropped at work today. I was still torn about whether to take the Wisconsin gig or throw Julia into the fire. Deep down, though, I knew the right decision.

"He's leaving it up to you two?"

"No," I clarified. "It's up to *me*. And that's fucked up. I wish he would've just made the damn decision."

"What did Julia say?"

"She tried to seem gracious, said she'd be willing to go, but I know better. She's been missing Newport Beach like crazy ever since we got here. She's only just now acclimated somewhat to being in Chicago—finding places to get her healthy food and stuff. Having to go to Wisconsin for two months would kill her spirit, whether she knows it or not."

"So, you're gonna volunteer?"

"I think I have to. I don't want to—not in the least. Unlike Julia, I actually love it here. There's no part of me that wants to leave, aside from missing you guys."

Catherine exhaled. "I think it's really crummy of your boss to put you in this situation. What about a coin toss?"

"That still leaves the possibility that Julia will have to go. She'd resent me too much."

"So, in that case, there doesn't seem to be all that much to discuss here. Seems like you've made your decision. You don't want to hurt Julia, so you're hurting yourself instead."

I sighed. "The girl broke up with her boyfriend to date me, and I haven't committed to her, even though she seems pretty damn emotionally committed to me, and now I'm gonna ship her off to Wisconsin? That would be messed up. Don't you think?"

"I agree that you have little choice here if you're looking to take Julia's feelings into consideration." Catherine paused. "What about Molly? What does she think?"

That question filled me with dread. "I haven't told her anything yet. This just happened today. Molly's at work right now."

"Whatever happened with the conversation you were supposed to have with her?"

Cringing, I closed my eyes. "It backfired. Long story short, I'd built up the nerve to tell her I wanted to take a chance on us, but before I could say it, she told me the damn doctor had asked her to date him exclusively. She said she was going to go for it."

"What was your response?"

"I kissed her."

She laughed. "You what?"

"I kissed her. And it was the best damn kiss of my life."

"I'm sorry. I'm so confused."

"Me, too, Catherine."

"Okay, back up."

"Molly is supposed to tell him tomorrow night that she's going to take him up on his offer. Once she announced that, I decided I wasn't going to stand in her way. You told me yourself to act based on the vibe she gave me. Well, she made it pretty damn easy. But...since she was still technically single, and I might not have another chance to kiss her, I asked if I could do it just once. She said yes. It was amazing. The end. That was last night."

"So, in forty-eight hours, you decided to go for it, got your heart broken, kissed the girl anyway, then found out you're moving to Wisconsin for two months. I'd say you deserve a drink tonight, little brother."

I opened the fridge and grabbed a beer. "Popping it open right now."

"Is simply saying no to this transfer an option?" she asked.

Opening the bottle and taking a sip, I shook my head. "Not if I want to keep my job. And certainly not if I want to be considered for the promotion I've worked so damn hard for."

"Okay." My sister let out a long breath. "Let's step back and take a look at this situation with a wider lens."

"Alright."

"Molly made her decision. She's going to date the doctor. You're not that into Julia anymore. Might this temporary move to Wisconsin be a good thing? You won't have to be around to witness Molly moving on, and it will resolve your situation with Julia without you having to let her down. Maybe once you reset and head back to California after Wisconsin, you'll be able to move on from all of this, too?"

"You make my mess of a life sound so simple."

"Why does it have to be complicated?"

"Well, there *is* a small complication: the timing. I'll likely still have to come back to Chicago to finish off the assignment here when Wisconsin wraps. By that time, God knows what I'll be coming back to. But you know... the more I think about it, the more I realize it doesn't matter how I feel right now. I have to go to Wisconsin." I downed a long sip of my beer and repeated, "Dammit, I have to go."

CHAPTER
TWENTY-ONE

Molly

My father's advice had rung through my mind ever since I'd left him. I'd told Will I was going to give him a decision tonight, but was that really necessary? Why did we need to rush things? If I wasn't sure, I most definitely needed to do as Dad said—take more time before making a commitment.

Looking in the mirror, I unbuttoned the top of my blouse and pulled it aside. The mark Declan had left on my neck was still there. I would have to cover it up with makeup before my date. The hickey would be one of many things I'd have to deal with before tonight. I didn't feel ready to face Will without talking to Declan one more time.

Declan had texted that he was coming home from work and hoped to catch me. I wondered if he wanted to talk about what happened between us on Monday.

On the surface, that kiss seemed like a simple goodbye gesture, a gratuitous opportunity to take advantage of the situation. But the *way* he'd kissed me told a different story. It was desperate and full of passion and unlike any kiss I'd ever experienced. And it left me feeling more confused than I had before.

I thought about the conversation I'd had with Dad. There was more than one way to hurt someone. If I was going to commit to a man, I needed to be certain I wouldn't be thinking of another. At this point, I didn't see how my telling Will yes could automatically turn off my feelings for Declan. How would I feel if the tables were turned—if Will agreed to be my boyfriend, yet held complicated feelings for another woman? I would hate it.

My thoughts were interrupted by the sound of the front door opening. I stayed in my room, anticipating that Declan would come find me.

A minute later, through the mirror, I saw him standing in my doorway. His melancholy expression, though, was not what I was expecting.

I turned to face him. "What's wrong, Declan?"

He plopped on my bed, lying flat on his back and scrubbing over his face. "I don't know how to say this."

My heart sank as I walked over to sit on the edge of the bed. "What's going on?"

My mind raced. Is he going to tell me he has feelings for me? Did our kiss change things? Did something happen with Julia? What he actually said, though, was far worse.

"I have to leave Chicago, Mollz."

"What? Did something hap—"

"I'm being reassigned to an account in Wisconsin. The guy running it left our company, and my boss needs someone there ASAP to take over. He wants it to be me or Julia, and he left me in charge of deciding who goes."

Him or Julia?

My heart pounded. "So why isn't *she* going?"

He shut his eyes briefly. "Julia can barely handle Chicago. She does nothing but complain about how much she misses California. This assignment is in the middle of nowhere. I'm pretty sure those two months would kill her."

"You're leaving?"

He nodded. "Yeah. I have to, Mollz. But it's the last thing I want."

"I can't believe this. I always knew your time here was limited, but I feel like we just got robbed."

"Me, too. I've been really down all day. Once I told Ken I'd do it, I fell into a horrible funk." He sat up so he was right next to me. "There's a little silver lining, I guess. Depending on when things wrap up there, I might be coming back to finish off the Chicago gig before I have to head back to California."

That gave me a glimmer of hope. "So you might be back?"

"I'm not sure how it's going to play out, but that's a definite possibility. I did talk to my boss about the company covering my rent here for the remainder of the time I'd committed to. I didn't want to put you out. He agreed to reimburse me for it." Declan placed a piece of my hair behind my ear. "Can you keep my room here open? That way I know I'll have a place to stay when I come back."

It still felt surreal. "Of course, Declan. Of course."

He shook his head as he stared down at my bedspread. "This is shitty timing—literally kissing and running." He looked up at me and flashed a crooked smile that made my heart ache. Then he took my hand in his. It was an innocent gesture, but it made me warm all over.

I looked down at our entwined hands. "No matter how confused we might be, Declan, you're one of the best friends I've ever had. I hope we don't lose touch, because the thought of that makes me so very sad."

He squeezed my hand. "I promise to stay in touch, Molly. I would love that."

"You've helped get me through a really tough time in my life. Your friendship, your breakfasts for dinner, your smile..." I grinned. "I've felt more alive since you've moved in than I have in years."

He studied my face. Maybe that was a little much to admit.

"This sucks," he muttered.

The room fell silent.

"When do you have to leave?" I asked.

"He wants me out there by the beginning of next week."

I did the math. I was off for the next three days but had to work Saturday through Monday. That meant I only had a couple of days to see him before he left.

I wanted to cry. "That's so soon."

He frowned. "I know."

"What about you and Julia? Where does this leave that relationship?"

He shrugged. "In limbo, I guess—but that's not far from where it already is. I think the distance will be good for us. I'm glad we hadn't made any kind of commitment before this happened."

Declan would surely want to be free to date whomever he pleased in Wisconsin. The thought of that made me nauseous, once again reminding me of my feelings for him.

"I wish I could say 'fuck the job' and stay. I really do. I love it here, and no part of me is ready to leave." He exhaled. "I've come so damn far with this company, and if I pushed back on this, it would make me seem like I wasn't a team player. It would hurt my chances of promotion."

"I totally get it. Now is the time in your life to work hard so you can play later."

He let go of my hand and laid back down, staring at the ceiling. "My need for success is deeply rooted. My parents are very old-fashioned—particularly my father. I grew up being told I needed to be successful because I'm a man, whereas they were fine with my sisters just marrying and settling down. The ironic thing is, my sisters all excel in their careers. But even so, my father has always put added pressure on me because I'm the only boy. I disappointed him when I chose not to go to law school like he wanted, so I've tried so damn hard to show him I can make my mark in an industry of my own choosing, not the one *he* chose for me."

"Your dad is a lawyer?"

"Yeah. I never told you that?"

"No."

"Yep. So he wanted me to follow in his footsteps, but it never felt right. When I finally decided to go into marketing, I promised I would prove myself to him, prove that I could carve out my own success."

"You talk so much about your sisters, but you don't talk much about your parents."

"It's a bit of a sore spot. But it's also what motivates me."

"I get it."

He looked over at me and smiled. "You have a way about you that makes me want to share things I don't normally talk about. I'm gonna miss talking to you—in person. I promise we'll keep talking."

"I'm gonna hold you to that."

He nodded. "You're still going out with Will tonight, right?"

I sighed. This news about Declan leaving threw a wrench into my plans to talk about my conflicted feelings with him this evening. "Yeah. I'm supposed to meet him at his place."

"And you're gonna answer his little proposal?"

I hesitated. "I don't know."

"I have a confession..." he said.

"Alright..."

He sat up again to face me. "That kiss... I don't regret it. Not for a second. It was an asshole thing to do, though. You'd just told me you'd made a decision you felt good about, and I went a little caveman, because I was feeling jealous."

I smiled and let him continue.

"I didn't have a right to toy with you like that. And I'm sorry."

"I don't regret the kiss," I immediately said. "Maybe I do regret letting you suck on my neck so hard, because now I have to wear this shirt buttoned all the way up tonight. I look like a nun." I unbuttoned the top two buttons and pulled the material back to show him the bruise. "No offense with the nun comment."

"None taken." Declan ran his finger along my skin. "Shit."

The brush of his fingertip made me shiver.

"But damn, I do like seeing it on you. Sorry not sorry. Is it wrong that I kind of want Dr. Dick to see it?" he asked. "It's like I've brainwashed myself into thinking the competition we created between me and him is real."

If only he realized how *real* it had been for me all along. All I wanted to do tonight was hang out with Declan because our time was so limited.

I'd almost suggested canceling my date when Declan said, "Go have fun tonight. Don't let my news about leaving get you down. Order the most expensive fucking thing on the menu. Get a little tipsy—but not too drunk. And go with your gut, Molly. If you don't feel like you're ready, don't tell him anything tonight. You don't owe anyone an answer on any timeline."

"That's the same advice my dad gave me." I smiled.

"Well, great minds, then."

• • •

I didn't end up having dinner with Will after all. He was called in for an emergency at the hospital and had to cancel at the last minute. That was a relief—which had made me question my feelings all over again. I'd gone back home and found Declan out, so I'd used the quiet to think about things some more. I'd decided that in order to really assess how I felt about moving forward with Will, I needed Declan to be gone. It wasn't fair to make a decision right now when all I could think about was him leaving.

Anyway, Will and I had rescheduled our dinner to lunch this afternoon. We were meeting at a place near my apartment, which made me feel a lot more comfortable than the dinner at his place we'd originally planned. So far, we'd only shared a few kisses on the nights we'd had dates, but the natural progression of a physical relationship was looming, and I didn't want that pressure before I had my head screwed on straight.

It was Friday morning. Declan was at work, but we had planned to hang out tonight, since it was my last evening off for a few days. He'd be leaving on Monday.

When I went out to the kitchen, I noticed a single pink M&M on the countertop along with a note.

Mollz, I realized that before I leave I should probably give you back your pink M&Ms. But I've decided to leave them around the apartment in various spots so when I'm gone you'll think of me and smile whenever you find them. It'll be like I'm still here. (Not.) This is your first one. I hope you have a good day. See you tonight.

CHAPTER
TWENTY-TWO

Declan

"You know what? I'll take these, too." I pointed to a colorful bouquet of flowers. I'd stopped at a fresh fruit stand to pick up some strawberries for the dessert I planned to make Molly.

The old woman who worked there smiled. "Good choice. These just came in. The colors are so pretty, aren't they?"

"They are. I'm not usually a flowers guy either."

The woman *tsk*ed. "Uh-oh. You must be in the doghouse then? What did you do?"

I laughed. "No, I'm not in any trouble."

"Just bringing them for no reason?"

"Yeah, I guess. I'm making my...friend dinner and thought they would be nice to put on the table."

The woman bagged the strawberries, and I paid. As she handed me the flowers, she winked. "Good luck with your *friend* tonight."

The fruit stand was the last of five stops I'd made on the way home. Since tonight would probably be the last meal I'd get to cook for Molly, I'd decided to leave work early and surprise her by making appetizer-sized portions of all of her favorite dishes. I knew that would make her smile, which in turn, had me in a good mood. It was the first time I'd been able to put thoughts of leaving Chicago out of my mind. In fact, I felt so chipper as I walked home, I didn't even realize I was whistling.

About a block from the apartment, I stood at the crosswalk waiting for the red light to change. While I whistled the old "Don't Worry, Be Happy" song, I happened to glance across the street at the Italian restaurant Molly and I had ordered from a few times. And my whistling came to an abrupt stop.

Molly.

She was inside the restaurant, sitting at a table right up against the front window. And she wasn't alone. *Will* sat across from her. The light I'd been waiting on turned green, and people all around me started crossing. But I couldn't move. I just stood there staring. Molly was smiling—she had a big, real smile that lit up her beautiful face. The douchebag across from her leaned in and said something, and her head bent back in laughter.

Ever see a car accident on the side of the road? You know you shouldn't look, yet you can't stop staring—even when what you see causes an ache in your chest. Yeah, that's not what this felt like *at all*. This felt like I'd been the one who crashed the fucking car into a tree going eighty miles an hour. My chest tightened, and my throat constricted, making it hard to suck air into my lungs.

Fuck.

Fuck.

Fuck!

My Molly. With Will. And she looked...happy. As much as I wanted that for her, it was physically painful to see another man making it happen. Two minutes ago I'd been bringing home flowers and whistling, yet now my whole world had come crashing down on me. I'm not an idiot—I'd known I had strong feelings for Molly. But now I realized I felt a lot more than that.

I'd fallen in love with her.

• • •

A text came in as I folded another pair of pants into my suitcase.

> **Molly: Should be home about 7:30. I went over to my dad's this afternoon to check in on him, and we lost track of time. Want me to pick up anything on the way back?**

After I'd gotten home earlier, I'd sat around moping, trying to figure out what to do. Nearly four hours later, the decision I'd come to felt a little rash, but deep down I knew it was the right thing...for both of us.

Rather than tell Molly I'd moved up my flight, I chose to wait until she got home. I didn't want her rushing back and taking time away from her dad.

> **Declan: No, all good. Enjoy your time with your father.**

An hour later, I was zipping my last suitcase closed when I heard the front door open. I'd meant to go out into the living room and greet her so we could talk before she noticed all my luggage, but she came to my room before I could finish.

"Hey, what do you say we..." Molly's voice trailed off, and her brow furrowed as she took in the suitcases on my bed. "You're packed already?"

"Yeah."

She walked over to an open, empty dresser drawer and shut it before opening the one underneath.

Empty.

She quietly shut it and moved on to the one underneath that.

Again empty.

"What's going on, Declan? You didn't leave any clothes out."

She'd asked the question, but her face told me she already knew the answer.

I sat down on the bed and patted the spot next to me. "Come sit."

During the months I'd lived here, there were probably half-a-dozen times I should've lied to her—like when I'd admitted Julia and I had fooled around, or better yet, when I'd told her I had feelings for her. But I'd been mostly honest. So the bullshit words I spoke now tasted extra sour coming out of my mouth.

"There's been a change in plans. The guy working with our Wisconsin client had an emergency. So my boss told me I need to be there sooner."

Molly looked panicked. "When?"

I swallowed. "Tonight. I'm booked on the last flight out of O'Hare. It leaves a few minutes before eleven."

"But...but...that means you have to leave for the airport by, like, eight thirty?"

"Eight fifteen, actually. I have a car coming for me."

"Oh my God, Declan. No! That's too soon. We didn't get to spend any time together."

I looked down and nodded. "I know. I'm sorry."

Molly looked at her watch. "Why didn't you call me or text me earlier? I would have come home instead of going to see my dad tonight."

"Your time with your dad is important. I didn't want you to rush."

"But my time *with you* is important, too." She reached over and took my hand. It felt so damn right, which made what I was doing even harder.

I cleared my throat. "Come on. Why don't we go out to the kitchen? I made you dinner and have water boiling. Let me feed you one more time before I have to go."

Molly and I were both quiet as I led her out of my bedroom. I'd changed my plans from making appetizers to making fresh gnocchi, so they only needed to boil for three to four minutes. The water was already simmering, so I turned it up to a boil before starting to heat the cream sauce.

"It'll only take five minutes. I picked up some of the wine you like. You want a glass?"

Molly sat down at the table. Her face was glum, but she nodded and attempted a smile, though she failed miserably.

"Here you go." I set a glass of her favorite white in front of her.

The mood in the room was somber as I pulled together dinner. I made two plates and placed them on the table.

"Eat up," I tried to joke. "This could be your last good meal for a while now that you'll be cooking for yourself."

Molly pushed the pasta around with her fork. Finally, she looked up at me. "What were you going to do if I didn't get home?"

"What do you mean?"

"I told you I'd be home around seven thirty. But what if my train got stuck or something? Were you going to leave without saying goodbye?"

I hadn't poured myself any wine, but I changed my mind now and filled a glass. "I don't know. But you made it home. So it doesn't really matter, does it?"

Molly surprised me by raising her voice. "Yes. It does freaking matter!"

I put my hands up. "Okay...okay. I guess I would've called you to say goodbye then?"

She shook her head. "Really? After the last few months you would have just walked out the door—without even saying goodbye to me in person?"

I dragged a hand through my hair and shook my head. "I don't know, Molly. It didn't happen like that, so I can't really be sure what I would've done."

Molly pushed her chair back, the bottom of it scraping against the tile as she stood. "Yes, we can be sure. Because you just told me you would've left without saying goodbye!" She turned and marched off toward her room.

"Where are you going?"

"To be alone. Since you don't care if you say goodbye to me in person, we don't need to spend this time together."

"Molly, wait!"

Her response was a door slam—so hard it made the walls in the living room shake. I closed my eyes. *Fuck.*

I sat in the kitchen for a few minutes. But then I caught the time on the microwave and a wave of panic hit me. *Nineteen minutes.* I had nineteen goddamned minutes left with Molly, and whether she was pissed off or not, there was no way in hell I was going to spend them alone. So I walked to her bedroom, knocked gently, and waited.

No answer.

So I knocked a second time and creaked open the door. "Moll—"

"Go away."

The hurt in her voice was palpable.

"I'm coming in."

I gave her ten seconds to stop me, but when she didn't, I opened the door the rest of the way.

Fuck. She was crying.

I shut my eyes and swallowed before walking over to the bed and sitting beside her.

"Molly, I'm so sorry. I didn't mean to upset you. I just...I have no idea how to do this. I don't know how to say goodbye to you. These last few months you've become such an important part of my life."

Her shoulders began to shake a few seconds before the sound came.

"Come here..." I turned her and wrapped her in my arms. Stroking her hair, I spoke softly. "Don't cry, sweetheart. Please don't cry."

"I'm going to miss you so much."

"I know. And I'm going to miss you." I cupped her face in my hands, wiping away the tears on her cheeks. "I might be leaving, but I'm leaving a piece of me behind, Molly." I looked straight into her eyes. "And I'm taking a piece of you with me. We'll always have that. We won't physically be in the same place, but it doesn't change how much I care about you."

Molly sniffled. "Will we talk every day?"

I smiled. "Dr. Dick will probably hate that. So absofuckinglutely."

She laughed through her tears. All I wanted to do was kiss her beautiful, red, blotchy face, but I knew that would make things harder. "Seriously, Moll." I took her hands and weaved her fingers with mine. "Thank you for the last few months. I don't know how you did it, but I feel like you've changed me as a person."

Molly nodded. "I know what you mean. I feel the same way."

Before we could say anything else, my cell phone buzzed in my pocket. I wanted to ignore it, but I had a feeling it might be the driver, so I begrudgingly let go of one of her hands and dug it out.

I frowned reading the text. "My car is here. It's a few minutes early. There's nowhere to park, so he's going to circle the block until I come down."

Renewed tears began to fill Molly's eyes. I pushed a lock of hair behind her ear. "No more crying, beautiful. We're not even going to say goodbye. I'm coming back in a couple of months, remember? So it's more of an *I'll see you later.*"

Though it was true that I might be back, things wouldn't be the same. She'd have spent a lot of time getting closer to Will, and...well, this would likely be the end of who she and I were to each other at this moment. I kissed her forehead. "I'll see you soon, Mollz."

I was super proud of her for not crying again as she walked me to the door. I gave her one last hug and wheeled my bags out. "Take care, sweetheart."

It took everything in me to put one foot in front of the other and walk away. My heart wanted to stay so badly. But somehow I managed to get into the waiting car. Inside, I stared straight ahead, even though I felt Molly's eyes on me at the window. I knew she was waiting for me to look back. But I couldn't do that to her. It would only make it harder if she saw the tears on my face. So I looked down. *Goodbye, Molly.*

CHAPTER
TWENTY-THREE

Molly

A week later, my father was at the hospital for a scan. It was my day off, so I went with him. I wanted to spend as much time with him as I could, and I also wanted to give Kayla some time to run her errands. She'd been by his side nearly every minute since his diagnosis.

They'd taken Dad back a few minutes ago, so I sat in the empty waiting room by myself. While I was thumbing through a magazine, Will walked in, carrying a coffee in each hand.

"Hey," I said. "I didn't think you were on today."

"I'm not. I came to keep you company." He leaned down and kissed my cheek before taking the empty seat next to me.

"You did? Thank you. That's so sweet."

He extended a hand with one of the Styrofoam cups, then pulled it back and switched. "Actually, this one's yours. It's black. Mine has cream and sugar."

His thoughtfulness made me feel guilty. I'd mostly avoided him over the last week, since Declan had left.

I hadn't felt up to spending time with another man. In fact, it had been an effort to get out of bed most days, so pretending to be happy was more than I could handle.

Will peeled back the plastic tab on the top of his coffee. "How's your dad doing?"

I sighed. "He's lost a lot of weight, and his skin tone is off. But he's doing his best to be in good spirits."

Will nodded and took my hand. The gesture was sweet, but it also reminded me of how tightly Declan had held my hand on that last evening before he left. Which in turn, made me feel even guiltier. I was sitting next to a man who was trying so hard to be here for me, yet I was thinking about someone else.

"I hope you don't mind me saying this, but it looks like you've lost some weight, too," he said. "I've heard you tell more than one new father that it's important to take care of the caretakers. I'd like to do that for you, Molly. You don't need to carry this all on your own."

God, I'm an awful person. The guy I was supposed to be dating had offered to take care of me because I was sad. And part of the reason I was sad was because of another man.

I squeezed Will's hand. "Thank you. That means a lot to me."

Over the next half hour, our conversation moved to lighter topics. We talked about work, who was secretly sleeping with whom this month, and Will kept me entertained, telling me about all of the bizarre things he'd seen shaved into a woman's private area over the years.

"Someone really shaved the Chanel logo down there?"

"How could I make this shit up?"

228

I laughed and realized it was the first time I'd done so in a week. But then my cell rang, and my smile wilted. Declan's name flashed on the screen. And I wasn't the only one who noticed.

Will eyed me and sipped his coffee. "Aren't you going to answer that?"

I shook my head. "I'll call him back later. He knew my dad had an appointment, so he's probably checking in to see how things went."

Will nodded, but said nothing.

Since I'd been dodging him, he didn't know Declan had left. I figured it might be a good time to fill him in.

"He moved to Wisconsin," I said.

Will's brows lifted. "Declan moved?"

I nodded. "He had a change in his work assignment."

"Is this a permanent move?"

"No. But Declan actually lives in California. He might come back for a few weeks after he's done in Wisconsin, but then he'll be going home to Newport Beach for good."

"I didn't realize he didn't live here."

Of course, since I'd used Declan to make Will jealous, I hadn't mentioned that tidbit.

"Yeah. He was never here permanently."

Will quietly sipped his coffee some more. The next time he spoke, he shifted in his seat to look at me. "How do you feel about that?"

"About Declan being gone?"

He nodded.

My relationship with Will had started with a lie— Declan and I pretending to be a couple. If we had any real chance of things working out, I needed to be honest. So I was, even if it wasn't what he wanted to hear.

"I'm sad he left. We had grown close. But he's a good friend, and we want to keep in touch." I paused. "Will that upset you?"

Will looked into my eyes. "Is that all you are now? Just friends?"

Whether my heart wanted more or not, that was what we were now. So I nodded.

Will shook his head. "Then, no, I won't let it upset me. I'd be lying if I said I wasn't a little jealous of your relationship with him. But if you say you're only friends, that's good enough for me. Right now you need all of your friends to support you, even if one happens to be too damn good-looking for my liking."

I smiled. "Thank you for understanding, Will."

He squeezed my hand. "Just remember, I can be here for you, too. All you have to do is let me."

CHAPTER
TWENTY-FOUR

Molly

Iopened the Advil container and out came a pink M&M. I couldn't tell you how many times I'd stumbled on candies all over the apartment. I always thought of Declan and smiled when it happened; he was right about that.

He'd been gone a month, and I still missed him. So much. The only difference between now and the time right after he left was that now I was forcing myself to move on—spending time with Will and allowing him to be there for me in every way. I hadn't been able to do that with Declan around.

I popped the pink M&M in my mouth before pouring some water to take two of the actual pills. Then I picked up the phone and texted Declan.

Molly: Got the one you left in the Advil bottle. Made me smile :-)

He responded with a photo of himself getting ready to bite into a big hunk of cheese.

Declan: Say cheese.

Molly: When in Wisconsin...

Declan: You feeling okay?

Molly: Yeah. Why do you ask?

Declan: The Advil?

Oh. Duh.

Molly: Just a headache. Stressful day.

A couple of seconds later, my phone rang.

I picked up. "Hey."

"Everything okay?" Declan sounded concerned.

"Yeah. Nothing terrible. Just visited Dad. He wasn't feeling well, but at least he hasn't had to be hospitalized. Now I have to go to work tonight, and it's the last thing I want to do. I'm so tired, but I'm going to jump in the shower and push myself to go."

"You don't ever call out, do you?"

"No. I feel too guilty about leaving my co-workers high and dry at the last minute."

"I bet they do that to you all the time."

I took a moment to ponder that. "You're right. It happens way more than it should."

"You're long overdue. I think you should call out and just rest tonight."

I bit my bottom lip. "I don't know if I could go through with it."

"Yes, you can. And I hereby declare today National No Fucks Given Day. I think it should be celebrated at least once a year. Today is that day for you. Mark the calendar to remember it next year."

I laughed. "And what does this *holiday* consist of?"

"Whatever the hell you want. That's the beauty of it. So take the night off. Give yourself a break. Seriously, when was the last time you called out of work?"

"Never."

"You're kidding. Never? Not even once?"

"Literally never. I have never called out of work in my entire life—not because of sickness or anything else."

"Molly. Fuck. It's time. You owe it to yourself. Do it. Call the hospital. Do it now and call me back."

"You're serious?"

"Yes. I am dead serious. I know it will be hard for you, but it's a good exercise in putting yourself first. Sometimes that's necessary. Didn't that therapist you see want you to be less rigid? This is the perfect exercise for that. Now, go make the call, then take a nice, hot shower to decompress. Call me back after. I need to know you actually did it."

I took a deep breath in and let it out. I couldn't believe I was considering it. If Declan wasn't pushing me, I would never have thought to do this.

"Okay." I exhaled. "Okay. I'll call them now."

"Good girl. I'll talk to you in a bit."

After we hung up, I stared at the phone for a while, having an internal debate. But then I came to the conclusion that the longer I debated, the less notice I'd be giving my colleagues, and that was bad. So I forced myself to make the call.

My hand trembled as I dialed the number. When my co-worker Nancy answered at the nurses' station,

I forced out that I wasn't feeling well and wouldn't be coming in for my shift tonight. It hurt my chest to lie. She sounded sympathetic and said I must *really* be sick if I was calling out, because I'd never done so before. I didn't say anything in response to that, because I couldn't lie any more than I already had. I simply thanked her and hung up. But after, I felt...a small sense of relief.

I took the long, hot shower Declan had suggested. I probably didn't need to shower now that I wasn't going in to work, but he was right. It did relax me, and by the time I got out, I no longer felt as guilty as I had before.

After I dried myself off, I dialed Declan back.

He answered, "Have we lost all our fucks yet?"

"We have. Or at least we're trying to. It's done. It was very uncomfortable for me, but I feel a lot better since I showered."

"Woohoo! Welcome to the dark side."

I chuckled, twirling a piece of my wet hair. "What's next?"

"You've got the entire night off. The possibilities are endless."

I knew Will was working at the hospital tonight. He'd probably text me as soon as he realized I'd called out to see if I was okay. Would I lie to him, too? I suppose I could be honest and tell him I wasn't really sick, just needed a mental break. That *was* the truth.

There was a knock at the door.

"Hang on. Someone is at the door."

When I opened, I found a delivery man standing there. "Delivery for Molly?"

I narrowed my eyes. "I didn't order anything."

"I did," Declan said in my ear.

234

My jaw dropped. "Declan, you what?" I took the bag from the man and ran to get my wallet, but he held his hand out. "Tip is taken care of." He nodded. "Have a great night. Enjoy."

The smell of marinara wafted in the air. I knew that smell. This food was from my favorite Italian place down the street.

"How did you manage this? I didn't even know Nonna's delivered."

"I called while you were in the shower. And...well, they deliver if the owner's daughter has a crush on you."

"Ah." I felt a twinge of jealousy and shook my head to ward it off.

"I knew you'd sit around for hours debating what to eat. So I made it easy. It's not my gnocchi, but it will have to do. Besides, I couldn't find any place fast enough that delivered breakfast for dinner."

"I'm too spoiled with your French toast anyway. No one could top it." I sighed as I opened the bag and took out the aluminum containers. In addition to the gnocchi, he'd ordered me cheesecake. "Declan, seriously, this was so sweet of you. I can't even—"

"Okay, so dinner's sorted. No Fucks Given Day is in full effect. Now we have to figure out the rest of your night." He paused. "I assume you want to be alone if you're not feeling great?"

He might have wondered whether the man I was dating would be coming over. Declan never asked how things were going with Will, so I never offered the information. Did it bother him? There were things I avoided asking him too—like if he'd met anyone or screwed anyone since arriving in Wisconsin. Perhaps he was aloof with me because he didn't want to share what was going on with *him*.

"Will is working tonight," I reported.

"Ah. Good. Okay. Well, I can't be there to keep you company either, of course, but I can still provide compelling dinner conversation."

I smiled. "That sounds perfect."

Declan stayed on the phone with me for over an hour while I ate the delicious dinner he'd ordered. While we'd talked briefly a few times a week since he'd gone, I hadn't spent this kind of time with him in a while. And it made me really miss him.

After we got off the phone, I was on my way to my room when I took a little detour, instead opting to enter Declan's room and lie in his empty bed. To my surprise, even though he'd been gone a month, his sheets still smelled of his cologne. I hugged his pillow and nodded off, feeling rested and truly cared for.

• • •

Later that week, Will visited my apartment for the very first time. You'd think in all the weeks I'd been seeing him, he would have come by at least once. But I'd never suggested it while Declan was living here, and I'd done a great job of avoiding the situation like the plague. So him coming over was long overdue.

When I opened the door, Will looked so handsome and held a huge bouquet of flowers. He handed them to me before pulling me into a hug. "Hey, gorgeous. How are you?"

I sniffed the arrangement of lilies and hydrangeas. "I'm good. Thank you so much for these."

"Well, this is a pretty big occasion, finally getting to see your apartment." He looked around. "Nice place."

"Thank you." I walked over to my sink and pulled a vase from under it.

Will leaned against the counter as I arranged the flowers. "You said your roommate recently left, right?"

I swallowed the lump in my throat. Will obviously never knew my mystery male roommate and Declan were one and the same. I hated lying to him, but I couldn't risk admitting everything now.

"Yeah... He left, and now I have to find someone else. But he paid the rent through the end of his original commitment, so I still have a couple of months before I have to find someone."

"Well, this will be a nice break from having to share your space," Will said as he continued to scope out the place.

"I definitely prefer living alone, but finances mandate that I have a roommate."

Will flashed a sympathetic look. "I get it. It's expensive to live in the city, and this is a nice place in a great neighborhood. Before I paid off my student loans, I always had to have roommates, too." He smiled. "In any case, I'm happy to have you all to myself tonight." He reached out to draw me close. "Come here."

I thought he was going to kiss me, but instead he flipped me around and placed his hands on my shoulders.

"What are you doing?"

"You seem tense. I want to help." He began to massage.

I closed my eyes and relished the feel of his strong hands on my neck and then my back. I thought about how lucky I was to have these hands on me; they brought life into the world almost every day, and now they were taking a break from that just to make me feel good.

"You know what sucks?" he asked as he continued to rub my shoulders.

"What?"

"I really wish I could cook. I have this urge to make you dinner tonight—to take care of you—but I can't cook to save my life." He lowered his hands and circled his knuckles against my lower back.

It felt damn good. I closed my eyes again. "You have so much going for you as it is. If you were a great cook on top of everything else, that would almost make you too good to be true."

He laughed. "I don't know about that."

"I do."

"I have an idea," he said, turning me around to hold me. "How about we order from that great Italian place down the street, and I'll pretend I made it? I'll serve it to you."

My face felt momentarily hot. Food from Nonna's reminded me of my remote dinner with Declan. Not sure why I felt guilty, but I did. But that was silly. I needed to just enjoy this moment.

"I think that sounds amazing," I finally said.

When Will left to go pick up the takeout, I used the bathroom and refreshed my makeup. I put on some of Will's favorite jazz music, and as the minutes passed, I began to feel excited about his return.

After he got back, Will plated our takeout, insisting that I let him cater to me while I sat at the table.

"Why are you being so nice to me tonight?" I asked.

"Because I know you're under a lot of stress, and I want to take your mind off it," he said as he used tongs to scoop out linguini. "I work so much, and our schedules don't always match up, so I need to take advantage of any opportunity I get to show you how much you're starting to mean to me."

That made me feel warm inside. "You're starting to mean a lot to me, too."

Will brought our plates over to the table. "Wine with dinner, right?"

"I would love some." I stood. "I can open it."

He held out his hand. "No, I'm serving you, remember? Let me."

He walked over to the counter and took two bottles of wine he'd purchased out of a paper bag.

"I wasn't sure if you'd be in the mood for red or white. So I bought a sauvignon blanc and a cabernet."

"White is great."

"You got it." He winked.

I pointed. "Opener is in the second drawer to the left."

Will grabbed the opener and took out two of my nicer wine glasses. Those were the ones I reserved for guests, so I supposed it was fitting to use them tonight.

"Huh," he said, examining the glass.

"What?"

"There's a pink M&M in one of these glasses."

My heart clenched. Declan had showed up to say hello—or maybe *fuck you* to Will. This evening was probably the longest I'd gone without thinking of him.

Will put the M&M in his mouth and chomped it. That seemed wrong, symbolic in some way, like he was eating the last of my lingering feelings for another man.

He approached with the two glasses of wine. "Here you go, lovely."

"Thank you." I took a long sip.

We listened to jazz as we devoured the delicious food. As always, we talked a lot about work during dinner.

After, Will refilled our wine glasses before we moved over to the couch. It was relaxing to just sit with him and listen to music without having to say much.

"Can I confess something?" I asked, looking at his gorgeous face.

He grabbed my hand. "Of course."

"I used to have the biggest crush on you—before we started dating."

Will smiled and squeezed my hand. "I love that."

"It was mainly based on your looks and my admiration for how you handle your patients. But my impression of you is nothing compared to the reality. You're a good doctor, but more than that, you're a great man, Will."

"Well, see? Now I have to kiss you." He leaned in and took my mouth with his.

The taste of wine immediately registered as our tongues danced. Will was an amazing kisser. When I finally managed to pry myself off of him, I rubbed my swollen lips.

He set his wine glass down and pulled me in to rest my head on his chest. He kissed the top of my hair. "Tell me what you're thinking."

My voice was muffled as I spoke into his chest. "I don't know... I'm excited. Excited for the future, I guess, but also scared of the next several months in terms of my father."

He rubbed the top of my arm. "I think you need something to look forward to."

I looked up at him. "What do you mean?"

"Let's make a pact. If things are going well with us in six months, we'll take our vacation at the same time and go somewhere amazing."

He wants to go away with me? "I can't tell you the last time I took a vacation," I said.

"It's been a couple of years for me."

I felt giddy. "Where would you want to go?"

A smile crossed his face. "I'm thinking something like...Hawaii. What do you say?"

Hawaii? Hawaii with Will sounded like a dream. But there was one not-so-little problem. I wasn't sure I could afford it.

As if he could read my mind, he said, "I'd be paying, of course."

I shook my head. "You don't have to do that. I can save for it. I—"

"I want to. That's not up for debate. If I can't spend my money on someone I care about, who can I spend it on? This will be an epic trip, and I don't want you to have to worry about the financial aspect. I just want us to have fun."

My mouth hung open. "Well, I don't even know what to say."

His brow lifted. "Say you'll come with."

"Yes!" I sat up to hug him. "Yes, of course I will—assuming the situation with my dad allows."

"I don't want you to stress about that either. If we book tickets, I'll get insurance in case we have to change our plans."

Amazing. Will seemed firmly in the commitment camp tonight, and it felt like I'd won the lottery.

CHAPTER TWENTY-FIVE

Declan

I wasn't quite sure what to do with myself.

It was Thursday evening, and I didn't have to be back at work until Tuesday morning. Labor Day was typically a three-day weekend, but Border's Dairy had also closed on Friday to give their workers a gift since they'd had a record-setting year of profits. Of course, I could work through it, like I did most weekends, but the last week or so I'd been feeling pretty down, and I figured maybe I should get out for a change of scenery. A woman in the accounting department had invited me to go to some big lake with her and her friends. She seemed nice and was good-looking enough, but the last thing I needed was to get involved with a third woman.

Julia and I had kept in touch, and she'd been bugging me to take a trip back to Chicago for the long weekend. She'd even gone so far as to say she'd *make it worth my while*, which should have had me jumping at the opportunity since it had been forever since I'd gotten laid. Yet it did the complete opposite. The time away from Julia had made me realize we didn't have a long-term future. I didn't think about her all the time like I should have—unlike *the other* woman in my life whom I should *not* have been thinking about, yet consumed my daily thoughts.

Molly.

Six weeks away from her had made me realize what I felt was no joke. I'd always been a driven person—able to see where I wanted to be in six months, a year, and even five years. But since I'd left Chicago, I couldn't figure out where to go for the fucking weekend. I could no longer imagine where I wanted to be in six months, because it was too painful to imagine that wherever it was, Molly wouldn't be with me.

Rather than sit in my hotel room and wallow, I decided to take a walk. There was a bar a few blocks away. Maybe I'd go in and grab a beer. The Spotted Cow had looked like an old-man's bar from the outside, but inside, the place was filled with women. In fact, as I moseyed up to an empty stool at the corner of the bar, I realized I was pretty much the *only* man here.

The bartender was probably in her early sixties. She had flaming red hair and the brightest green eyes I'd ever seen. She placed a napkin in front of me.

"You're not from around here, are you?"

I hadn't said a word yet, so her assessment wasn't based on my accent. I shook my head. "I'm not. But how did you know that?"

She chuckled and held out her hand. "Lucky guess. My name is Belinda. What can I get you, cowboy?"

I shook. "I'll take a beer—Stella, if you have it. And I'm Declan."

"Alright, Declan. Give me a minute."

When she returned with my beer, she slid it over and leaned her elbows on the bar. "Were you looking for some company for the night?"

My brows drew together. Was she *propositioning me*? Is that what this place was? Why it was filled with women? "Umm...no, not really. I'm working in the area. I needed to get out of my hotel room. Just figured I'd have a drink, I guess."

Belinda nodded. "Okay then. Just didn't want you to be disappointed if you were looking to meet someone." She lifted her chin toward the door. "Don't get me wrong, you're welcome here. But the bar across the street might be more of what you were expecting."

I looked around, confused. Two women stood nearby, and one rubbed the other's arm. I scanned around the room a bit more, and there were an awful lot of women standing really close together. Squinting, I noticed two making out in the corner. *Oh shit.*

Belinda watched me take it all in. I chuckled, shaking my head as I took a slug of my cold beer. "And here I thought you were pimping."

"Excuse me?"

"You asked me if I was looking for some company."

Belinda bent her head back in laughter. "Honey, you don't have enough money in the world to take one of these women home tonight."

I smiled. "That's fine with me. I got enough woman problems."

She shook her head. "Don't we all, honey. Don't we all."

A lady sitting a few seats over held up her hand, so Belinda excused herself. She returned fifteen minutes later and swapped out my empty Stella for a full one.

Leaning on the counter, she said, "Okay. So lay it on me."

"What?"

"Your woman problems."

I smiled. "Thank you, but it's okay."

"Listen, sweetheart, I've spent my life dealing with women—lived with a half dozen I loved, and owned this bar for three decades. And I also got twenty years on you." She winked. "So trust me when I say you don't have a problem I haven't come across. You obviously aren't looking to get lucky, or you would have left after you realized that isn't happening here. So I'm thinking you're having a few drinks and looking for some mental clarity. But alcohol doesn't give you that." She stood tall and patted her chest. "A bartender does."

"That's very kind of you. But I'm good...really. My problem doesn't have a solution, so I don't want to waste your time."

"Every problem has a solution. Sometimes we just need to pull our heads out of our asses to see the answer."

I laughed. "You don't beat around the bush, do you, Belinda?"

"Nope. So let's hear it. What's on your mind?"

I supposed there was no harm in talking with Belinda. She didn't know Molly or Julia. So I took a deep breath and tried to figure out where to start.

"A few months ago, I had a thing for a woman I worked with. Her name is Julia. We were on assignment, living in Chicago for six months. I was sharing an apartment with Molly, who had a thing for this guy at her work, Will. I came up with the bright idea for me and Molly to make Julia and Will jealous by pretending to be dating."

"Oh boy, this sounds like a hot mess already."

I smiled. "Long story short, I got the girl I wanted. Molly got the guy she wanted. But then I realized I didn't want the girl I had. I wanted Molly."

"So you're one of those, huh? The type who only wants the things he can't have?"

I frowned. "Honestly, I would love to say you're wrong. But I think that was part of what attracted me to Julia originally. She was beautiful and unavailable, and maybe that was a challenge I wanted. Does that make me a total asshole?"

She nodded. "Pretty much."

I laughed. "Thanks. Anyway, it's not like that with Molly. Molly is..." There wasn't a simple way to describe what she meant to me. But eventually, I looked at Belinda and came clean. "...Everything. Molly is everything."

Belinda smiled warmly. "Yeah, I had one of those once."

I took a swig of my beer. "What happened to her?"

"Passed away twelve years ago. Car accident." She glanced away for a moment. "Still think about her every day."

"I'm sorry."

Belinda cleared her throat. "Thank you. So, does this Molly girl love this Will guy?"

I shrugged. "I'm not sure."

"But she picked him over you?"

"It wasn't really a pick-one-over-the-other-type thing. She knows I live on the opposite side of the country, but more than that, I never really gave her the chance to choose me because I never told her how I feel. I don't think I can give her what she deserves."

Belinda wrinkled her forehead. "You don't have a dick or something?"

I laughed. "No, I'm good in that department. I just mean...Molly's special. And I..." I shook my head. "I'm not reliable like Will. He's a doctor, lives in Chicago with her, and has his shit together. She deserves someone stable."

"You switch jobs a lot or something?"

"No. I've been with my company for five years."

"So why can't you be stable like this Will guy?"

"It's...complicated."

"No shit. Life always is. It's why those who persevere reap the rewards. You know what people who take the easy way out and don't push through their problems get?"

"What?"

"They get what they deserve."

I sighed. "Yeah."

"So what's really going on, Declan? It sounds like you got a good job, and you claim your dick works well enough, so what part of you isn't reliable?"

I was quiet for a long time. Belinda waited patiently, watching me. I could've thrown a twenty on the bar and walked out. But I was going to have to admit to someone what I feared. So why not Belinda? Chugging the rest of my beer, I blew out a jagged breath.

"My mother is bipolar."

"Okay..."

When I said nothing more, she prodded.

"Did your father leave your mom high and dry, and that left a bad taste in your mouth for commitment or something?"

I shook my head. "Nope. He stuck by her side. They've been married for thirty-five years. I'm the youngest of five kids."

"So what am I missing?"

"My father's a good man. He wouldn't walk out on my mother. But it changed his life. He carries a pretty damn big burden every day. When I was younger, my mom spent months at a time in bed and couldn't hold a job. So he worked a lot, and when he wasn't working, he was trying to help out with one of the five kids, or he was taking care of my mother."

She nodded. "That sounds tough. But you can't spend your life avoiding commitment because your father had to carry more than his share. That's got nothing to do with your life and your relationships."

"That's not what I'm worried about."

"Then you're gonna need to spell it out for me. Because I've spent thirty years listening to people half in the bag tell me their problems. And I'm having a harder time following you after just two beers than any of them. What's got you afraid to go after the woman you love?"

I'd never said the words out loud before. But fuck it... Looking Belinda directly in the eyes, I said, "I suffer from depression. Started in high school, though, if you asked most of my classmates, they'd tell you I was the life of the party. But I went through some rough times before I spoke to one of my sisters about it and sought help. It's pretty much under control now, though I take medication and go to therapy to keep it that way."

"Okay, well, none of us is perfect. But it sounds like you're managing things."

I shook my head. "When my mom started out, her doctor thought it was just some depression, too. It took years for her illness to show all its signs."

"So you think because your mom got worse, that might happen to you?"

I nodded. "Bipolar disorder is hereditary."

CHAPTER
TWENTY-SIX

Declan

"**H**ey, Dad."

"Declan! What are you doing here?" My father took off his glasses and pushed up from his recliner, swamping me in a bear hug. "I thought you were gallivanting around the country for that fancy job of yours?"

I smiled. "I'm still working in Wisconsin—just came home for the long weekend. Sorry I didn't call. It was a last-minute decision." *As in, I woke up this morning and went to the airport without even having a plane ticket or knowing the flight schedule.*

"You never need to call. But you just missed your mother. She went over to visit your aunt Gloria. She had some surgery on her foot, so your mom has been helping her out every day."

I dropped my duffle bag on the floor and took a seat on the couch opposite my father's favorite chair. "I didn't know that. How's she doing?"

"Eh. You know your aunt Gloria... She makes a federal case out of everything and loves the attention. But the doctor says she's healing just fine."

That sounded about right. Aunt Gloria did love having people fuss over her. "How about Mom? How's she doing?"

"Good, good. Got some arthritis starting up lately. But that's normal at our age."

I nodded. "How about her...mental health?"

My father's brows dipped down like he had no idea what I was talking about. "Your mother's fine."

Dad liked to pretend there was nothing wrong, so Mom's condition wasn't something we talked about with him—especially not me, since I was the youngest. It had been my sisters who first explained things to me when I was eight or nine and started to realize other moms didn't spend two months in bed, followed by three months of singing, crafting, cooking, and incessant housecleaning at all hours of the night.

I raked a hand through my hair. "I know we don't talk about it, but I worry about Mom's mental health."

"You don't need to worry about that."

"Yeah, I do, Dad."

He leveled me with a warning look. "No, you don't."

I sighed. My dad was a good dad—a great dad, even. When I was a kid he would come home after working a sixteen-hour day and still throw a ball around with me in the yard. He showed up to every baseball, hockey, and swim-team event, and never even missed a painful recorder concert. He made sure we had dinner on the table every night, even if Mom was in bed, and he quietly picked up all the slack during her dark times.

But what he didn't do was talk about it. And to this day, I wasn't sure who he was trying to protect—my mother or me and my sisters.

"Dad... Can we talk about it for a minute?"

My father stood. "There's nothing to talk about. I'm going to make us some tea."

I followed him into the kitchen. Leaning against the counter, I watched as he busied himself filling the pot and getting the mugs ready with tea bags. If I didn't push, this conversation wasn't going to happen. In fact, it might not happen even if I did push. Yet I needed to try. It was long overdue.

"Did you know how Mom was before you got married?"

"I'm not talking about this."

"But I need you to."

"No. You don't." The kettle started to whistle, so he lifted it and poured the water into the mugs. After he steeped the tea, he put sugar on the table and took a seat.

"Dad..."

He let out a loud sigh. "What difference does any of this make to you? Your life is what it was regardless of what I knew and didn't know, and I think we gave you a pretty damn good childhood regardless."

"You did. Absolutely. I had a great childhood."

"Then why do you need to poke around? None of it will change anything. Let sleeping dogs lie, son."

I took the seat across from him and waited until he looked up and gave me his full attention. Then I took a deep breath. "I...I sometimes worry that my depression might progress into something more, or maybe I haven't developed all the symptoms I'm going to have yet. Bipolar is hereditary. I know you know that."

My father closed his eyes. "*Shit.*" He took a minute and then nodded. "Are things getting worse for you?"

"Nothing I can't handle. I still struggle with some lows at times, but my doctor has been great, and once he adjusts my medicine, I'm able to snap out of it. I don't spend months down followed by months of manic highs or anything...yet."

"How's your sleeping?"

"It's good. No trouble there."

My dad stared down into his mug. Eventually, he sighed. "Your mother and I got married very young. I was twenty-one, and she was twenty. She'd always had a lot of energy at times, where she wouldn't require more than a few hours of sleep, but then there would come a point where she would crash."

"So you knew about her bipolar disorder before you got married?"

My father frowned. "No. I knew she was different. But I didn't know the extent of things. It took about five years before it progressed to the level that we couldn't chalk it up to mood swings anymore."

I'd done enough reading on the subject to know the average age of onset was twenty-five, so it seemed my mother fit right into the norm.

"Would it have...changed things if you knew?"

My father's forehead creased. "What are you asking me?"

I shook my head. "I don't know, Dad."

My father stared at me for a while. "I'm not going to sugarcoat it. Living with someone with bipolar disorder can be very difficult. But there's never been a single day I regretted asking your mother to be my wife."

I looked down. "I know you had Catherine before you were twenty-five, so maybe *regret* isn't the right word."

"No, it's definitely not the right word. But I think I understand what you're getting at. If I'd fully known about your mom's condition, would I have walked away, and the answer is absolutely not."

I shook my head. "How can you be so sure?"

"Because I'd take three-hundred-and-sixty-four bad days a year just to have your mother for one good one, Declan. Your mother makes me happy. We have our ups and downs, maybe more so than most, but she's the light of my life. I'd have thought you knew this, considering how many kids we have."

That made me chuckle. "Yeah... I guess so."

My dad touched my arm. "Have you spoken to the doctor about your concerns?"

"No."

My father nodded. "You know you need to, right?"

I blew out a deep breath. "Yeah, I do."

"Good. There are a lot of things in life we can't control. But you can't sit around waiting for something that might not even happen. Because then you're not really living—you're standing still."

I sighed. "I know."

My father studied me. "You do, huh? Then I want you to promise me something."

"What's that?"

"You won't sell yourself short. I'm assuming there's a reason you wanted to have this talk today. And that reason looks good in a skirt."

I smiled. "Her name is Molly."

"Well, Molly would be very lucky to have you. Just like you are, son. No matter what road life takes you

254

down. Trust me, I know that firsthand. Sometimes a bumpy road takes you to the best places."

Though I didn't necessarily agree with him, I knew my father meant well. So I pretended he'd helped me solve my dilemma. "Thanks, Dad."

• • •

My time in California was limited. But there was no way I could come all the way home and not see my favorite sister. On Sunday, I decided to take a road trip to the convent to visit Catherine. She was four hours north in San Luis Obispo.

When I arrived, some of the nuns were playing basketball on the court near the front of the property. It was a riot to see them bouncing the ball around on the pavement, most of them in knee-length skirts or longer. If anyone thought all nuns did was sit around and pray, this proved them wrong. Some of these ladies could put me to shame on the court. Catherine was always telling me about their outings, too. They took exercise classes together, went to speak at schools, and volunteered in so many places. It was a very active lifestyle. Which was a good thing because if I were forced to be celibate, I would definitely need distractions, too. But let's be real, that would *never* be my reality. I didn't know how my sister did it. But this was the life she chose to lead.

I always had to wait outside until Catherine came out to get me. Since she didn't have a cell phone, I had to dial the main line and request that someone tell her I was here.

Catherine finally emerged and reached out her arms to greet me as I stood at the base of the steps.

She gave me a hug. "How was the ride, little brother?"

"Long, but worth it to see you, Sister-Sister."

She wore a simple, gray dress and small cross around her neck. Catherine's order was less strict than some. They didn't have to wear the traditional habits. Let's put it this way: they were as stylin' as nuns were going to get.

I gestured to the court. "How come you're not out there playing?"

"It's my turn to cook dinner tonight. I had to start preparing it." She shrugged. "I played yesterday."

I asked the question I always did when I came to visit. "I got my car running out front and ready to go. Are you sure you don't want to skip this joint and never look back?"

She rolled her eyes. "Not a chance."

Of course I was kidding. She knew that now. Although a few years ago, I might have been serious.

Catherine had been very careful to choose an order that allowed her to see her friends and family. Some nuns in other convents were kept apart from their loved ones. While I had to make an appointment, I was grateful to be welcome here. I couldn't imagine not being allowed to see her.

We walked through the grassy field that surrounded the place.

"I was surprised when you told me you were back here for such a short time," she said.

"Yeah. Well, I needed a break from Wisconsin."

She cocked her head. "Too much...dairy?"

"Nah. The cheese is the best part." I laughed. "Not *enough* of everything else, like my fam."

256

"When do you go back?"

"Tomorrow." I sighed. "I wish I could stay in California a few more days, though."

"You miss home that much? That's why you're here? It's an awfully long way to come for just a few days."

"Well, I needed to do some soul searching. And I wanted to talk to Dad, in particular—and see you, of course."

Catherine was the only one I'd spoken to at length about my bouts of depression over the years. But even so, I'd never expressed my deepest underlying concern to her: that I feared turning into our mother. Catherine didn't realize the extent to which it plagued me.

A look of concern crossed her face as she gestured toward a bench near a monument of Holy Mary. "Let's sit."

I looked up at two birds congregating on the Blessed Mother's head and finally said, "I'm going to talk to Dr. Spellman. I keep waiting for things to get worse."

She tilted her head. "Worse how?"

I looked my sister in the eyes. "You know..."

Catherine adjusted the gold cross around her neck. "No, I don't. What are you saying?"

I hesitated. "I feel like it's only a matter of time before I'm cleaning the bathroom floor with a toothbrush at two in the morning, Cat. What if I wind up with bipolar disorder like Mom?" I swallowed.

She frowned. "Just because you struggle with depression, that doesn't mean you have exactly what Mom has."

"Last month they had to adjust my meds again. I missed a few days of work and was feeling really down."

"Okay…well, that still sounds like depression. You know medications need to be adjusted from time to time. That's true for almost any condition."

"Or my illness could be progressing. I talked to Dad, and Mom didn't change overnight."

She let out a long breath. "You can't jump to a conclusion like that just because you needed a medication adjustment. But let's walk down that path for a moment. What happens if things turn out to be the worst-case scenario and you're diagnosed as bipolar someday? What are you really worried about here?"

"I don't want to be sick, Cat."

Her eyes narrowed. "Having depression or bipolar disorder doesn't make you sick. It just means you have something you need to learn to live with." She paused. "But what's wrong with the idea of being sick anyway? We all become sick, whether mentally or physically, at some point. No one escapes this life unscathed."

"Yeah," I muttered as I looked up at the birds again, listening to them chirp.

My sister placed her hand on my arm. "No one would ever know you sometimes suffer on the inside. Most people probably think you're a carefree, happy-go-lucky guy. You can hide a lot behind a smile."

"Yeah, I try."

"You shouldn't have to work so hard to please others or give them an impression of you that's not real. But you're not alone in that. Many people hide their depression behind larger-than-life personalities. You never know what someone is going through on the inside."

That reminded me of Molly. She knew a lot about me. But she knew nothing about my struggles with

258

depression. And that was my fault. While she was always open about her anxieties, seeing a therapist and such, I'd never even hinted at my own struggles. Not only had I been dishonest with her in that sense, but I now realized how much my having to hide that part of me ultimately impacted my relationship with her.

"I had a realization at this lesbian bar back in Wisconsin..."

Catherine's eyes widened. "I'm not going to ask what you were doing at a lesbian bar." She laughed. "But tell me more."

"My worry about ending up like Mom is the driving force behind a lot of my actions, particularly the way I handled the Molly situation. I think it's why I let her slip away so easily, why I didn't admit my feelings or fight harder for her. I sabotaged myself, so I wouldn't have to deal with telling her about my worst fears."

"You worry about turning into Mom, but you do realize the likelihood of that is slim, right? Just because you're her son doesn't mean your experience will be the same. Everyone is different."

"I get that. But seeing how much Dad had to struggle with it when we were growing up has made me fearful of being a burden to someone. Shit, even if I was *half* as bad, that would still be pretty terrible. I'm young. Anything can happen."

"Dad loves Mom. He doesn't look at her as a burden."

"Yeah, you know, I didn't have a true understanding of that until I talked to him yesterday. But he didn't know Mom was sick when he chose to be with her forever. By the time things got bad, he'd already committed."

"What's your point? That you should stop yourself from ever falling in love and warn people away from you, on the off-chance you end up like Mom?"

"Well...yeah. I guess that's what I'm saying."

"Don't be foolish, Declan. I think you need to be treated for health anxiety, too. You can't throw your entire life away out of fear. I guarantee you the fear of ending up like Mom is far worse than the reality of *being* Mom or living in Dad's shoes. Yeah, she's had some rough episodes. And it was hard for all of us growing up—embarrassing and humiliating when it happened in front of our friends. But she was untreated for a very long time. You have a good handle on things. And despite all of the bad moments with Mom, there have been a lot of wonderful moments too. Life has ups and downs. And if you love someone, you deal with it all."

I kicked some grass. "I get what you're trying to convey. But I'd still feel guilty allowing someone in my life when I struggle to feel normal sometimes. I don't want to put that on someone else or make them feel inadequate when I inevitably fall into a depression they can't get me out of. I don't want that person feeling like they're not enough to make me happy, because the truth is, when I get that way, *nothing* makes me happy, not even the people I care about."

Her brow lifted. "But it always passes, doesn't it?"

"It does." I nodded and exhaled. "Yeah. It always has so far."

"Well, there you go. It's fleeting, not a permanent part of you."

"I guess so." Something about that statement comforted me, allowed me to momentarily see my depression as something outside of myself—something that latches onto me but isn't constantly attached. *Not a part of me.*

My sister tilted her head. "You said a moment ago that you struggle to feel normal. What *is* normal anyway? Is *normal* some societal expectation that we all have to be perfect? Happy? Successful? I personally think it's more *normal* to have flaws." She stared off for a moment. "I grew up being told that women were supposed to get married and have children, right? It wasn't popular to say you didn't want that. And when I announced that I wanted to give up all of my material possessions and serve God, everyone—including you— thought I'd lost my mind, or that it was a phase. Not everyone has the same view of what's normal. Freedom for me was giving up material possessions to live my life for a greater purpose. It's what makes me happy. And I had to put aside my guilt about hurting others to achieve what I wanted."

"It took me a while to accept that you're where you were meant to be," I said.

"My point is, Declan, you shouldn't let your guilt or fear about anything dictate your decisions. God is the only true judge. And He leads you to the people and places you were meant to encounter. People like Molly. But He also chooses which crosses you will bear and never gives you anything more than you can handle." She looked into my eyes. "You can handle this. You can handle anything as long as you put your faith in Him."

I wished I had the kind of faith my sister had. But trusting that all was going to work out without any visible evidence was always a hard sell.

• • •

On Monday night, I headed straight to my new favorite bar after landing in Wisconsin. It wasn't like I had anything else to do here.

Belinda was wiping the counter down when she spotted me approaching. "Boy, you must really like it here. I can't seem to get rid of you."

"Yeah, well, turns out, I like the music and the company."

She winked. "And you don't have to worry about getting hit on."

"I guess that's true, too."

"What can I get ya tonight?" she asked, her red hair seeming even brighter than the last time.

"A time machine?" I chuckled.

"Uh-oh. That bad, huh?"

Earlier today, while waiting for my flight, I'd made the mistake of going to Molly's Facebook page and had seen a new update: *In a Relationship with Will Daniels.* It was official. There were also some new photos they'd taken together during a jazz concert.

I'd avoided asking Molly about the status of things with Will during our phone conversations because I didn't want to hear it. But now I knew they were exclusive—i.e., *You missed the boat, Declan.* That boat was so far offshore now, it wasn't even funny.

I spent the next several minutes unloading to Belinda, as had become my habit, telling her about my trip and Molly's new Facebook status.

She cringed. "Ouch. Okay. But there's always hope, right? This doesn't mean it'll always be that way. Relationships are hard, man. This dude can easily screw up. You might still have a chance someday."

I shook my head, staring into my glass. "I don't know what I hope anymore, Belinda. Maybe she's better off with him. But..."

"But you still want that time machine." She smiled sympathetically. "Okay, let's talk about this. What would you do differently if you could go back and change things?"

I laughed under my breath. "A fuck ton."

"Like..."

"I had multiple opportunities to tell her how I feel, and I blew them all. I'd take one of those moments back. I think I'd take the risk despite all of the fucked up voices in my head telling me not to."

"And there's no way you can do that now? Tell her how you feel?"

"She'll think I'm only doing it because she's unavailable now. She's already seen what happened when I started dating that other girl, Julia. That one *was* about the game—or maybe I started falling for Molly. My feelings for Molly are different, but I'm just not sure she'd see it that way. And that's my fault. I waited too long." I sighed. "Plus, she's getting serious with this guy now. I don't want to mess anything up for her, if she's truly happy." I downed the rest of my drink and slammed the glass on the bar. "It just sucks."

Belinda poured me another drink and said, "Okay. Wanna know the best advice I have right now?"

I took a sip and let out a small belch. "Yup."

"Never be too far away. If you care about her, just stay in her life. That way, if there's ever an opportunity, you won't miss it. You can't spot the cracks in the foundation if you're too far away from the house. Get what I'm saying? Don't be afraid to ask how things are going with this guy, because the biggest clues will come straight from the horse's mouth. Stay the course, my friend. If it's meant to be, it will."

Will. I chuckled at the irony of that last word. I nodded as Belinda moved down the bar to attend to a couple of ladies on my right.

As much as I hated being stuck in Wisconsin, there were some benefits. It allowed me a neutral place to work on my own shit, see a doctor, and deal with my hang-ups without any distractions. But Belinda was right. If I wanted a chance with Molly, I couldn't distance myself because her being with another man upset me. That was a pussy thing to do. I needed all the information I could get.

It was a good thing the bar was only a short walk from my hotel because I'd definitely had too much to drink. That also meant I wasn't of sound mind when I texted Molly on the way home.

Declan: I fucking miss you.

It was late. I had no idea if she was in the middle of one of her shifts. But she responded just a few minutes later.

Molly: My father was just admitted to the hospital and needs to be on life support.

CHAPTER
TWENTY-SEVEN

Molly

"**I** need some fresh air."

Will nodded and stood. "Let's get coffee and take a walk around the hospital."

"Would you...mind staying here?"

"Oh. Yeah, sure. Of course. I'll text you if anything changes, or if Sam comes in for rounds early."

I smiled sadly. "Thanks, Will. I appreciate it."

He kissed my forehead. "I'm sorry, Molly. I wish there was something I could do. It's killing me to sit here and do nothing. I hate feeling so helpless."

I knew Will meant every word. He was a very caring doctor, which is one of the things I admired most about him. So many physicians stopped seeing patients as people, focusing instead on the clinical symptoms of an illness. But not Will. He got to know his patients and their families and had so much empathy.

"Thank you for being here. I know you should be home sleeping because you have to work tonight."

His forehead wrinkled. "No, I shouldn't be home sleeping. I'm right where I'm supposed to be, Molly."

I walked through the corridors of the hospital in a complete daze until I stepped outside into the cool, early-morning air. It hit me that I didn't remember anything after walking out of the ICU double doors a few minutes ago. The trek along the fourth floor, down the elevator, and out through the lobby were lost inside my head. I took a deep breath and decided to follow the trail around the hospital that I sometimes walked on my breaks with other nurses.

Last night, Kayla had called at a little after eleven o'clock. She said she was riding in the back of an ambulance on her way to the hospital. She and my dad had dozed off on the couch while watching a movie, and when she went to wake him to go upstairs to bed, he was unresponsive. The paramedics performed CPR when they arrived and were able to get a weak pulse, but things weren't much better now, almost six hours later.

Kayla had run home a half hour ago to check in on my half-sister and give her an update before bringing her back to... I couldn't even finish the sentence in my head. Bring her back to what? Say goodbye? That thought was still unfathomable.

When she called, I'd been at Will's apartment freaking out about the possibility of finally having sex with the man I'd been dating for a few months. At the time, it had felt like the biggest decision I'd ever had to make. But now, just hours later, my father's wife was looking to me for guidance on his health, and I could no longer imagine I'd thought my sex life was important enough to waste precious time fretting over.

My head was a jumbled mess as I rounded the rear corner of the hospital. When my phone buzzed in my hand, I held my breath. Seeing Declan's name, I let out a sigh of relief, glad it wasn't the hospital, or Will, calling with bad news. I swiped to read the message.

Declan: Just checking in on you.

I smiled halfheartedly. After the bombshell one-line message I'd sent to him on my way to the hospital earlier, I'd given him an update and promised I'd call if anything changed. But I really wanted to talk to him right now, so rather than text a response, I hit *call*.

He answered on the first ring.

"Hey—how are you?"

His voice wrapped around me like a warm blanket, and I felt my shoulders relax a little. "I've been better," I said. "It's good to hear your voice. I'm sorry for calling so early. I hope I didn't wake you."

"Are you kidding? I was pacing, not sleeping. How's your dad?"

"He's...not good." I felt my eyes well up with tears. "I don't think he's going to make it too much longer. He has a DNR—a signed do-not-resuscitate order—so he didn't want to be put on life support. Without any help, his pulse is weak and his breathing is slow."

"Jesus, Mollz. I'm so sorry. I knew he was sick; I just didn't know this would happen so quickly, or I wouldn't have left." He paused. "I should've stayed. I should've fucking stayed."

I smiled. Though I couldn't see him, I knew Declan had just dragged a hand through his hair. "You had to work. No one knew how fast we were going to get here."

"Is he...comfortable?"

"I think he is. He's not awake to tell us, but his face is relaxed. He actually looks very much at peace right now."

"Good. Good. Are you at the hospital still?"

"Yeah. I needed some fresh air, so I decided to take a walk—do a lap or two around the building."

"Is Kayla with you?"

"No, not at the moment. She went home to talk to my half-sister."

"Shit. I wish I could've jumped in the car when I got your text last night. But I'd been drinking and couldn't. You shouldn't be alone."

"I'm not. Will is here with me."

There was a long moment of silence before Declan spoke again.

"Right, of course. I'm glad you're not alone."

I needed a few minutes of escape. "Tell me about Wisconsin."

"Are you changing the subject because you need a break?"

I smiled. He knew me so well. "Yeah, I am."

"Okay, well...let me see, where should I start? Oh, I know—I met a woman."

My heart sank. "You did?"

"Yep, her name is Belinda. She's sixty-one and a lesbian."

I chuckled, feeling instantly relieved. "Do you work with her at the dairy company?"

"Nope. She owns the bar down the street from my hotel. I really like it there. The people are great. I don't know why I never went to a gay bar before."

"Probably because you're not gay."

"Oh yeah, that might be it."

Declan spent the next ten minutes telling me about random people he'd met in Wisconsin. His physical descriptions were amusing because he likened everyone to a different cartoon character. From the way he spoke, I envisioned the state of Wisconsin much like Narnia—except I'd pass over the state line rather than through a closet and suddenly everything would be animated.

Only Declan could make me laugh right now. I sighed. "God, I needed this."

"What? To hear about my boring life in Wisconsin?"

"Just to forget for a few minutes."

He sighed. "I wish I was there with you."

As I turned the corner to return to the front of the hospital, my heart nearly stopped seeing Will walking toward me. He must've noticed the color drain from my face, because he held up his hands.

"Everything is fine. Everything is fine. Kayla came back, so I gave her and your sister a minute alone with your dad. She promised to text if anything changed."

"Oh…" I let out a jagged breath. "Okay, thanks."

Remembering I was still on the phone, I returned to my conversation, "Sorry. I panicked there for a minute. I thought something happened with my dad."

"Yeah, I heard. Is that Will?"

"Yes."

An awkward silence ensued. "Do you want me to let you go?"

"Yeah, I guess I should."

"Okay. But keep in touch. Promise, Mollz?"

"I will."

"Bye, sweetheart."

"Bye."

After I swiped the phone off, Will handed me a coffee. I hadn't even noticed he had one in each hand. "Who was that?"

"Declan."

He frowned, but tried to cover it. "How's he doing?"

"Good. He texted me last night to check in when we'd just gotten to the hospital, so he was worried."

Will nodded. It dawned on me that I'd asked him to stay behind while I went out to get air. He probably thought I'd done that so I could sneak off to talk to Declan. That hadn't been my plan, but talking to Declan had made me feel better than I had since last night—and that had me feeling a little guilty. Will had been so amazing when it came to my father. He'd been pretty amazing, in general, the last few months.

"I hadn't planned on talking to Declan when I stepped out from ICU. That's not why I asked you to stay."

Will searched my eyes a moment before nodding. "Okay."

I nodded back. "How's Kayla now?"

"She seems more pulled together than she was earlier. I'm sure she's trying to put on a strong front for Siobhan."

"Yeah, of course."

"You want to take another lap to give them a little time with your dad?"

"Yeah. That might be a good idea. My sister needs to prepare."

• • •

Robert Emerson Corrigan died at 6:38PM. Will and I knew it was about to happen, so he'd taken my little sister down to the cafeteria and left Kayla and me to stay at Dad's bedside as he took his last breaths.

Being a nurse, that hadn't been the first time I'd stayed with someone while they passed away, but doing it for someone you loved—your own father or your husband—was definitely a first for Kayla and me. The steady decline of his vitals had told me it was going to happen soon, but nothing could've prepared me for the moment the doctor pronounced him gone.

"Time of death, 6:38PM."

Kayla and I had clung to each other in the minutes that followed. I'd managed to stay strong until a howl escaped her—then we both fell apart. She wanted to say her goodbye first because she needed to go break the news to Siobhan. So I waited by the nurses' station to give her time alone. Then, when she was done, I went in.

Taking my father's hand, I stared down at his now-lifeless body. It was surreal that he was gone. I'd only just reconnected with him, and now I'd never see his smile or hear his laugh again. Tears streamed down my face.

"Hi, Dad. I don't know if you can still hear me, but I have so much I didn't get a chance to say." I shook my head and swallowed the lump in my throat. "You were a good man. I know I didn't always make you feel like I believed that, but you were. You were kind and patient, forgiving and honorable. I was stupid to let so many years go by without having you in my life, and I'm so glad we had these last few months to get to know each other again." I wiped tears from my cheeks. "I know I can't take back what I did, but I want you to know that I've learned from my mistakes. Time is too valuable to not be with the people you love, and I love you, Dad, with my whole heart. I also love Kayla and Siobhan. I know how deeply you care about them both, so I'm going to make sure to be a part of their lives from now on. I know you'd want that for all of us. They're forever my connection to you. Thank you for bringing them into my life." I stood and leaned over and kissed his forehead. "I love you, Daddy. I'll see you again one day."

Will was waiting outside of the curtain when I came out. After I spent some time with Kayla and Siobhan, he drove me home. On the way, I called my mom and texted my closest friends, including Declan, to let them know Dad was gone. When we finally walked into my apartment, it had felt like a year passed since I'd left yesterday. I looked at the time on the clock as I set my purse down on the kitchen counter.

"Oh my God, Will. It's almost eleven o'clock. Your shift started at eight, didn't it?"

He rubbed my arms. "Kurt Addison was on tonight. He owed me a favor, so he's going to stay until I get there. I'll go in and relieve him in a little while, and then I'll work on finding people to cover my shifts for a few days."

"You don't have to do that."

He kissed the top of my head. "I want to. This is going to be a tough week for you."

I leaned against his chest, suddenly exhausted.

"You haven't eaten anything in more than twenty-four hours," he said. "Do you want me to make you something?"

I shook my head. "I'm too tired to even chew. I think I'm going to take a quick shower though."

"Okay. While you do that, I'll make you some soup." He winked at me. "There's no chewing involved."

I took a long, steaming-hot shower and slipped into a furry bathrobe. My face was puffy from all the crying, and I left my hair wrapped in the towel because I was too lazy to brush it. Basically, I looked like hell, but didn't have the energy to care.

In the kitchen, Will had set two bowls of steaming soup on the table. He pulled out a chair for me as I padded into the room.

"I found chicken noodle and tomato soup. I figured the tomato soup involved less chewing, but seeing that it expired a year and a half ago, I thought you'd be better off with a few noodles."

I smiled and sat down. "Thank you."

"Oh, and I almost forgot..." He turned around and grabbed something from the counter. "You also had this hidden behind the cans." Will placed a shot glass filled with M&Ms on the table. "Do you hide candy for emergencies or something?"

My heart felt heavy. Yet again, Declan had found a way to remind me of him—not that my thoughts were ever too far away.

"I guess I just forgot I put them there," I said.

After we ate our soup, I couldn't wait to curl up in a ball in my bed. Will climbed in behind me and snuggled for a while, but eventually he had to leave for the hospital. He must've thought I was sleeping as he ever so carefully slipped out from the room. Rather than let him know I wasn't, I kept my eyes closed and stayed quiet.

I hadn't slept in more than a day and a half; I was physically and emotionally exhausted, yet I couldn't fall asleep. I kept thinking about how much time I'd wasted, how many years I'd kept my distance from my father—and now he was gone. It was a real reminder that life moved fast, and it was so important to spend as much time as possible with the people you loved. I couldn't go back, but I could make that a priority in the future.

CHAPTER TWENTY-EIGHT

Molly

My father knew a heck of a lot of people.

Three days later, my sister Lauren had arrived from London, and we sat in the front row of the funeral parlor as what seemed like an endless stream of people stopped by to offer their condolences for the second day in a row. I was pretty sure anyone who happened to have a heart attack this afternoon might be shit out of luck, because every doctor and nurse in the county was at the wake. My dad and I had worked at two different hospitals, and the turnout was bigger than I'd anticipated. Even my mom came, which made me happy.

The wake started from two to four in the afternoon, followed by a three-hour break, and then another session from seven to nine in the evening. In between, Kayla had arranged for us to have dinner in a private room at a nearby Italian restaurant. Since my dad was an only child, and both of his parents were already deceased, most of the family there was Kayla's. Again, Will stayed by my side the entire time.

"How you holding up?" He leaned over after we finished eating and kissed my temple.

"I'm good. But I can't believe I have to go through this again tonight."

Thankfully, this evening was the last of the sessions. Tomorrow would be the funeral.

"I'm sorry I can't stay," he said. "I'll be there all day tomorrow with you, though."

"Don't be silly. First of all, you have been here for me every step of the way. I'm not even sure when the last time you slept was. And you definitely don't need to apologize for having to work tonight. You don't need to come back and babysit me tomorrow. You've done enough, Will."

Will weaved his fingers with mine and brought my hand to his lips. "I just want to be here for you."

I cupped his cheek. "You have been, and I really appreciate it. Thank you, Will."

The evening session of the wake was much of the same. I'd never met half the people who came up to talk with me, and that was a constant reminder of how long I'd kept my life separate from my father's. At one point, I stood between my sister Lauren and my dad's wife. I looked toward Kayla to introduce her to a nurse who had worked for our dad when we were little, and when I turned back, instead of yet another healthcare worker, I found my sister shaking hands with a man.

"Declan? Oh my God! What are you doing here?" I launched myself into his arms.

He chuckled as he stumbled back, unprepared for my enthusiastic greeting. "Of course I came. How could I not with a welcome like that?"

I attempted to dial it back as much as I could. "I had no idea you were coming."

"My flight was delayed. I was supposed to be here for the afternoon session."

"Well, this is a welcome surprise. Thank you so much for coming all the way back."

We talked for a few minutes, until Declan noticed he was holding up the line. "I'm going to pay my respects and go sit in the back," he said. "Find me later when you're free?"

"Yeah, of course."

Unfortunately, *free* didn't happen until almost an hour and a half later when things were coming to a close for the evening. But my spirits had greatly improved since Declan arrived. Every once in a while, I would look over my shoulder to make sure he was still there, and each and every time, he smiled at me. It was like the shot of medicine I needed to keep going.

When the line finally slowed, Kayla rubbed my arm. "It was nice of Declan to come. Your father really liked him."

"He liked Dad a lot, too."

"I hope you don't mind me saying this, but the night the two of you came to dinner, your father told me he thought he'd just met his future son-in-law."

"Dad said that?"

Kayla nodded. "He did. I thought I saw something special between you, too."

I looked over at Declan. He was still seated in the back. But this time when he smiled, he held up a bag of M&Ms and let them dangle. It made me chuckle.

When I turned back to Kayla, she smiled warmly. "You two have fun tonight. You need a break."

• • •

Resting my head on the back of the seat in Declan's rental car, I sighed. "What a long day."

He reached his hand across to squeeze mine. "You must be so tired."

I yawned. "I am."

"What can I do?" he asked.

"I just want to go home."

Declan flashed a warm and comforting smile. "Let's do that then."

He started the car and took off down the road.

He turned to me. "Have you eaten?"

"I could really go for some breakfast for dinner right now."

His brow lifted. "You got eggs and bread?"

"My fridge is totally empty."

"I'll stop at the market and run in real quick."

I smiled. "Thank you. You're the best."

During the ride, I stared out the window. A sudden wave of sadness hit me. I'd somehow been able to block out the reality of my father being gone today, even at the wake. But in the quiet of this car, everything seeped in. It started to rain, and that just amplified the mood.

When we got back to the apartment, I took a long, hot shower. When I ventured out into the living area, it seemed like no time had passed since Declan left for Wisconsin. While I crashed on the couch, he stood at the stove, preparing his famous French toast. The smell of cinnamon wafted through the air. And on this miserable day, finally there was a moment of joy.

I breathed in, savoring the scent. "I still can't believe you came all this way."

"Not coming was never an option, Mollz."

A smile spread across my face as I watched him flip the toast. "This is exactly what the doctor ordered: breakfast for dinner and getting to hang out with you tonight."

He turned around. "Well, not sure which *doctor* we're talking about, but I'm not sure Dr. Will would have ordered *me* here with you tonight."

I blushed, feeling suddenly guilty. "Probably not."

"Speaking of which, if my sleeping here is going to cause any complications, I can stay at a hotel."

I sat up. "Are you kidding? This is your home. You've paid your rent. The room is still yours. Not to mention, I don't want to be alone tonight."

"I get that, but will he come by? You never told Will I was your roommate all that time. So my being here wouldn't make sense to him. I don't want to get you in trouble."

I knew Will wouldn't be happy with this, but no way would I tell Declan to leave. I shrugged. "He's working all night. He's not going to come here. And if for some reason he did, I'd tell him the truth—that you came into town and you're staying here. He would have to accept that, because he knows you and I are still friends."

Declan nodded. "Okay, sweetheart. I just don't want to make things complicated."

It was the second time this week that Declan had called me sweetheart. Maybe I needed to evaluate why I loved it so damn much when a man who wasn't my boyfriend called me sweetheart. But I was too tired to obsess over it right now.

"You're not making anything complicated, Declan. You're making it a lot easier for me tonight because I don't have to be alone."

PENELOPE WARD & VI KEELAND

He smiled. "Well, I'm happy as hell to be home."

Home. I wasn't sure he realized what he'd just said. "Home, huh?"

He paused. "It's funny. That just came out. But I guess I do view this as home. My second home, at least."

Declan arranged two plates of cinnamon French toast with hefty sides of bacon. The appetite I'd lost earlier was back with a vengeance, and suddenly I couldn't get enough food.

We sat down, and he grinned as he watched me. "I'm glad to see some things haven't changed."

In no time, there wasn't a morsel left on my plate. But we continued to sit across from each other in comfortable silence. I finished off the last of my orange juice.

"Did you tell Julia you were back in town?" I asked, still feeling a twinge of jealousy at the mention of her name.

He shook his head. "No. She doesn't need to know I'm here—not looking to start anything up there again. Better to leave well enough alone. I only came for you."

My chest tightened. "When do you have to go back?"

"Unfortunately, my flight leaves tomorrow night. So, I'll be here for the funeral, but I have to be back in Wisconsin right after. The following morning I have an important presentation. I wish I could stay longer."

I frowned. "Me, too."

Silence settled over us, and the high I'd been experiencing started to wane.

Declan sensed it. "Do you want to talk about today?"

I shook my head. "No, even though maybe I should. Rehashing this day is the last thing I want. It was grueling, and I am absolutely dreading tomorrow." I kicked his foot playfully under the table. "Let's talk about anything but death, okay? Tell me more about cheese and lesbian bars."

So Declan told me a few funny stories about life in Wisconsin, and I got lost in his humor. With each minute that passed, I was more and more grateful that Declan was here with me tonight.

"I'm not the only one who appreciates you being here," I said. "My dad's wife thought it was really nice that you showed up, and made a point to tell me how much my dad adored you."

Declan reached across the table and squeezed my hand. "I really liked him, too. I wish I'd had a chance to get to know him."

"Even though he didn't know you very well, my father sensed that you were good people, you know? Just like I did when I first met you. I think he loved the fact that you're so outgoing and pleasant. Seriously, Declan, whenever you're around, you just light up a room."

The expression on his face changed after I said that—darkening, as if somehow my compliment had upset him. It was strange.

My eyes widened. "Did I say something wrong? That was meant to be a compliment, you know."

"No." Declan leaned back in his seat and let out a long breath. "Of course it was. That was a nice thing to say." He wiped his forehead, and his face turned red.

Something was off. I leaned in. "Are you okay?"

He blinked repeatedly, as if he didn't quite know how to respond, then attempted to brush it off. "Now is not the time to be talking about me. That's not why I'm here."

"I want to know if something is bothering you, Declan." My heart started to race. "Besides, the last thing I want to talk about is *me*. So please, tell me what's going on."

He looked down at his hands and circled his thumbs. "It's nothing."

The more he tried to downplay it, the more worried I became.

"Your face dampened the second I said you light up a room. It triggered something. Please tell me why."

He swallowed. "Okay... There *is* something going on with me. But I just don't feel like tonight is the right time to get into it." Exhaling, he said, "Maybe we can talk about it over the phone when things calm down for you. I don't want to—"

"I don't know if you realize how much I care about you," I interrupted, my choice of words surprising me. "If something is bothering you, Declan, I need to know. Now. Please? It's okay. Do I look like I'm going anywhere tonight?"

He stared into my eyes for what seemed like an unusually long time. Then he finally nodded. "Let's go over to the couch."

My heart sank. My imagination ran wild as I waited for him to sit down with me. Had something happened back in Wisconsin? Had he gotten someone pregnant? That last thought was really random, but anything was possible. He took our plates to the sink before joining me on the sofa.

We sat close and faced each other.

"There's something I haven't told you," he began. "Something I didn't fully realize about myself until recently."

My heart pounded. "Okay..."

Declan didn't say anything for a full thirty seconds.

"Getting these words out is harder than I thought." He took a deep breath in and blew it out. "Okay. I'm just gonna come out and say it." He closed his eyes. "There are times when I don't feel right, when I get down." He paused. "I suffer from depression, Molly. It's something I've been treated for since high school. My mother also suffers from...bipolar disorder."

Wow. Okay. Hadn't seen that coming.

"I've always worried that my depression might be the beginning signs of bipolar disorder," he continued. "It isn't easy to diagnose because it progresses over a long period of time. I only recently discussed that worry at length with my doctor. He doesn't seem as concerned as I am, but he also couldn't tell me definitively that my worries are unfounded. I take medication for the depression, and for the most part, it helps. Though sometimes I go through these terrible low periods where I struggle, and then my doctor usually adjusts my medication. The night you came home from staying at your dad's for a week, I was in one of those rough patches. The toughest part is not being able to get myself out of it right away when it happens."

I let that sink in. It pained me to know he'd been suffering in silence and hadn't felt like he could tell me. Moreover, it hurt because I'd been too damn wrapped up in my own shit to figure it out, even though I'd seen the signs. I knew something was bothering him when I came home from my dad's, but I never imagined it was coming from *within* him.

"Are you feeling okay right now?" I asked.

"Yeah, I am. While I'd always had it in the back of my head that my issues could spiral into something more serious, lately I'd really begun to worry I was turning into my mother. The worry itself became a problem for me, and I needed to admit that to myself and to my doctor."

"So you said you spoke to your doctor?"

"Yeah. I spoke to my doctor back in California. We've started doing some Zoom therapy sessions, and he's put a lot of my fears to rest. He seems to think if I were bipolar, it would manifest differently. He believes I'm just depressed. Though, of course, he can't be fully certain."

"You never talked much about your mom. Now I realize it's a delicate subject."

"Growing up with her mood swings and episodes was really hard. It's never been easy for me to talk about. And believe me, the last thing I wanted to do was bring all of this up *tonight*."

I reached for his hand. "I'm so glad you did." I felt like I was finally getting the missing piece of a puzzle. As close as he and I had become, I'd always had the sense something was missing. Now I knew.

"Declan, you have no idea how much it means that you're sharing this with me right now. I've always wondered if there were parts of yourself you never showed me—almost like you were too good to be true." I laughed a little.

He smiled. "Yeah, I get it. I've grown pretty good at hiding a lot behind a smile. Sometimes I think I overcompensate and try to make people laugh so they aren't busy looking any deeper at me. Not many people are able to tell when I'm covering my feelings, but I had an inkling you could see through my bullshit that night you came home from your dad's. I didn't want to burden you, even though I knew you'd be supportive."

"I know how hard it can be to talk about things like this."

He nodded. "You've always been honest about your own anxieties. It just took me a while to get to that place."

I exhaled. "I wish I'd known so I could have helped."

"The fact that you know now and I don't have to hide it anymore makes me feel better."

Over the next half hour, Declan talked a bit more about his mother and the challenges of growing up with a parent who had a mental illness.

"Again, I'm so glad you told me."

"Me, too." He flashed a hesitant smile. "I've taken the past few weeks to deal with my shit in a way I should've been doing for some time. I even went back to Cali for a few days."

"Oh, wow. I didn't realize that." I smiled. "Are you sure you're feeling okay tonight? You must've traveled all day and then you sat at a wake for hours."

He took my hand. "I feel especially good tonight because I'm with you—even under the horrible circumstances that brought me here. I really missed you. I don't think I realized how much until I saw you tonight."

His words nearly melted me. *What is going on?* I thought I'd started to get over Declan. Things had been going so well with Will. But right now, all I could see, all I could feel was Declan.

I wanted to say so much, but the only words that came out were, "I missed you, too."

Declan took a deep breath in and smacked my leg. "Enough about this now, okay? We need to talk about happy things for the rest of tonight."

"For the record, talking about the tough stuff isn't hard for me. I love learning more about you, even if it's painful."

He looked into my eyes. "It wasn't that I didn't think you'd accept me or anything like that. I was in denial myself and didn't want to deal. My doctor feels like I might have a form of PTSD from my childhood, in terms of things I witnessed with my mom. And even though clinical depression is my main issue, my fear of turning into my mother has affected the way I deal with certain things—like my relationships, the decisions I make..." He stared into my eyes.

Was he talking about *us*? His decision not to pursue anything with me? Or was he referring to Julia?

Rather than ask him to clarify, I said, "Promise me something."

"Yeah?"

"Promise me that now that I know, you'll lean on me. Promise me you'll call me anytime you need to talk about how you're feeling."

Declan smiled. "Okay, I promise."

I'd thought I cared about Declan before tonight, but experiencing this raw and vulnerable side of him was a level of intimacy we'd never shared before. All of the complicated feelings I'd ever had for him lit up inside me like a fire reigniting.

CHAPTER TWENTY-NINE

Declan

I woke the next morning feeling all sorts of fucked up.

Fucked up because I'd poured my heart out to Molly like that.

Fucked up because my feelings for her were at an all-time high.

And fucked up because I woke up in her bed.

Nothing happened—physically, at least.

After our talk last night, my heart felt ready to explode. She'd made me feel so accepted, so cared for. It made me regret not opening up to her a long time ago.

As much as I'd wanted to do something fun for her, we were both exhausted. She'd leaned against me at one point while we were on the couch, and I ended up holding her until we fell asleep. When I opened my eyes and realized we were still on the sofa, I woke her so we could go to our respective bedrooms. Then she'd told me she didn't want to be alone. I didn't have to think twice. I followed her to her room and held her again until we fell asleep together in her bed.

So here I was the next morning, feeling fucked up for once again having way-more-than-platonic feelings for Molly. Except this time was even *more* screwed up because she had a boyfriend.

As she slept, I could see her phone blowing up with messages—Will checking in on her. I didn't know what to do. I was leaving tonight, and I'd be leaving a piece of my heart behind. Something had shifted between us. As strong as my feelings had always been for Molly, they'd never felt quite like *this*.

• • •

The plan was for everyone to meet at the church to say their final goodbyes to Molly's dad before heading to the cemetery.

Molly had seemed completely numb the entire morning. I couldn't blame her. It didn't matter what I said or did today, I couldn't take the pain away. We arrived early, and I gave her some space to comfort her little sister, but I never veered too far from her, in case she needed me. I planned to be here for her until the moment I had to leave for the airport.

A few minutes before the mass was to start, Molly came in my direction. Her eyes were glassy and distant. I knew she was still trying not to feel anything. She sat down next to me in the pew and leaned her head on my shoulder. I wrapped my arm around her and held her close. She felt limp, as if I were the only thing keeping her from collapsing.

I would never have let her go were it not for a firm tap on my shoulder. I turned around to meet Will Daniels' incendiary glare.

"I can take it from here."

I wasn't about to argue in a church. Plus, hell, I was the one in the wrong. I had my arm wrapped around *his* girlfriend. Molly looked panicked, like she had no idea how to handle the situation, so I made it easy for her. It was the absolute last thing I wanted to do, but I stood and held out my hand.

"Hey, Will. Good to see you."

He hesitated, but shook. "I didn't realize you were coming, Declan. I thought you were living out of state."

"I got in last night for the wake."

Will frowned, and his eyes shifted to Molly. He was clearly agitated, but when he looked down and saw her face, he thankfully put our pissing match aside and crouched down to speak to her at eye level.

He cupped her cheeks and looked into her teary face. "Oh, Molly... It's gonna be okay. Not right now, not an hour from now, maybe not even in a few days—but I promise it will get easier. Today is the hardest part, and you're entitled to feel every moment of it. You don't need to hold it in. Let it out, honey."

The tears she'd been keeping at bay streamed down her face. Will leaned forward and pulled her into a hug. Standing there, I felt like a third wheel. So I did what I thought was right, and I let them have a private moment. I took a seat a few rows back and watched as he helped dry her tears, and then she leaned on him as he walked her to the front row.

Throughout the mass, I mostly stared at the back of their heads. It hurt like hell for another man to be sitting in my spot, giving my girl comfort. But in the end, Molly was most important, not my own selfish desires.

After the service, the pallbearers carried the casket out of the church, and Molly and her family followed directly behind. I kept my head down as she and Will passed so I wouldn't make things uncomfortable. Outside, a hearse and a stretch limousine waited. I figured Will and Molly would ride in the limo together with her family, so I was surprised when I saw him kiss her forehead, pull his keys out of his pocket, and head to the parking lot alone. Molly looked around, and when our eyes met, she smiled sadly. I walked over, figuring I should probably say goodbye now.

I rubbed her arms. "How are you holding up?"

"I'm really glad that's over."

"Yeah, I bet."

Over her shoulder, I saw Kayla helping her daughter and two older women into the limousine. When she was done, she scanned the crowd.

"I think Kayla might be looking for you."

"Do you think she'd be upset if I told her I didn't want to ride in the limousine with them?"

"I think you should do whatever is going to be easiest on you. It looks like she has family with her, so she won't be alone."

Molly held up a finger. "Will you give me a minute, please?"

"Of course."

I watched as she walked over to her dad's wife, and they spoke. Molly pointed to me, and Kayla's eyes lifted to meet mine. She smiled. They hugged before Molly made her way back over.

"Are you going to the cemetery?" she asked.

"I was planning on it."

"Can I ride with you?"

I was surprised, but wasn't going to turn down a few more minutes alone with her. "Of course."

Cars were lining up behind the limousine with their headlights on. I noticed the second car back was Will, and his eyes were on us.

"Does Will know you're riding with me?" I lifted my chin and pointed to his car. "Because he's watching us right now."

Molly sighed. "No, I should probably go tell him."

I nodded. "Why don't I go get the car from the parking lot?"

"Okay, thank you."

When I pulled the car around, Molly climbed in.

"Everything go okay?"

She shrugged. "He said it was fine."

The hearse at the front of the long line of cars pulled away from the curb, and the procession followed. Molly stared out the window as we started to drive.

"Can I ask you something?" she said.

"Of course. Anything."

"What scares you the most about dying?"

I glanced at her and back to the road. "I don't know. I don't think you're in physical pain once your heart stops beating, and I like to think that there's an afterlife of some sort. So I'm not necessarily afraid of the physical notion of death. I think what probably scares me the most is dying with regrets."

"Like what?"

I shrugged. "I don't know... I guess if I looked back and realized I'd worked really hard, but it was at the cost of neglecting the people I love. Or if I didn't have a wife or a family for some reason." I paused and glanced over at Molly again. "If I missed important opportunities because I was too afraid to take a chance."

She nodded and continued to stare blankly out the window. "I don't think my father had too many regrets...

290

maybe some with how he handled things after he left us, but I feel like he made peace with that recently."

I reached over and took her hand. "I think you gave him that peace, Molly."

She sighed. "I'm so glad I had these last few months with him."

I nodded. "I think it meant the world to him, too."

A few minutes later she said, "Will told me he loved me a few days ago. It was the day before my dad died."

It felt like I'd been punched in the gut, and all of the air was sucked out of my lungs. I had to take a minute to be able to respond. "Were you...happy about that?"

"He's been really great through all this. I know you had your doubts about him in the beginning. I did, too. But I do think he cares about me."

"Are you...in love with him?" I held my breath.

"I like him a lot." She looked down at her hands on her lap. "But I couldn't say it back. Not yet. I care about him, and we have a nice time when we're together. We have a lot in common." She shook her head. "I don't know. Maybe my emotions are just all over the place because of everything going on with my dad and that's making me unsure of my own feelings."

I might not be certain about most shit in life, but one thing I now knew is that when you're truly in love, you know it. And even if Molly wasn't going to be with me, I never wanted her to settle for anything less than she deserved.

"I think you know it when you're in love, Molly."

"But how? How do you know?"

Just as she asked, we arrived at the wrought-iron gates of the entrance to the cemetery. The funeral procession slowed as we followed the hearse to Molly's dad's gravesite.

I was grateful that I didn't have to think and could just follow the car in front of me because my mind was preoccupied with how to answer her question. Too soon, the hearse slowed and pulled to the side. Panic set in as I realized Molly and I were just about out of time together.

Once I parked, Molly turned to face me. She shook her head. "I'm sorry for being so random and asking you the meaning of life on the way here. I guess seeing my father come to his end has made me realize it's about time I find my beginning."

People in the cars parked ahead of us began to open their doors to get out. Molly put her hand on the door latch. "Thanks for driving me, Declan."

As she started to get out, I yelled to stop her. "Wait!"

She turned back.

"You know you're in love if every little thing you've ever been scared of suddenly doesn't seem half as terrifying as not spending the rest of your life with that person."

Molly's eyes filled with tears as we stared at each other, almost trancelike. I wanted so badly to tell her I knew what love was because she was the love of my life. But the moment came to an abrupt halt when someone knocked on the passenger window.

Will.

I shut my eyes. *Fuck.*

Molly's face was somber. "Thank you again so much for coming, Declan."

I lifted her hand to my lips and kissed the top. "Of course. I'll always be here for you, sweetheart."

CHAPTER
THIRTY

Molly

"A re we okay?"

I stopped tracing figure eights in the condensation on the bottom of my glass and looked up at Will. "I'm sorry, what did you say?"

He smiled sadly. "Come here." We'd been sitting next to each other on my couch, and he gave my arm a little tug and pulled me onto his lap. Pushing a lock of hair from my face, he looked into my eyes. "Is everything okay with us?"

"Yeah, sure. Why wouldn't it be?"

He shook his head. "I don't know. You've been distant. I know it's only been a week and a half since your dad passed, and you have every right to be down, but for some reason, I feel like it's more than that."

I had felt off lately. And while a lot of that obviously had to do with my father, some of it also had to do with Declan. I hadn't heard from him in the days after the funeral, and when I'd finally checked in, he wasn't his normal self. His messages were polite and all, but sort of distant. Which made me realize my concern for Declan seemed an awful lot like Will's concern for me.

I hated to lie to Will, but I also didn't think I should share my concerns about another man, especially Declan. So I went with a partial truth. "I'm sorry if I've seemed far away. Losing my dad has led me to a lot of thinking, and I feel like it's hard to escape my head—if that makes any sense."

"Of course it does. But I hope you know I'm here to talk, if you want to try to work out some of whatever is on your mind—no matter what the subject."

"I do know that, Will. You've been amazing through this—so patient and supportive."

He cupped my cheeks. "That's because I love you."

This was now the third time Will had said he loved me, and I hadn't returned the sentiment. I felt more and more pressure to say it back, but I couldn't without being sure.

I turned my face in his hand and kissed his palm. "Thank you."

A little while later, Will had to go to the hospital for his shift, so we said goodnight. After I shut the door, I felt a little relieved to be alone. I could stare off into space as much as I wanted; I wouldn't have to pretend I was okay or explain why I wasn't. So I poured myself a glass of wine, hoping it would help me unwind, and picked up the photo album that had been sitting on the living room coffee table since before my dad's wake. My little sister had made photo collages to display at the services, so I'd borrowed an old family album from my mom with pictures of my dad and me.

I sighed as I flipped through the pages—my father and me fishing, my father trying to teach me how to play softball, my father with nail polish painted halfway up his fingers because he'd let four-year-old me give him a manicure. Mom, Dad, my older sister, and me pumpkin picking—page after page of memories I hadn't remembered from my childhood. When I got toward the end, warm tears slid down my face. And when I turned the very last page, I saw a photo I definitely hadn't been expecting.

Instead of more family pictures, it was a piece of paper with a selfie of Declan printed on it. He was making a funny face with his eyes crossed, cheeks hollowed out, and his lips puckered. He was also holding up a three-pound bag of M&Ms. I laughed out loud reading the note scribbled next to the photo.

Dry your eyes, my beautiful girl. I know it wasn't easy flipping through those pages. But you made it, so you deserve a reward. Now get your lazy butt up and look under the couch.

Amused, I practically jumped out of my seat and crouched down. Sure enough, there was an unopened, three-pound bag of M&Ms. Snatching them up, I sat back on the couch and took out my phone to text Declan.

Molly: I just found my M&Ms! How did you know I'd need them, and when did you put them under my couch?

A few minutes later, the dots on my phone started to jump around, and I got more excited than I'd been in weeks.

Declan: I did it when I was home for the funeral last week—before you woke up. Are those the only ones you found so far?

Home. Yet again, he'd referred to here as his home. I wondered if he realized it.

Molly: I've found the loose ones you hid. But this is the only one with a picture of you. Are there more?

Declan: I guess you'll figure that out at some point...

I laughed and started to text back. But at the last minute, instead of pressing *send*, I hit *call.*

"Did you believe the green ones made you horny?" he said in greeting, rather than hello.

I chuckled. "No, but I do think Twinkies will outlast the apocalypse."

"Interesting. If you could only leave the house with one item when the apocalypse hits, what would it be?"

"I have no idea. Maybe a flashlight or a lighter? How about you?"

He answered confidently. "Ketchup. A big-ass bottle."

"Why in the world would you bring ketchup?"

"Why in the world wouldn't you? That shit is good on everything."

I laughed. "God, Declan. This conversation is ridiculous, and yet it's exactly what I needed."

"Sadly, that isn't the first time I've been described that way by a woman."

There had been background noise, but it suddenly went quiet. "Did you just turn off the TV?"

"No, I'm at the bar down the block from my hotel."

"The lesbian bar?"

"Yeah. I've made some good friends."

That made me smile. Declan could make friends anywhere.

"Well, I won't keep you long, then."

"Don't worry about it. I just stepped outside so I can hear you better."

"I wanted to say thank you for doing that—for knowing I'd get to that last page of the photo album and need some cheering up."

"Anytime, sweetheart. Anytime."

Hearing him call me that sent a flush of warmth rolling through my belly.

I laid back on the couch and held the bag of M&Ms to my chest with my cell phone at my ear. "How are things in Cheeselandia?"

"Actually, it's getting a little creepy."

"Oh? How so?"

"I'm starting to get a pretty full arsenal of cheese jokes."

"Cheese jokes? You mean your jokes have grown corny?"

"No, as in *literal* cheese jokes. What did the cheese say to itself in the mirror?"

"I have no idea. What?"

"You're looking *goud-a*."

I laughed, which, of course, just encouraged him.

"What do you call cheese you stole?"

"What?"

"*Na-cho* cheese."

"I hope these aren't part of the big marketing plans you've been working on."

"If I don't get out of here soon, they might be."

"Speaking of which, when are you done?"

"The end of this month."

"Oh, wow. So you'll be back in Chicago in just a couple of weeks?"

Declan was quiet for a moment. "Actually, I may be going back to California instead."

"What? Why? I thought you were coming back to help finish off the project you started here?"

"I was, but...I think it's probably best if I go back to Cali."

"Is your boss pushing you to do that?"

"No...I think it would be... I don't know. I haven't decided yet for sure."

I felt a sudden sense of panic. "But if you don't come back to finish the project in Chicago, when would I see you again?"

Declan sighed. "I don't know, Mollz."

"You have to come back."

He was quiet for a long time. "I better go. Belinda is probably going to wonder if I skipped out on my tab."

"Oh...okay."

"You take care of yourself, okay?"

"I will. You too, Declan."

After I hung up, I felt a heaviness in my chest. What if Declan didn't come back to Chicago?

CHAPTER
THIRTY-ONE

Declan

Sweat dotted my forehead as I let the music take me away. Once again, I was the only guy in sight at The Spotted Cow. "Whatta Man" by Salt-N-Pepa played as I moved and grooved amidst a sea of women. They'd played that song especially for me. I was honored. It was the Saturday before I was set to leave Wisconsin later in the week. Belinda had hired a DJ as a little going-away present for me. It was definitely the best goodbye party I could've hoped for. Drinks on the house weren't half bad either. It was a much-needed night of escapism, because the days since returning from Chicago hadn't been easy.

The disappointment in Molly's voice when I'd told her I likely wasn't coming back had killed me. Her reaction made me doubt my decision. But I knew I couldn't handle watching her with Will again. It was one thing to know that with each passing day, Molly was getting closer to him. But seeing and experiencing it wasn't something I wanted to put myself through. Not to mention, it was going to look suspicious if I showed up there again so soon. He'd give her shit about it, and I didn't want to cause Molly stress. Whether or not she realized it, my heading straight back to California was the right decision. I still second-guessed it every chance I got, though.

When the song changed to a slower one, I left the dance floor and headed for the bar.

Belinda smiled from ear to ear. "Damn, boy. I've never seen you dance like that."

I grabbed a napkin and wiped my forehead. "Yeah, well, I'm trying to forget about shit, you know? Dancing my troubles away."

"When is your flight again?"

"Thursday night. You'll still be seeing me until then."

Belinda pouted. "I'm sure gonna miss you."

"You need to take a vacation and come out to California."

"I promise you, I will." She smacked me over the head with her dishrag. "What's going on, Dec? I know you're not devastated to leave Wisconsin. So there's got to be something else you're trying to forget. You've seemed down ever since you came back from Chicago."

I hadn't gone into much detail since returning from Molly's dad's funeral. But what did I have to lose now? "Can I tell you something I've never told anyone before?"

"Of course. But is the only reason you're telling me because you're half in the bag?"

I laughed. "No. I swear."

"Okay. Just didn't want you to regret it." She leaned in. "What's the big secret?"

300

"I think I'm in love."

"With me?" she said without batting an eyelash.

That made me cackle. "Well, with you, yeah. That's a given. But I was referring to someone else in this case."

She smiled knowingly. "Molly..."

Letting out a long breath, I nodded. "Yeah."

"You're only now just realizing this?"

I sighed. "I always knew I cared deeply for her. But after this last trip to Chicago, I'm a hundred-percent sure I'm actually *in love* with her. And I don't know what to fucking do about it."

"So you realized you're in love with Molly, but you're not going back to Chicago." She scratched her head exaggeratedly. "Yeah...that makes a lot of sense."

"I know it doesn't seem right. But the situation isn't that simple."

"If you love someone, you have to tell her."

"Not if I don't think I'm what's best for her. If you love someone, you want what's best for *them*." I paused. "I told you about my depression. What if I can't get a handle on it, or what if it gets worse over time?"

"Have you told her about it?"

I sighed. "I told her during this last visit. She was wonderful and supportive."

"So what's the problem?"

"The problem is, even if she accepts it, she may not really understand what she'd be getting herself into."

She shook her head. "No one knows what they're getting into long term or what the future holds. That's a risk you take for love. I'll bet she's stronger than you think. And if she loves you back, she'll accept that you have some bad days."

The wheels in my head were still turning against me. "Okay...well, even if you're right, she's currently with someone else."

"What does she say about her feelings for this other guy?"

"Last I checked, she hadn't *told* him she loved him, even though he'd said those words to her. But that doesn't mean she won't get there."

Belinda's eyes popped wide. "Uh...hello? That's a pretty big clue that she *doesn't* love him."

"That could have changed by now, though." I leaned my head in my hands. "Regardless of her feelings for him, I have no clue if she feels the same way about me as I do her. She cares about me. We're good friends. And she's attracted to me—or at least she was at one point. But that doesn't mean she feels as strongly as I do."

"So ask. What's the worst that could happen?"

I sighed. "I'm afraid of turning her life upside down. She's been through a lot recently. I don't want to cause trouble or confuse her if she's in a happy, stable situation."

Belinda shrugged. "She couldn't tell you for sure that she loved this guy..."

"She was also in a weird place when she admitted that. Her father had just died—not sure she could feel anything at all."

Belinda leaned her chin into her hands and smiled. "Is she the first girl you ever loved?"

There was no question. "Yeah. Without a doubt."

"What made you certain you love her?"

I sighed. "There was a point at the church when I had to sit behind her and her boyfriend." I shook my head. "It felt so unnatural...so painful. I felt like part of my heart was beating inside her, and I couldn't get to it. I wanted so badly to be the one comforting her. And I felt literal pain. But it didn't hit me until I was on the plane coming back here that the feeling of pain? It was actually love."

Belinda shocked me by wiping a tear from her eye. "Declan, you have to tell her."

My eyes widened. "Oh my God. I can't fucking believe I made you cry just now."

"I'm crying because what you said is beautiful. And I'm crying because I feel really bad that I'm gonna have to beat your ass in a minute." Her tears gave way to laughter. "Dec, it would be tragic if you let her go without a fight."

"I can't let her go if I don't have her in the first place."

She rolled her eyes and whacked me with her dishrag again. "You know what I think?"

"What?"

"I think you're scared. You said you don't want to cause confusion, but if causing confusion is a concern, a part of you must know she has feelings for you—feelings that would mean she has a choice to make."

That definitely made some sense. "Maybe..."

"By not saying anything, you stay in this safe place—she remains in your life, but never the way you hoped. You're letting fear make all of the decisions here. Get your head out of your ass and see it for what it is."

I chuckled. "Damn. I'm losing my straight-shooting therapist in a few days, aren't I?"

Belinda held up a finger and left me momentarily to visit the DJ. When she returned to her spot behind the bar, Melissa Etheridge's "I'm The Only One" started playing.

She spoke over the music. "Listen to the words of this song. This is the attitude you need to take with Molly. There is no other person who will love her like you do, even if life ain't perfect all the time. You're the *only* one, Declan. You know that deep inside. And the first way you can prove that is to risk getting your heart broken. Silence is regret. Inaction will always translate to regret in the end. If you never say anything, you'll never know."

I rubbed my temples. Belinda had given me way too much to think about tonight. She knew it, too, because she stopped talking and poured me another drink.

CHAPTER
THIRTY-TWO

Molly

It was one of the most grueling natural labors I'd witnessed in a long time. It was also another testament to the fact that Will Daniels was one damn amazing obstetrician.

"It's a boy!" Will proudly proclaimed through his surgical mask as he pulled the baby out of our patient, Karma's, womb. She'd been in labor for over twenty-four hours and had refused all drugs. Karma and her husband, Joshua, had chosen not to find out the baby's sex, so they were just realizing they had a son.

"I can't believe it!" Joshua proclaimed.

The excitement of a new baby being brought into the world never got old. It didn't matter how many night shifts I'd endured. Each new life was just as amazing as the last.

Several minutes later, someone asked, "Do you have a name?"

The new mom smiled. "Declan."

That stopped me in my tracks.

Declan.

Tears formed in my eyes. Declan had confirmed that he'd chosen not to come back to Chicago after his Wisconsin gig, and I hadn't been able to get over it.

I didn't understand why his not returning had this sort of impact on me. I mean, him going back to California was always the plan. But I knew there was a good chance I might not see him ever again.

I wiped my eyes. "Declan is a beautiful name."

Will returned from washing his hands, took one look at my face, and squinted. He obviously knew I'd been crying but didn't pry.

Will Daniels was a good man. I knew that now more than ever. He was the whole package. The real deal. And he'd told me he loved me over and over. And yet...I still couldn't say it back.

We'd gotten into a couple of arguments lately regarding my moodiness and my inability to explain why I was sad. What was I supposed to say? *I'm sad because the guy you hate for me to be around may never be coming back? I'm sad because I don't quite know why I don't love you?*

But I realized it didn't matter why I apparently didn't love Will enough to say it. What mattered was being honest with him. And the truth was obvious. I couldn't return his sentiments, and I wasn't sure if I ever would.

Later, when he caught me in the break room, I couldn't seem to look him in the eyes. And in that moment, I knew I'd reached my breaking point. I couldn't do this anymore. Will Daniels might have been the perfect man, but he wasn't the perfect man for *me*. He deserved someone who could profess her love for him without hesitation. I knew there would be a line of women waiting to take my place the second he went on the market again. Why waste his time if this wasn't going to work out?

"Will...can we go out to the courtyard and talk?"

The look of disappointment in his eyes told me he knew exactly what was about to go down. He nodded and followed me outside.

And I broke up with one of the greatest men I'd ever met. Only time would tell if that was the biggest mistake of my life.

• • •

The following evening was my night off, and I decided to do something I'd been putting off; I invited my little sister, Siobhan, over for a sleepover. She'd just turned ten and was still struggling after Dad's death. According to Kayla, Siobhan felt less alone around me because we had the loss of our dad in common. Kayla thought it would be a good idea for us to spend a little more time together. Hence, the sleepover. It was a nice distraction for me, as well.

While we noshed on pizza on the living room floor, my sister stuck her little nose where it didn't belong.

"What happened to your two boyfriends?"

My eyes went wide. "Excuse me?"

"You have two boyfriends, don't you? Will and Declan? They both came to Daddy's funeral."

My sister was more astute than I'd thought. And apparently, she thought I was polyamorous.

How to answer... "While in a fantasy world, a woman might be able to have two boyfriends and get

307

away with it, in this world, most of the time, you only have one. Will was my boyfriend. Declan is my friend. Neither is currently my boyfriend."

She tilted her head. "Why?"

No way was I getting into this with a ten-year-old.

"It's complicated. But let's just say, I didn't love him the way I should have."

She crossed her legs. "Why not?"

I blew a breath up into my hair. "I'm not sure. You know if you *do* love someone, but...it takes a little longer to figure out if you *don't* sometimes." Wiping my mouth with a napkin, I said, "Most of the time, it's just a feeling. And once I realized Will wasn't the one for me, I didn't want to waste his time."

"So how do you know if you love someone?"

That reminded me of my dad's funeral and Declan's words that day after I'd asked him the very question my sister had just asked me. "You know you're in love if every little thing you've ever been scared of suddenly doesn't seem half as terrifying as not spending the rest of your life with that person."

If I stopped to analyze what I'd been feeling these past several days, it was fear—fear that I'd lost Declan. From the moment he'd told me he wasn't coming back to Chicago, I could focus on little else.

Oh my God.

I finally answered her. "Siobhan, I think there's more than one way to know you love someone. And one of those ways is losing them. Sometimes we don't realize we love someone until it's too late. Until they're gone. I think that might be what's happening to me."

Her eyes practically bugged out of her head. "You love someone? Another guy? Number three?"

I shook my head and laughed. "No. Not number three. I love Declan." I paused, gauging to make sure. *Wow. Yeah. It sure is.* "It's Declan."

She gasped. "Are you gonna tell him?"

I shook my head. "Maybe? I don't know. I need more time to think about it. I only now just figured it out."

"Okay." She smiled and resumed eating her pizza as if this whole thing was no big deal.

It was to me.

We watched a movie after that and shared a giant tub of popcorn. But all I could think about was my realization about Declan. What did it mean? He was leaving Wisconsin for California in a few days. I still had a life here. Furthermore, what if he didn't love me back? Then it wouldn't matter how I felt.

I could only hope for some sort of sign in the days to come. I needed guidance on how to proceed. But I was especially glad I'd let Will go. Now I knew the source of my inability to love him. *I loved someone else.*

$$\bullet \ \bullet \ \bullet$$

Later that night, Siobhan had gone to Declan's room (yes, it would always be "Declan's room") to sleep, and I'd retreated to my own bedroom.

About ten minutes into my nighttime skincare routine, I heard my sister call me from across the hall.

"Molly!"

"Yeah?"

"Can you come here?"

When I entered the room, she was holding a piece of paper. "I found an M&M under the bed when I went to put my shoes there. So I went looking for more of them and found this."

I took it from her. It was Declan's handwriting.

And there were expletives.

Shit.

A bunch of sentences had been scratched out with a single line through them.

I read the note.

Fuck it. Let's just try it.
I can't stop thinking about what it would be like to fuck you, Molly. But it's so much more than that.
Maybe we should take it day by day and see where it goes.
I'm crazy about you, Molly. So let's just do this.

What? My heart clenched. "Pretend you didn't see this, okay? Go to bed, and we'll talk in the morning."

"Okay." She shrugged. "'Night, Molly."

"Goodnight."

I took the note to my room and sat on the bed, rereading it over and over.

When did Declan write this?

I wracked my brain and couldn't figure it out. But the timing didn't matter. This proved he *had* wanted to be with me at one point, even though something had stopped him from telling me. This was all the answer I needed. I'd gotten the very sign I'd asked for. Now... what was I going to do about it?

CHAPTER
THIRTY-THREE

Declan

I had no idea if I was making the right decision. Sitting on the runway, I stared out the window while my heart pounded in my chest.

What if I'm too late?

What if she tells me she's in love with him?

What if she can't see a future for us as more than good friends?

The other alternative should have brought me relief...

What if she loves me back?

But instead, that thought made me sweat even more.

What if she loves me back?

What if she gave up the opportunity for a stable life with a decent guy, and all I could give her was long periods of darkness where getting out of bed to go to work was the best I could do?

What if things got worse and someday it affected my job, and I couldn't even provide for us?

I stared at the cabin door. I was sitting in row seven, and people were still boarding the plane. The seat next to me hadn't even been filled yet. If I wanted to, I could grab my bag from the overhead compartment and bolt out the door. Molly had no idea I was coming, so it wasn't like she'd be disappointed.

Beads of sweat trickled down the back of my neck even though the AC was blowing right on me. I continued to watch passengers pass, inwardly freaking out as the plane filled up and my time to escape ticked away. At one point, a gigantic man stopped at my row of seats. He had to be at least six foot six and easily three-hundred pounds of muscle.

He lifted a suitcase into the overhead compartment and stepped into the empty aisle seat next to me. Buckling, he apologized. "Sorry if I encroach, man. I usually try to fly first class for the wider seats, but they didn't have any open."

"No problem."

I kept staring at the cabin door.

"Nervous flier?" he asked.

I guess the guy noticed the anxiety wafting from every one of my pores. I let out an exasperated sigh. "Not usually."

"Well, the weather's supposed to be good today. Should be a smooth flight. Try not to stress."

I nodded.

But a minute later, my leg started to bop up and down. The gap between people boarding began to space out. *We're almost done.* Any minute now, that damn door was going to slam closed. I unbuckled my seatbelt and stood, then abruptly sat back down and raked my hands through my hair.

"You sure you're alright?" my seatmate asked. "You're making me a little nervous the way you're acting."

Shit. I guess I'd be freaked out watching someone act sketchy on a plane these days, too. "Sorry. Don't mean to worry you. I just...I'm going to see someone, and I'm not sure I'm making the right decision."

The tree trunk of a man actually looked a little relieved. He nodded. "Must be a woman?"

"Yeah..."

"Well, that explains why you look terrified." He smiled. "You look like you might shit your pants. When I was six years old, my old man and my mom got into an argument. My old man was a big dude. He made me look tiny. He'd fucked up yet again—lost half his paycheck gambling, and Mom chased him out of the house. I'd been sitting out front on the porch, and he took the seat next to me and cracked open a beer. To this day, I've never forgotten what he said."

"What?"

"He said, 'Son, when you find a woman who scares the living hell out of you, marry her.'" The man chuckled. "My wife is five foot nothing, and I'm terrified of that little lady. Sometimes being scared of a woman can turn out to be the best thing in your life."

I smiled halfheartedly. "Thanks."

He nodded.

A few seconds later, the urge to flee felt like it was crushing my chest. I turned to my seatmate.

"Can you do me a favor?"

"What's up?"

"Don't let me get off this plane."

He arched a brow. "You sure about that?"

I blew out a deep breath. "Absolutely."

Tree Trunk folded his arms across his chest and stretched his thick legs out to block my passage. "You got it."

• • •

I decided to check into a hotel. It felt weird while I was in Chicago, but I didn't want Molly to feel pressured by me staying with her. If we had our talk and she told me she didn't want to be with me, what would happen? I'd say goodnight and go to sleep in the room next to hers? That felt wrong. So I'd checked into a Hampton Inn around the corner from the hospital where she worked. Since it was late, I decided to try to get a good night's sleep and wait until tomorrow to make contact. I wasn't sure if she was working or not, so I thought I'd call around the time she normally got off.

But *get a good night's sleep* turned out to be an unrealistic expectation. Instead, I tossed and turned all night, still unsure if I was doing the right thing. I wanted the best for Molly, and in the end, that might not be me.

The morning light didn't bring much clarity either. I went downstairs to the free breakfast at 6AM for some much-needed coffee. After sufficiently caffeinating, I stared down at my phone, trying to decide what to text to her. In the end, I went with simple.

**Declan: Hey. Are you just getting off work?
I was hoping we could talk.**

I felt like I was in middle school as I watched the message go from *Sent* to *Received* to *Read*. My pulse raced, and I started to perspire again. At least I probably wouldn't have to wait very long. Molly was usually pretty fast at responding to texts.

But a half hour later, she hadn't written back. Rather than sit around and wait for my phone to chime, I hopped in the shower and started to get ready for work—which was a whole different can of worms. My boss, of course, knew I was coming back to Chicago. Two days ago, I'd told him I wanted to check in on how things were turning out before deciding whether or not to stay. He'd been great about the last-minute change. But he'd left it up to me to let Julia know, and I hadn't done that yet. Obviously, I had some loose ends to deal with there, too.

By eight forty-five, it was time to leave for the office, and I still hadn't heard from Molly. I knew she'd read my text, so I assumed maybe she was stuck in a delivery or something. I hated to leave for work without talking to her, but the ball was in her court now.

At the office, I found Julia in the conference room. The walls were all glass, so I could see in from the hall, but she was busy and didn't notice me at first.

"Knock, knock," I said opening the door.

"Declan!" Her whole face lit up. "What are you doing here?"

It looked like she'd been prepping for a meeting. A projector was set up at the head of the table, and she was placing packets of papers in front of each seat. But seeing me at the door, she stopped and rushed over. Since the conference room was a fishbowl, she looked outside in the hallway to check whether the coast was clear before reaching up and wrapping her arms around my neck. Julia pushed her tits up against my chest and came in for a kiss. Luckily, I managed to turn my head in time, and her lips landed on my cheek instead.

Ben, one of the two junior account executives they'd sent to replace me, came walking down the hall, so I lifted my chin and cleared my throat. "Ben."

Julia probably assumed that was why I'd avoided the lip-lock and stepped back.

"Hey, Declan. How are you?" Ben said. "Julia didn't mention you were coming."

"She didn't know."

Julia beamed. "He surprised me."

Great. Now she thought I'd wanted to *surprise her* rather than avoid talking to her.

"Does that mean I'm heading back to corporate early?"

I nodded. "It might. I told corporate we'd get together and see where things are and how many hands we need here before the launch."

Julia's eyes sparkled. "Oh, I know exactly the hands I need and where."

Shit.

I was relieved when people started to file into the conference room for the meeting. It gave me a chance to escape Julia's claws, but also and more importantly, to check my phone. Julia loved to put on a good show, so I took a seat and let her bask in the limelight while I surreptitiously stared at my cell, hoping to see a new message pop up.

The meeting lasted more than two long hours, but it wasn't until five minutes before the end that my phone finally buzzed. My blood started to pump. But it was only Belinda checking in on me. I didn't want to disappoint her, so I responded as vaguely as I could without lying.

Belinda: How you doing, cowboy?

I texted back.

Declan: Hanging in there. Waiting to talk to Molly now.

Belinda: Go get 'em, loverboy. Let all us girls know how you make out. We're rooting for you.

Great. Now I was going to let down an entire lesbian bar if I struck out with Molly.

After the meeting broke up, people who had come in late stopped to say hello and welcome me back. When it was just Julia, me, and the two other account execs from corporate, she turned her focus back to me. "Why don't you and I get an early lunch to catch up?"

"Umm…" I glanced down at my phone, which still had no new notifications, and nodded. "Sure. That's a good idea."

We walked to a deep-dish pizza joint two blocks from the office. Julia requested a booth, and a waitress came over to deliver waters and pass us each a menu. The minute she was gone, Julia got up from the other side of the table and slid into my side of the booth.

"What are you doing?" I looked over at her, confused.

She grinned, and suddenly I felt a hand on my thigh beneath the table.

"Uh, that's not a good idea."

She slid her hand up farther and cupped my junk. "No one can see."

317

I covered her hand and removed it from between my legs. "Do you think you can sit on the other side so we can talk?"

She pouted. "All business and no fun makes Declan a dull boy."

But when I didn't acquiesce, she rolled her eyes and sighed. She also moved back across from me.

"Listen, Julia. You're a great girl, but..."

She blinked a few times, and then her head reared back like she'd been slapped. "You've got to be kidding me."

"What?"

"You're going to give me the *it's not you, it's me* speech?"

"Well...I...we..." I sighed and ripped the Band-Aid off. "I'm sorry. I met someone. And I'm really crazy about her."

"In Wisconsin?" She folded her arms across her chest. "That was fast."

I shook my head. "No, here in Chicago."

"What do you mean here in Chicago? How long have you been back?"

"I just got in last night."

"So how did you meet someone here in Chicago?"

I dragged a hand through my hair. "I'm in love with Molly."

Her entire face twisted. "Molly? As in your roommate?"

I nodded.

"When did this happen?"

God, this sucked. But I owed Julia the truth. "I guess it happened over time, while I was living here. It was slow, but then it sort of hit me all at once."

She shook her head. "So you're telling me while we were hooking up, you were falling in love with another woman?"

It sounded awful when she said it like that, but it was also the truth. I hung my head and let her get it out. She had every right.

Julia raised her voice. "I broke up with my boyfriend for you!"

"I'm sorry. I liked you. I really did. This thing with Molly—it was very unexpected."

"You know what else wasn't expected?"

She stood, pulled her pocketbook onto her shoulder, and took two steps to my side of the booth. Then she picked up the large glass of ice water the waitress had left and dumped the entire thing onto my lap before storming out.

Well, that went well.

• • •

The next morning, I woke with a bad feeling in my gut. I still hadn't heard from Molly, even though I'd sent a second text last night. Again she'd read my message, but hadn't responded. I started to get worried, so I'd followed up with a call. But that went straight to voicemail. It wasn't a good sign when the woman you flew into town to profess your love to wouldn't even text or call you back.

Though, for some reason, being back in Chicago had a surprising effect on me. I'd started to feel surer than ever that I needed to come clean with Molly and put my heart on the line. So rather than send a third text that would keep me staring at my phone all day, I decided to go find her.

Molly's normal shift ended at seven, so I went to the hospital and waited out front. A slew of people dressed in scrubs walked in and out, but there was no sign of the woman I'd come to see. Just as I was about to leave, I noticed a familiar face come through the door.

"Emma?" I called.

Her brows pulled together for a second before she recognized me. "Declan, right?"

I nodded and walked toward her. "Yeah. How you doing?"

Emma had been walking with another nurse, and she turned and told her she'd see her tomorrow.

"What are you doing here? Is everything okay? Are you visiting someone?"

I shook my head. "I'm actually looking for Molly. Did you happen to see her today? I'm not sure if she's working or not."

Emma frowned. "She wasn't on last night. Though I saw her name on the schedule earlier in the week, so I asked our supervisor. She said Molly had requested a few days off."

"Oh? Is she okay?"

Emma looked at me with what could only be described as pity. "Yeah, I texted her to check in and ask if everything was alright. She said she went out of town for a few days—a mini vacation of some sort, I guess."

"Out of town? Did she say where?"

Emma shook her head. "We were really busy last night, so I didn't get a chance to text back. Once I knew she was okay, I figured I'd check in with her when I got off today."

Well, this news sucked, but I guess that's what I got for showing up unannounced. "Thanks, Emma."

"Do you want me to let Molly know you're looking for her when I text her later?"

It dawned on me that Molly had found time to text her friend back, but not me. My theory that she was busy went flying out the window.

"No, it's okay. Thanks."

"Alright. You take care, Declan."

She turned away, but I needed to know one more thing. "Emma?"

She turned back.

"Did you happen to see Will Daniels on tonight?"

She frowned again. "No, he wasn't on either. Sorry."

After that, I wasn't quite ready to go to the office. I decided to take a ride out to the lake. When I got there, I sat on the concrete wall that ran along the sand and looked out at the water.

Where was I going from here? Back to California? It was screwed up, but the place where I'd lived my entire life no longer felt like home. I used to think home was where all of my shit was stored. But now, home felt more like where my heart resided. And that was in Chicago with Molly. Leaving here would be leaving it behind. I couldn't imagine ever having another use for it, so maybe it didn't matter where the hell I left it.

I wound up sitting on that wall for hours. I didn't even call or text Julia to let her know I would be late to the office. I doubted she was anxiously waiting for me to show up anyway, unless perhaps there was another glass of ice water nearby. At noon, my phone buzzed in my pocket. It was the first time in the last few days I hadn't gotten that rush of excitement, thinking it might be Molly. Because now I knew she was most likely away with Will. Nevertheless, I dug out my cell.

Belinda's name flashed on the screen. I debated not answering, because what was I going to tell her? That I'd waited too long and failed? I hated to disappoint yet another person. But before I could decide, it stopped ringing. A moment later, it started to ring again, and the same name flashed on the screen.

So I took a deep breath and swiped to answer.

"Hey, Belinda."

"Where the hell are you, cowboy?"

"I'm in Chicago, down by the lake."

"Well, I just opened up for the day, and guess what? A gorgeous woman was my first customer. Little thing made my heart do a pitter-patter."

I smiled. "That's great, Belinda."

"It sure is. Beautiful woman walks into a lesbian bar and smiles at me. I was thinking this was my lucky day. So you know what I did?"

"What?"

"I hit on her. Used one of my best, tried-and-true lines."

"Good for you."

"Not really."

"How come?"

"Because this woman sitting here at my bar isn't looking for Mrs. Right."

"Sorry, Belinda."

"Don't be sorry. What you need to be is back here in Wisconsin."

I wasn't following. "Why do I need to be back there?"

"Because the woman sitting at the end of my bar who just turned me down cold is your Molly."

CHAPTER THIRTY-FOUR

Declan

I'd started driving the rental car from the lake toward the airport. But as I did the math, I realized even if I were lucky enough to catch a flight right away, between returning the rental car, the time it takes to board and disembark, picking up another rental car on the other side, and the forty-five minute flight, I'd barely make it there any faster than I could drive. So instead of exiting for O'Hare, I headed north toward Madison. I couldn't risk that a flight might get delayed or that there wouldn't be any seats left until late tonight.

When I started, the GPS said the drive would take me about three hours, but apparently they didn't know what speed I'd be going. Because two-and-a-half hours later, I was parking outside The Spotted Cow.

I had no luggage, no hotel, and a rental car that was supposed to be in another state, but none of that mattered. I'd asked Belinda to stall Molly for as long as she could, but not tell her I was in Chicago. My heart pounded in my chest as I opened the door and saw Molly sitting in my usual seat.

It felt like it took forever to get to her, even though she was just at the end of the bar.

Molly jumped down from her stool and landed clumsily on her feet. "Oh my God, I thought you'd never show."

Unable to touch her fast enough, I wrapped my arms around her and drew her in close. "I can't believe you came here." I squeezed. "God, Molly, I missed you."

"It was a spur-of-the-moment decision. I had to see you."

I moved back to look at her face. "Why didn't you tell me you were coming to Wisconsin?"

She shrugged and smiled. "I don't know. I guess I didn't want you to say anything that might change my mind. I wanted to get to you before you could talk me out of it. I needed to see you before you left for California."

I pulled her in for another hug and spoke in her ear, "I have so much to say to you. But we need to go somewhere and talk privately."

When our eyes met again, she asked, "What took you so long to get here? Where were you tonight?"

"Well, funny you should ask..." I laughed. "It took me forever to get here because I was driving back from Chicago."

Her eyes widened. "What?"

"I went to see you."

"Are you kidding?"

"No. You can't make this shit up. I was looking for you. You weren't answering my texts. I was losing my mind, Molly."

She put two and two together. "Wait, does that mean you've already checked out of your room here?"

I chuckled. "Yup. I'm homeless as of right now."

Belinda interjected, "No, you're not. You're going to my place. I'll spend the night at my sister's. Been meaning to catch up with her anyway."

"I can't let you do that. We can go back to the hotel. I'm sure they have a vacancy."

Belinda slapped her dishrag against the wood of the bar. "No way I'm gonna let you do what you need to do tonight with bedbugs as your audience." She reached into her pocket and removed one of the keys from her keyring. "Take my damn key and go upstairs."

Belinda lived right above the bar in a loft-style apartment. While I'd never been inside, I suspected it was nice. I also suspected I'd be wasting my time if I believed she'd take no for an answer tonight. And it was a relief not to have to waste time finding a room.

"I won't fight you on this, Belinda," I said. "Thank you."

While Molly gave her a hug goodbye, Belinda flashed me a thumbs-up. I guess I officially had her approval.

Placing my hand on the small of Molly's back, I led her out of the bar.

As we climbed the stairs to Belinda's, my heart raced. I gathered my thoughts and wondered what had prompted Molly to come all the way here. Was she freaked out that she might not see me again, or was it something more?

I turned the key to enter Belinda's apartment.

"Wow. Nice place," Molly said.

Belinda had plants throughout the space, and the bright décor was just as vibrant as she was. It was one big space with a kitchen that opened to the living room, and a large bed in the farthest corner of the room. Everything was meticulously clean.

Molly looked around, and then finally at me. "I'm so confused, Declan. I thought you were never going back to Chicago. Obviously, I wouldn't have come here if I knew you were headed to me."

I placed my hands on her shoulders. "I wasn't planning to go to Chicago. But then I got my head out of my ass and realized I would regret it for the rest of my life if I didn't come see you." I took a deep breath. *Here goes.* "Things with Will and you are at a point that if I waited any longer, I would never get a chance to tell you how I feel—"

Before I could elaborate, Molly interrupted me. "There is no more Will and me, Declan."

I cocked my head. "What?"

"I broke up with him."

My heart felt ready to explode, bursting with hope. "When was this?"

"A couple of days ago."

"What happened?" I tried to seem sympathetic, though I wanted to dance.

"I realized one night—when I randomly started crying at work because someone named their baby Declan—that I'm...totally in love with you." Her chest heaved.

She's in love with me?

Molly is in love with me?

I should've immediately told her I loved her back, but my overwhelmed brain wasn't there yet. It hadn't caught up with my heart and was still processing.

"Why didn't you call me?" I asked.

"Because I didn't know if you felt the same way, and I wasn't sure it was right to tell you. That is, until I found a note you'd left under your bed. Well, actually Siobhan found it."

Note? "What note?"

Molly took a piece of paper out of her purse and handed it to me.

I recognized the rambling thoughts I'd written down the time I was going to ask her to take a chance on me. I'd never imagined those scribbled words would lead her to me tonight.

"I wrote all that down the night you told me you were going to start dating Will. All day I'd tried to figure out how I was going to tell you I wanted us to take a chance and go for it. But when you made that announcement, you seemed so optimistic... I decided I shouldn't tell you what I was feeling. But I've regretted that decision every day."

Molly wrapped her hands around my face. "I would've chosen you, Declan. There's no doubt in my mind. I wish you'd told me."

Placing my hands over hers, I said, "I didn't want to turn your life upside down when you'd made the decision I thought you wanted. My fears crept in fast. I convinced myself you were better off without me. Better off with him."

"Why would you ever think that?"

It was hard to admit that my insecurities were to blame. "It had a lot to do with my fears about turning into my mother—how my future might affect you. I hadn't told you about my depression at that point. I didn't want to burden you with my issues. Not to mention, at the time, you were going through a lot with your dad, and I didn't want to make things harder."

She shook her head. "You could never be a burden to me. When you care about someone, you take all parts of them. It doesn't scare me, Declan. And even if it did, it wouldn't stop me from wanting to be with you. No one is perfect—certainly not me. As long as you let me be there for you and don't shut me out, we can make it through anything."

Her words brought me immense relief. "I know you mean that." I nodded. "And I'm trying to work through my fears."

We stared into each other's eyes until Molly finally spoke.

"The day you hid the note under your bed... Maybe at that time I thought Will was what I wanted, but there's never been a moment I wasn't thinking about you, hoping *we* could be together. I was kidding myself believing things could work out between Will and me. This entire time, I've been falling in love with you. My inability to tell Will I loved him had nothing to do with my feelings for him, and everything to do with the fact that I love *you*." She laughed. "It just took me a while to figure it out."

I placed my forehead against hers. "I believe you've now told me you love me twice, and I haven't said it once." Not wanting to flub this, I kissed the top of her head and geared up to pour my heart out. "Molly, I love you so much. It's why I went to Chicago—to tell you. Up until now, I'd been afraid you'd tell me to go back to Cali. I wasn't gonna fight it if you were truly happy with him. But I'm so glad I went with my gut. If I'd known you felt this way about me, I would've been there a hell of a lot sooner."

"It's okay. We both had to figure this out in our own way."

"We've been trying to get to the same place—to each other—but we've had a lot of missed connections along the way."

"What now?" she asked.

"You tell me," I said.

Molly reached up on her tiptoes to speak over my lips. "I want *you* right now. I feel like I've been waiting forever."

"Pretty sure if I don't get to feel what it's like to be inside you, I'm gonna explode." I savored the sweet taste of her lips. Then I lifted her into my arms and carried her over to the bed, collapsing on top of her.

The second our bodies hit that mattress, the bed bounced us around as if we were in the middle of the goddamn ocean.

"What the fuck?" I yelled.

Molly fell into a fit of laughter. "What is this, 1985?" she cracked.

Belinda had a freaking waterbed! "What the fuck is she thinking?" Then I noticed something else. "Listen." I paused with Molly still under me. "Do you hear that?"

It was the sound of the ocean. Belinda had some kind of setup where as soon as the bed moved, it triggered the sound of waves and seagulls.

It was fitting, with how topsy-turvy our relationship had been, that our first time would be in a waterbed that mimicked the ocean. Honestly, it didn't matter where we were.

I began to devour Molly's neck, speaking into her skin. "I can't believe how long I've had to wait for this. You taste so fucking good."

She gripped my back, digging her nails into me. "Please don't go back to California..."

"I don't want to be away from you." I spoke over her lips. "We'll figure it out, baby."

We began to rip off each other's clothes. With the sounds of the ocean still playing, we were now totally naked as Belinda's waterbed tossed us around.

Desperate to taste Molly, I lowered my head to her pussy and spread her legs. She gasped as I began to lap at her tender clit. There was no easing into it. I was so hungry for her. Molly tasted sweeter than anything. Pushing her legs wider, I devoured her, harder and faster, before inserting my tongue. She pulled at my hair and guided my face deeper into her.

"Declan," she panted.

All she needed was to say my name. I slid up to meet her lips. Molly moaned over my mouth, and within seconds, I was inside of her. My eyes rolled back. She was so wet and ready that I nearly came the second her pussy wrapped around my cock. This was something I never thought I'd get to feel. What started out slow soon turned into hard and fast, made even more intense by the rocking motion of the "water." But I needed to feel her without the distraction of the bouncy bed.

I pulled out and led her onto the floor, grabbing a pillow to support her head. As I hovered over her, Molly placed her hand around my engorged cock and once again led me into her opening. She was so incredibly wet and warm. I'd always imagined what it might feel like, but this was better.

She tightened around me, and I nearly came. When she wrapped her legs around my back, allowing me even deeper into her, I almost lost it again.

Molly circled her hips to meet my thrusts. I closed my eyes in euphoria, unable to believe I'd almost let her go, almost never experienced this moment. The idea of that caused me to move even faster. She was every bit mine now.

Her hands wrapped around my ass as I pumped into her.

Molly's screams of pleasure echoed throughout the big loft as she suddenly let go. It took everything in me not to explode, but I held on until the moment I felt her orgasm pulsate around me. I'd never made a woman come that fast before. It was beautiful to see her come undone.

I lost it soon after, diving into her in one hard thrust as I came.

We lay limp on the ground, quiet and sated.

I wanted to be with her like this every day, and that meant we needed to figure a lot of shit out. But I wouldn't let it ruin tonight; this moment that was everything.

• • •

A few days later, Molly and I were back at the apartment in Chicago. We'd driven home the morning after our night at Belinda's and had been holed up together ever since. We spent the majority of time in Molly's bedroom "catching up" on lost time.

In our sex-induced haze, we were no closer to figuring out *how* exactly we were going to make this work. We both had jobs and family in different cities. I was supposed to start a new account in California at some point in the near future. Yet I didn't want to leave Molly.

But tough decisions would have to wait. Because today was a special day. It was my girl's birthday.

It was nearly 11AM. I left Molly sleeping and got up to make her French toast that I planned to bring into bed.

While the coffee was brewing, I decided to check her mail, which typically came early. Molly had mentioned she was waiting on a package to arrive today. Once downstairs, I found nothing but several envelopes in her mailbox.

As I made my way up the stairs, I sifted through her mail. There were a couple of bills and a birthday card from someone whose name I didn't recognize. Then I noticed a card from someone whose name I *did* recognize—Molly's dad.

I didn't know what to make of it. Maybe he'd planned to send it before he passed away. But I braced myself for the emotions that were sure to come once she saw it.

Back in the apartment, I left the mail on her counter and resumed making breakfast.

Molly appeared in the kitchen before I had a chance to bring her breakfast in bed.

"Hey, birthday girl," I said as I flipped a piece of French toast.

"Hey." She rubbed her eyes and yawned. "Whatever you're making smells amazing."

"It's your favorite. French toast. And it's just the start of a bunch of things I have planned for you today."

I wasn't sure whether to tell her about the envelope from her dad now or wait until she ate her breakfast. Given the potential for sadness, I opted not to tell her until she ate.

"Sit. I'll pour you some coffee."

Molly pulled out her chair and let me wait on her. I served us breakfast and sat across from her.

We ate in silence, but the thoughts in my head grew louder by the second. One of us needed to give up our job and move if we were going to be together. After a moment, I somehow once again shoved all of the unanswered questions to the back of my mind, reminding myself that today was not the day to stress.

We cleaned our plates, and I walked over to the counter. "So...I went to check your mail. I know you were expecting something. No package came, but I did see this." I handed her the envelope.

Molly examined it before her eyes widened. "It's from my dad..."

"Yeah."

She slowly opened the envelope and took out the card. She read the front and clutched it to her chest.

She handed it to me. "Will you read it to me?"

"Of course." I began to read her father's handwriting.

To my beautiful daughter,

If you're reading this, it's because I'm no longer on this physical Earth and had to miss your birthday. For that, I'm very sorry. I'm sorry for a lot of things when it comes to you. But perhaps I am most sorry for the fact that I didn't have enough time with you. I didn't get to fully enjoy spending time with the adult woman you've become, the one I've been so proud of. I would have taken you to your favorite Italian restaurant today and let you talk while I listened. There's nothing more I would want to do, especially at this moment—bed-ridden and unable to go out, let alone stomach something as delicious as one of those flatbread pizzas.

I worked very hard throughout my life, as you know, but in the end, I couldn't take my career with me. In retrospect, I wish I had spent more time with my children and less time working, as difficult as that is to do as a physician. If you have the opportunity in life to choose work or family, always choose family. Because not having spent enough time with mine is literally my only regret as I prepare to take the next step of my soul's journey.

Live each day as if it's your last, and make the most of your time with the people you love. Spend time getting to know your little sister. She's going to need your guidance and love. I am certain Kayla will remarry someday, and that's going to be extremely difficult for Siobhan. Unfortunately, because of me, you've been in that same predicament, and so you and Lauren will be able to comfort her in that respect. I love all of my children, but I worry the most about you, Molly. You're the one with the biggest heart. And I hope you don't have a single regret when it comes to me. I hope you let all of that go. I know you love me. Please don't ever doubt whether you showed me that sufficiently. You did everything you could in my last days to prove the love you had for me had never left.

I can only wish that you find a man who loves you half as much as I do. Please don't ever settle. You deserve someone who will love you with all his heart. And when you find *that person, you'll know. If you're trying hard to figure out whether someone is the right one, I'll tell you a secret: he's not. Unless we're talking about Declan. (Can you tell I like that guy?) I'm kidding, though. My opinion doesn't matter. Follow YOUR heart, my love.*

I have a few more cards written in my chemo-induced haze for your reading pleasure during subsequent birthdays. I wish I could have written you enough words to last a lifetime, but I hope you'll cherish the ones I do send. And please know that wherever I am, I will always be with you.

Love, Dad

Molly was in tears. My own eyes felt watery. A feeling washed over me, and I knew exactly what I wanted to do.

I walked over to my phone on the counter and dialed my boss, Ken, in California.

"What are you doing?" Molly asked.

"Taking your dad's advice and putting the person I love first. I don't want any regrets, Molly."

Ken picked up. "Declan. Good to hear from you. Any idea on your ETA?"

"Yeah. Um...that's what I'm calling about, Ken. We need to talk."

"What's going on?"

I looked at Molly and came out with it. "I'm really sorry to do this to you, but I have to give my notice."

Her mouth dropped open.

Ken was silent. "Really? What happened? You get hired by Integrity? I knew they were recruiting my people, but—"

"No. No, that's not it."

"Why are you leaving us, then?"

"I don't have anything lined up, but my girlfriend lives in Chicago, and I need to be where she is. I love her and don't want to be apart from her. So this is not a matter of money or anything else. It's just what I know is best."

Molly continued to sit there with her mouth hanging open. She clearly hadn't thought that I'd quit my job to be with her. But this was the right choice. I'd already known that in my heart. Her dad's letter simply gave me the final push.

"Well..." he said. "If I were your age, I might have given you a speech about this being one of the biggest mistakes of your life, but I've lived long enough to know sometimes you need to follow your heart."

I smiled. "Thank you for understanding. I hope you know that if you need my input on anything having to do with any of my previous accounts, I will always be available to you. I also hope I can count on you for a reference."

"Of course, Declan. You've been a model employee. I wish you the best and hope you remain happy with your decision."

I looked over at my girl and smiled. "I have no doubt."

After I hung up, Molly wiped her tears as she came over to embrace me. "I can't believe you just did that."

"One of us had to. And I would never expect you to leave your little sister." I lifted her up and squeezed her

336

tight. "I love it here, Mollz—because you're here. This was the decision I ultimately would have made, but your dad's words made it so clear that I couldn't wait another second."

She leapt into my arms again. "I love you so much, Declan. You make me incredibly happy. And I know my dad is smiling down right now."

I shook my head. "I hope this is enough to prove once and for all that I'm not gay."

EPILOGUE

Molly

It was Saturday morning, and Declan had just returned to the apartment. He'd gotten up early and left while I was still sleeping, so I was seeing him for the first time.

"How was it?" I asked, greeting him at the door by wrapping my arms around his neck.

"It was good. I met a kid today who reminded me a lot of myself."

"I'm really proud of you for doing this."

"Honestly, it's helped me more than it helps them. It's taken the focus off of me, and that can be a good thing."

I gave him a peck on the lips. "You've come a long way, baby."

Declan volunteered every Saturday morning at a teen crisis center in the city. He mentored kids going through tough times—many experiencing depression, something he understood firsthand.

"I think the biggest difference between me today and the man I was a year ago is that I don't doubt myself anymore, whether I'm worthy of certain things. Now I just choose self-compassion, even if things aren't certain. But you have to have a solid foundation to take that risk. You've been my foundation—the one sure thing that allows me to believe in myself."

I kissed him again. "Well, it's been my pleasure, Mr. Tate. You've brought a lot to my life, too, you know."

After Declan quit his job to stay in Chicago, he was unemployed for a few months. We'd made the most of that time. He'd kept the apartment sparkling clean and constantly cooked delicious food. I'd used my vacation time and we went out to California so I could meet Declan's family. It was definitely an experience getting to meet all of his sisters and taking a day to travel to San Luis Obispo to see Catherine at the convent. I'd laughed every time one of his sisters called him "Scooter."

Not only was it great to observe his family dynamic, but I got to know Declan's parents as well. We slept at their house and stayed up late talking with them on their back deck. I was surprised that Declan was so open with his mother. She even talked about her experience with bipolar disorder as it related to Declan's fears.

So between the California trip and getting Declan all to myself for a while, I'd cherished those first few months. But we were both relieved when he finally found a job at a local advertising firm.

Now, over a year later, things had settled into a routine. I had graduated to a level at work where I no longer had to work Saturdays or Sundays. I had a set schedule now of Tuesday, Wednesday, and Thursday. And I couldn't have been happier about that, because it had really sucked not getting to hang out with Declan on weekends.

I really appreciated lazy Saturdays like today. Now that Declan was home from his volunteer work at the teen center, I would have him all to myself.

"What's the plan today?" I asked.

"I have a few errands to run, actually. You good to hang out here for a bit while I do them?"

"I guess so..."

"Unless you haven't eaten yet? I can make you something for breakfast first."

"No. I ate a bagel while you were at the center."

"Cool. Perfect then. I shouldn't be too long."

"What do you have to do?"

"Just the usual Saturday stuff," he said. "Cleaners. Get to the bank before they close at noon. Stuff like that."

"Okay, well... Hurry back. Although, it's not like I don't have a ton of our laundry to keep me company while you're gone."

"How lucky am I that my girlfriend actually likes doing my laundry now when I used to use it as a punishment?" He winked.

"It's the least I can do, considering you do all of the cooking around here."

He brought me in for a kiss. "I love you. See you in a bit, okay?"

"Love you, too."

After Declan left, I went downstairs to the laundry room in our building. I threw a load of clothes into the washer and headed back upstairs.

When I returned to the apartment, I noticed an envelope laying on the ground outside the door.

I opened it, thinking it might have been one of those solicitations from cleaning services.

Instead it was a note—in Declan's handwriting.

Did you know it was two years ago today that I first left those cupcakes at your door? That was the same day you gave me a penis pass and let me move in. How about we mark the occasion by making this Saturday extraordinary? To celebrate, I'm sending you on a little scavenger hunt. So grab your tennis shoes and go to your first destination. Here's a clue: Because my girl loves to eat, it's the only place where the gnocchi has mine beat.

"Nonna's!" I said out loud, my voice echoing in the hallway.

Oh my gosh. What is this all about? Is he there waiting for me? I rushed inside and went in search of my tennis shoes.

The weather outside was perfect for a stroll through the neighborhood. When I arrived at Nonna's, I wasn't sure exactly what to do, though. As I entered the front door, it looked like they were just setting up for the Saturday lunch crowd. There was no sign of Declan.

The woman at the hostess station said, "Molly?"

"Yes. That's me."

She gestured to a table by the window. "Come sit."

"What's going on?" I asked. "Am I eating here?"

"Your boyfriend asked that we set you up with a snack-sized portion of your favorite gnocchi, along with a chocolate-covered cannoli. Enjoy, and then I'll provide you with an envelope that will lead you to your next destination, per his instructions."

This was one of the strangest experiences of my life, but I decided to go with it and enjoy every second. I sat alone, staring out at the people passing by as I ate my gnocchi and sipped the glass of white wine the waitress had brought me. A few people trickled in for an early lunch.

I tried to take my time, but I was anxious to get that envelope. I stuffed the cannoli into my mouth and finished it in three large bites. I left a ten-dollar bill on the table and, with my mouth still full, walked over to the waitress. "Thank you so much. That was delicious. I'm ready for my envelope now."

She handed it to me. "Have a great rest of your day, Molly."

"Thank you."

Outside on the sidewalk, I rushed to open it.

This is the point where you might need to go back and grab your car. Next destination is because I thank God every day that I met you. If my sister Catherine were here, this might be her favorite hangout. Hint: it rhymes with Notre Dame.

I paused. *Catherine.* Was there a convent nearby? A church?

Rhymes with Notre Dame.

Then it hit me: Holy Name! That was the large cathedral here in Chicago.

I speed-walked back to the apartment to get to my car, and then typed my destination into the GPS.

After a short drive downtown, I found a parking space and looked up at the grand structure with its massive bronze doors, wondering what I was supposed to do here.

Inside, the quiet space was a peaceful escape from the noise of the city. Surrounded by beautiful stained glass, I breathed in the soothing atmosphere.

"Are you Molly?" someone asked.

I turned to find a guy who looked about my age, dressed in Spandex and a hoodie. He must have been a bike messenger.

"Yes?"

"This is for you." He smiled, handing me an envelope. "But before you open it, sit for a while in the cathedral. Take a moment to quiet your thoughts and reflect with gratitude." He nodded and slipped away.

"Thank you. I will," I said, though he was already halfway out the door.

As I sat in the near-empty church, I looked over at an old woman in one of the front pews. I wondered what she might have been thinking about, whom she might have lost. I reflected on how fortunate I was. Even though I'd lost my dad too soon, I had a man in my life who loved me as much as my father had.

After several minutes of silent prayer, I stood up, feeling refreshed. Before I left, I lit a candle.

Back outside, I was met once again by the noise of the city. I opened the envelope.

Because you'll always be a daddy's girl. Think pink.

My eyes flitted back and forth as I processed that. *Think pink.*

The pink room in my dad's house! It had to be.

As I got back into my car, my heart beat faster in anticipation.

Once I got to Lincoln Park, the previously sunny weather turned drizzly as I made my way up the steps of my dad's house. The front door opened before I even had a chance to knock. It seemed Kayla was waiting for me.

"Hey, Molly." She smiled, looking utterly amused.

"So you're in on this little game, huh?"

She moved aside to allow me to enter. "The envelope is waiting for you on the bed in the pink room, but before you open it, there's a little surprise."

"Is Siobhan home?" I asked as I headed up the stairs.

"No. Your sister is at ballet."

"Oh. I'm sorry I missed her."

I spotted the white envelope on the bed and chills ran through me.

"So, before he died..." Kayla said, "your father left something else for you, in addition to the cards he wrote. Last weekend at dinner, I asked Declan's advice as to when I should give it to you, and he suggested today."

She walked over to the desk and handed me a small, pink-velour pillow. "Squeeze it," she said.

When I did, I heard my father's voice. *"Love you, my sweet Molly."*

I hugged it tightly as tears filled my eyes.

I squeezed it again. *"Love you, my sweet Molly."*

His voice sounded frail. He must have recorded it toward the end of his life.

I turned to her. "Oh my God. When did he do this?"

"I'm not sure exactly, but he left it in the box of stuff he gave me that was designated for you."

Wiping my eyes, I squeezed it a few more times, cherishing the sound of my dad's voice.

"I thought receiving that birthday card was amazing, but nothing beats getting to hear his voice again."

"I know he wanted to do a lot more toward the end—wanted to make an entire series of videos for you and your sisters—but he was just too weak and ultimately didn't want to be remembered that way."

"Can I take this home?"

"Of course you can. It's yours!"

I hugged her. "Thank you, Kayla. I have no idea what's coming next on this scavenger hunt, but I am certain nothing can beat this."

"Declan loves you so much. You got yourself a good man there."

"Tell Siobhan I'll call her to take her out next week."

"She'll love that."

I picked up the envelope before heading back downstairs.

As Kayla stood at the door and waved goodbye, I thought about how differently I viewed her now. I was grateful my father had gotten to spend his last days with someone who made him feel fulfilled.

In the privacy of my car, I opened the envelope to find out where I was headed next.

Because I know you need your favorite candy when you're emotional—and not just a small amount. A lot.

A lot. The bulk candy store!

I looked up the address and made my way there.

A bell dinged when I opened the door to Poppy's Candyland. A woman at the counter smiled at me.

"Hi...I'm Molly," I said. "I believe you might have an envelope for me?"

"Sure do." She handed me a plastic bag. "But first, feel free to peruse our candy selection." She winked and pointed to the left corner of the room. "The M&Ms are that way."

Heading over, I noticed there were two M&M compartments, one filled with primary rainbow colors, and one that contained all pink with a sign that read *Molly's*.

I broke out in laughter. *How the heck?* The amount of effort Declan had put into this scavenger hunt was unbelievable.

Filling my bag with my favorite pink M&Ms, I took it over to the counter so she could weigh it.

"No need to pay." She shook her head. "Your friend gave us more than enough to cover the cost of that bag." She handed me the envelope. "And here you go."

"Thank you so much." I smiled.

Back out on the sidewalk, I ripped open the envelope.

Because I miss you, it's time to go back to the place where it all started. See you soon.

As much fun as this had been, I was eager to get back to the apartment and kiss that crazy man for coming up with this idea.

Wearing a permasmile, I drove back in the direction of our apartment building.

Once back home, carrying my bag of M&Ms and my father's pillow, I reached the top of the stairs. A familiar sight brought a feeling of nostalgia—the same Tupperware container Declan had left at my door exactly two years ago. If it hadn't been for those cupcakes—those delicious cupcake tops I'd devoured—I might never have given in and called Declan to offer him the room.

I bent down to open the container. Six cupcakes with white frosting sat inside. And written atop them were six different words.

Will

You

Marry

Me?

Do

It!

Covering my mouth with my hand, I froze and stood up. When I turned around, Declan was behind me holding...a laundry basket. He'd apparently gone downstairs to fetch the clothes I'd abandoned upon discovering the first envelope.

His eyes widened, and he put the basket down. "Shit! How fast did you drive? You got here sooner than I thought. The clerk at the candy store texted me when you left. I was supposed to be standing behind the door on bended knee when you came inside. But I figured I'd fetch the clothes you left downstairs first." He exhaled. "Shit. The ring is on the kitchen counter. So much for a flawless proposal. Damn it, I—"

I practically leapt forward and cut him off with a long kiss. "This was perfect. Everything was perfect."

"Except my timing."

"We've always sucked at timing. But then we finally got it right. And by the way, you doing the laundry is almost as sexy as a choreographed proposal on bended knee." I shook my head. "I never dreamed this day was going to turn into a proposal. Oh my God, Declan."

As he squeezed me, I could feel his heart pounding.

"Can we at least pretend I got it right? Give me two minutes to put this laundry basket away." He lifted it off the ground. "I'll tell you when, and then you can come in. Okay?"

I laughed. "Okay, crazy man. Just tell me when."

He turned around. "You're gonna say yes, right?"

I wiped my eyes. "Yes."

"Okay, then I'll proceed."

He closed the door behind him. After about three minutes, I could hear him from behind the door. "You can come in now!"

When I opened, Declan wasn't on his knee, nor was there a ring in sight.

"This whole day has been about surprises," he said. "What's one more?" His eyes gleamed.

The next thing I knew, a dozen different voices shouted, "Surprise!" People emerged from every corner of the apartment. There were pink balloons and people rushing toward me. My mother. Kayla. Siobhan. Emma. And oh my God! Declan's parents. And two of his sisters!

It took me a few minutes to finish hugging everyone and wiping my tears. Then I went in search of Declan and couldn't find him anywhere. Until I looked down and found him on his knees.

He looked up at me. "If you think today showed how much I love you, think again. There is nothing I could do to demonstrate the depth of how I feel. Molly Corrigan, I wish I could say from the moment we met I've been in love with you. But that wasn't the case. You were my friend before you were ever my lover. I grew to like and respect you long before I fell deeply in love with you. But once that happened, there was no going back. Moving to Chicago was the second easiest decision I ever had to make. The easiest was deciding to propose to you today, the second anniversary of the luckiest day of my life." He opened the box, displaying a gorgeous, round, sparkling solitaire. "Will you marry me?"

I was too overcome with emotion to enunciate *yes*, although technically I'd already said it out in the hallway.

He placed the ring on my finger and stood, pulling me in for a hug. I'd nearly forgotten I was still holding the pillow from my father until Dad's voice rang out: *"Love you, my sweet Molly."*

Yup, Dad was here, too. I didn't think this day could get any better, but every moment kept showing me it could.

"Yes, Mr. Corrigan. I heard you. Don't worry." Declan smiled as he looked down at me. "I'll take good care of her."

ACKNOWLEDGEMENTS

Thank you to all of the amazing bloggers who helped spread the news about *Not Pretending Anymore* to readers. We are so grateful for all of your support.

To Julie – Thank you for your friendship and always being up for our little adventures!

To Luna –Thank you for your friendship, encouragement and support. Your strength and determination inspires us always.

To our super agent, Kimberly Brower – Thank you for always believing in us and working so hard on our behalf!

To Jessica – It's always a pleasure working with you as our editor. Thank you for making sure Molly and Declan were ready for the world.

To Elaine – An amazing editor, proofer, formatter, and friend. We so appreciate you!

To Julia – Thank you for being our final set of eyes.

To Kylie and Jo at Give Me Books Promotions – Our releases would simply be impossible without your hard work and dedication to helping us promote them.

To Sommer – Thank you for bringing Declan to life on the cover. Your work is perfection.

To Brooke – Thank you for organizing this release and for taking some of the load off of our endless to-do lists each day.

Last but not least, to our readers – We keep writing because of your hunger for our stories. We love surprising you and hope you enjoyed this book as much as we did writing it. Thank you as always for your enthusiasm, love and loyalty. We cherish you!

Much love,
Penelope and Vi

OTHER BOOKS BY
PENELOPE WARD & VI KEELAND

Park Avenue Player
Stuck-Up Suit
Cocky Bastard
Mister Moneybags
British Bedmate
Playboy Pilot
Rebel Heir
Rebel Heart
My Favorite Souvenir
Hate Notes
Dirty Letters
Happily Letter After

OTHER BOOKS BY
PENELOPE WARD

The Crush
The Anti-Boyfriend
Just One Year
The Day He Came Back
When August Ends
Love Online
Gentleman Nine
Drunk Dial
Mack Daddy
RoomHate
Stepbrother Dearest
Neighbor Dearest
Jaded and Tyed (A novelette)
Sins of Sevin
Jake Undone (Jake #1)
Jake Understood (Jake #2)
My Skylar
Gemini

OTHER BOOKS BY
VI KEELAND

The Invitation

The Rivals

Inappropriate

All Grown Up

We Shouldn't

The Naked Truth

Sex, Not Love

Beautiful Mistake

Egomaniac

Bossman

The Baller

Left Behind (A Young Adult Novel)

Beat

Throb

Worth the Fight

Worth the Chance

Worth Forgiving

Belong to You

Made for You

First Thing I See

CONNECT
WITH THE AUTHORS

Enjoy *Not Pretending Anymore?*
Then connect with the authors!

Join Penelope Ward's reading group
www.facebook.com/groups/PenelopesPeeps/
Join Vi Keeland's reading group
www.facebook.com/groups/ViKeelandFanGroup/

Follow Penelope Ward on Instagram
www.instagram.com/PenelopeWardAuthor/
Follow Vi Keeland on Instagram
www.instagram.com/vi_keeland/

Check out Penelope Ward's website
www.penelopewardauthor.com/
Check out Vi Keeland's website
www.vikeeland.com/

ABOUT
PENELOPE WARD

Penelope Ward is a *New York Times, USA Today* and #1 *Wall Street Journal* bestselling author.

She grew up in Boston with five older brothers and spent most of her twenties as a television news anchor. Penelope resides in Rhode Island with her husband, son and beautiful daughter with autism.

With over two million books sold, she is a 21-time *New York Times* bestseller and the author of over twenty novels.

Penelope's books have been translated into over a dozen languages and can be found in bookstores around the world.

ABOUT
VI KEELAND

Vi Keeland is a #1 *New York Times*, #1 *Wall Street Journal*, and *USA Today* Bestselling author. With millions of books sold, her titles have appeared in over a hundred Bestseller lists and are currently translated in twenty-five languages. She resides in New York with her husband and their three children where she is living out her own happily ever after with the boy she met at age six.

Made in the USA
Las Vegas, NV
06 November 2021